W9-ATQ-135

WITHDRAWN

Caravaggio's Angel

CARAVAGGIO'S ANGEL

Ruth Brandon

30036009999515

Constable • London

Constable & Robinson Ltd
3 The Lanchesters
162 Fulham Palace Road
London W6 9ER
www.constablerobinson.com

First published in the UK by Constable,
an imprint of Constable & Robinson, 2008

First US edition published by SohoConstable,
an imprint of Soho Press, 2008

Soho Press, Inc.
853 Broadway
New York, NY 10003
www.sohopress.com

Mixed Sources

Product group from well-managed
forests and other controlled sources
www.fsc.org Cert no. SA-COC-1565
© 1996 Forest Stewardship Council

FSC

A copy of the British Library Cataloguing in Publication
Data is available from the British Library

UK ISBN: 978-1-84529-697-1

US ISBN: 978-1-56947-519-5
US Library of Congress number: 2008018644

Printed and bound in the EU

1 3 5 7 9 10 8 6 4 2

For Lily and Tom

Author's note

I should like to thank Libby Sheldon and Sally Woodcock for their kind help regarding art-historical detail. Any mistakes are of course my own.

R.B.

1

To part is to die a little: Gloucestershire, September

It wasn't even my school fête. If I had children, which I don't, they wouldn't be at this school. An obese child of about ten looked up at me through round spectacles. Behind her, in a pen of hurdles, an exceptionally dirty sheep met my eye. Its greyish back glistened with moisture. 'Guess the weight of the sheep, miss?'
'What if I get it right?'
'You get a leg.'
'What of? That one?'
'Nah, it's in the freezer.'
I plucked a figure out of the air and handed over my fifty pence, wrote my name and phone number on one half of a raffle ticket and gave it to the child. Across the field, my friend Caroline and a comprehensively mackintoshed woman stood chatting outside the fancy dress tent, where Caroline's daughters were competing. I threaded my way through the stalls towards them. When I'd told her about Joe, she hadn't known what to say – the first time that had happened in twenty years of friendship. Condolences? Congratulations? Who whom? 'When was this?' she'd eventually asked, cautiously.
'Today. He left this morning.' It sounded completely unreal. Maybe it wasn't true after all.
'Where's he gone?'

I found this query, harmless enough in itself, oddly annoying – probably because I didn't know the answer. He'd just said, 'I'll be OK' – something I didn't doubt and hadn't asked. He was having his mail redirected. 'I don't think there's anyone else,' I said, in answer to the question she tactfully had not put. I didn't believe it, either. I asked if I could come and stay. Just for a little while, till my head got sorted.

'Long as you like. I could do with some adult company. David's away as usual.'

I floated numbly through endless meetings followed by a Hogarthian private view at which all the familiar faces seemed suddenly to transmute into gargoyles. A psycho-chemical bomb took me through the night, its effects lasting handily until well into Friday morning. Then there were some catalogue proofs to be checked before being rushed off to the printer. And finally I was off, into the Friday evening traffic, inching my way through a solid river of cars. Only when I turned off towards Cinderford and its shabby rows of coalminers' cottages did the flow eventually thin. I slowed down behind a meandering sheep and opened the window, trying to take deep, calming breaths. Then I shut it again. The air here, though pure, was noticeably chillier than London. All those exhaust fumes really keep you warm.

The green hills of the Marches rose all around, and a blue-black western sky promised another spectacular bout of precipitation. The field buzzed with excitement as people bought each other's pots of jam.

'Did you genuinely not have any idea?' Caroline asked when I arrived. 'Surely you can't really have thought it would last. He's such a bastard.'

'A charming bastard, that's the trouble.'

'Honestly, Reggie, you are so hopeless about men. I'm always amazed, someone as bright as you.'

It's true. Who else could have fallen for Joe's opening gambit? I'm on my second wife, he said the day we met, but I'm looking for a third. What could be more disarmingly frank? And what normally sane person would not have drawn the obvious conclusion – that no sooner would he have found his third than he'd be looking for a fourth, and then, probably, a fifth? Yet three months later he moved in. And now I was actually surprised, not to say distraught, that he'd moved out. And, doubtless, on.

'I knew things weren't that good, obviously. But it didn't seem particularly serious. No more than usual. I suppose I've been a bit distracted, trying to get the feel of things at the Gallery.'

'Of course, the new job. How's it working out?'

'Great – I'm really enjoying it. Or I will, once I get back to enjoying anything.'

'You will,' Caroline said firmly. 'That's the unnerving thing about you, Reg. The way you get on top of stuff. Look at you now.'

'What d'you mean, look at me now? I'm a wreck.'

'Of course you are. But imagine what I'd be like if David walked out. At my wits' end.'

If I were married to David *I'd* be at my wits' end, counting the minutes until he left the house in the morning so that I could awake from my stupor of boredom. Perhaps that was why Caroline chose to live in the country – it meant he'd be away more often than not. On the other hand, he was a good man. Unlike Joe. 'Luckily he never will.'

'I sincerely hope not,' she agreed gravely.

At least there weren't any children. When we'd first got together Joe had talked about our possible children. Don't you sometimes wonder what they'd be like. For a while I almost felt broody. It would still have been possible, just. But in the cut-throat world I then inhabited – I worked for an auction house, it was before I moved to the Gallery – children seemed unimaginable. In any case, even I, in my then state of besottedness, could see Joe was not ideal father material. He already had three offspring. He was fond of them, naturally, but it seemed fairly clear even then that the main impetus to procreation as far as he was

9

concerned was the primitive pleasure of peopling the world with Joe-lets. Later, as the years went on and we remained together, I began to think again. But by then he'd lost interest in that particular idea.

To breed or not to breed? As we climbed the career ladder, Caroline in her law firm, me in the auction house, our discussions led so invariably in that direction that it became almost a joke. Then she met David and had Rosie and Lina: pop pop. And David's lawyerly earnings (by then he was a full partner) meant she didn't need to work, so she declined the juggling act. Law may be lucrative, but it's a slog. So, of course, are babies, but at least they're your own slog. She decided she'd rather look after them herself than hand them over to some alien teenager. My job, on the other hand, was not a slog. It was demanding, but that's a different thing. By the time Caroline had Lina, I was authenticating and valuing and travelling all over the world. The day I realized the decision was out of my hands was a relief in a way. It was like losing your virginity (in the good old days when that mattered), or getting married. You can stop worrying about *that* and get on with other things.

Other things, other things, where were they now I needed them?

Next time I looked at the fancy dress tent, Caroline had vanished. There was a burst of applause from within: someone had evidently won something. Beside me, a second-hand book stall was piled with what looked to be the results of a house clearance – a tottering mound of sheet music, some battered cookbooks, a 1972 manual of antiques with price guidelines, a collection of postcards. Someone's grandparents must have died. There was also a heap of old magazines – *Life* and *Picture Post*. I glanced through them, caught as always by the photographs, and suddenly there it was: a pamphlet whose black-and-white cover showed an unframed picture leaning against a white wall, overprinted with a legend in bright red mock-handwriting: *Partir, c'est mourir un peu, Martyr, c'est pourrir un peu*. Inside, each page contained a photo of the same picture, in a variety of different locations.

Impossible. But when I looked again, the pamphlet was still there. I felt that all-over prickling, that sensation of total focus, that occurs when you find *it* – the real thing, lurking unsuspected. Still disbelieving, I picked the pamphlet up and turned it over. Surely it couldn't be?

It was. Slightly discoloured, but otherwise perfect: not a mark, not a tear, not a missing page. As incongruous as some brilliant Brazilian swallowtail suddenly caught in a flock of cabbage whites. I flicked through its pages. Lodged in the centre fold was a yellowing press cutting, the paper crumbling at the edges. It was in French, a paragraph clipped from the *faits divers*:

> *Yesterday, at 72 rue d'Assas, a body was found hanging, later identified as that of Robert de Beaupré, 22. Nearby was a copy of a pamphlet containing photographs of Caravaggio's 'St Cecilia and the Angel', which it may be remembered was recently stolen from the Louvre, together with a short note. M. de Beaupré was a member of one of France's most respected families. Why such a young man, with his life before him and everything to live for, should have met such an end, is something we shall probably never know. But perhaps his death is a measure of the degenerate influence of some of the so-called 'artistic' groups currently at work in our country, whose freedom of action may appear to some altogether excessive.*

I slipped the cutting back into the pamphlet and looked for a price, but there didn't seem to be one. Holding it out to the stallholder, a lugubrious man in a fawn cable-knit sweater that might have doubled as a pregnancy smock, I said, ever so casually, 'How much is this?'

He reached for it, turned it over unenthusiastically, flipped through it, considered: some weird collection of photos of the same picture. Was it possible you could be in the business and not recognize a nugget like this when you saw it? But perhaps he wasn't a professional, just a parent dutifully manning his allotted stall. 'One fifty?'

I wondered whether he meant one hundred and fifty, but didn't ask. No point putting ideas into his head. Instead, I fumbled in my purse and held out the coins. I could probably have got it for less, if I'd tried. He handed over the pamphlet without even bothering to meet my eyes, reflecting, perhaps, on the amazing things people will pay good money for.

Caroline came up. 'Something interesting?'

'Maybe.'

'Rosie won second prize.'

'So shall we go before that sky gets here?'

At Caroline's I had my assigned roles: godmother, gossip, cook. She turned on the news while I cut up apples. Every year she had this problem with excess apples, and every year, if I visited during apple time, I made her favourite dish – pheasant *à la normande*, with apples and cream. In the Middle East people were killing each other; in France, black and brown youths were rioting because *liberté*, *égalité* and *fraternité* only extended to those with pink skins. In Britain the government had problems with teenagers, and was considering locking up everyone between the ages of fourteen and twenty.

I was browning the pheasant when my mobile rang. My heart gave an almost clinical leap. He hadn't really meant it, it had all been a terrible misunderstanding.

An unknown voice said, 'Mrs Lee?'

Actually it's Doctor, or Ms, but I didn't quibble.

'You guessed the weight of the lamb,' the voice offered.

It seemed highly unlikely. 'Are you sure?'

'Quite sure. Your leg's waiting for you.'

I thought about the sad sheep and felt glad it was still, for the moment, intact. I also realized that this was the first time I'd thought about Joe since finding the pamphlet. Caravaggio's Angel to the rescue. Again.

My hero.

2

London, March

'How clever of you to have spotted it,' said the Director. 'I'm not at all sure I'd have realized, myself.'

'Oh, well, that picture's always been one of my favourites.'

'Really?' He raised his eyebrows. He didn't quite say *Extraordinary*, but I could sense it hovering there. The St Cecilia was popular with customers at the time: commissioned in 1605 as an altarpiece, it caught the eye of other potential buyers, and the artist made two copies, one for the private collection of his patron Cardinal Francesco Del Monte, one for Marcantonio Doria. But there's no denying it's one of his more run-of-the-mill productions. Perhaps he got bored, wanted to move on to something else.

That was one of the many mysteries surrounding *Partir, c'est mourir un peu*. Why, out of all the pictures in the Louvre, pick that one? It wasn't famous or symbolic like the Mona Lisa, which had been so resoundingly stolen from the same gallery twenty-eight years earlier. Far from it. At that time, no one thought much of Caravaggio – not even at his best. Nowadays, of course, the art world can't get enough of him. So modern, darling – that astounding naturalism and originality, that sense of theatre. And of course that undisguised sexuality – all those come-hither boys. But in 1937 the St Cecilia was a second-rank work by a little-regarded painter.

13

'I used to look at it when I went to stay with my grand-mother. My mother's mother. She lived in Paris.'

My grandmother lived on avenue Foch, and she's the one I have to blame for my monstrous first name. I think my parents hoped that calling me after her would encourage her to leave me something in her will. And so she did: five hundred pounds, or its equivalent in francs, like all the other grandchildren. I was fourteen at the time – I couldn't understand my parents' disappointment. Five hundred pounds seemed like a lot of money to me. But none of us ever saw any actual dosh. She very sensibly spent everything before she died. And more. The apartment only just covered the debts. So I was Regina in vain.

'Why don't we go to the Louvre?' said my mother one rainy afternoon. 'I haven't been there for years.' And there it was – love at first sight: my first experience of the trans-forming power of art. At that time I had a sort of ongoing romantic serial story that ran inside my head at night before I went to sleep, and from that moment the Angel was one of its chief protagonists (the other, I need hardly add, *not* being St Cecilia). Of course I knew nothing then about Caravaggio – least of all his supposed sexual ori-entation. I probably didn't know such a thing as sexual orientation existed. But whichever way that Angel swung he was a sexy creature. He appears in several of Caravaggio's pictures, doubtless one of his fancy boys. In this one he is naked to the waist, with pouting lips, gleam-ing muscular shoulders and macho black-feathered wings. He hangs in mid-flight in the picture's top left-hand cor-ner, while from the lower right St Cecilia gazes over her shoulder into his eyes. She is dressed as a Roman aristo-crat in a rich red silk dress, low-cut and trimmed at the shoulders with white fur, and surrounded by the instru-ments that denote her identity: in her hands a lute, at her feet a violin and an open music book, behind her a harp. A mysterious ray, possibly the light of holiness, emanates from the picture's top left-hand corner, suffusing the Angel and bathing St Cecilia in its glow. I remember thinking

14

what a ninny she looked. He was wasted on her. I couldn't take my eyes off him.

Later, when I did art history, I naturally gravitated towards Caravaggio. That's when I first came across *Partir, c'est mourir un peu*.

Everyone assumed the Surrealists had done it – everything about the affair carried their stamp. But they never claimed it, and no one ever knew for sure. In fact it was a while before anyone even noticed it had gone. The thief or thieves left an *On Loan* sign in the space where it had previously hung, and people thought no more about it. Then three days later two photographs were posted to *Le Figaro*. One showed the picture, still in its frame, leaning against the wall beneath the *On Loan* sign; in the second it was unframed but still on its stretcher, propped against the fountain in the Jardin du Luxembourg. Above it a board read: *Partir, c'est mourir un peu, Martyr, c'est pourrir un peu*, which might be translated as 'To part is to die a little, Martyrs get high a little'.

Over the next six weeks, fifteen of these teasing photographs appeared. The picture seemed to be engaged in a sort of dance, zigzagging from one side of Paris to the other: beside the canal de l'Ourcq, on a stone picnic table in the forest of Fontainebleau, at St Germain-en-Laye, propped against a baluster on the great terrace overlooking Paris, in front of a market stall in rue Mouffetard . . . By this time, of course, the police were involved. But they never caught the photographer/thief at his audacious work. It was whispered, though no one knew quite where the whisper started, that all the photos had been taken before anyone even realized the picture had gone. There was nothing on the usual art-theft grapevines – the inevitable gossip, of course, but no real substance. The insurance company offered a reward for any information leading to its recovery. But no one replied.

And then one day towards the middle of June, it re-appeared. When the attendant arrived, the canvas, no longer on its stretcher but otherwise undamaged, was waiting for him on a chair. Beside it was a sheet of paper. On one side, a typed message said *Thanks for the loan*; the other bore the familiar punning couplet: *Partir, c'est mourir un peu, Martyr, c'est pourrir un peu.*

The same day, an anonymous booklet appeared in all the left bank bookshops. On the cover, the mysterious legend was splashed redly over a hitherto unseen photograph of the picture, propped against an anonymous white wall. Inside, without comment, was the sequence of photographs that had been sent to *Le Figaro*.

About a month later, on 12th July, the affair took a further and decidedly sinister turn. That day the body of the Surrealist poet and painter Robert de Beaupré was discovered hanging in his studio at 72 rue d'Assas. On the table beside the body lay a copy of the pamphlet, and a note which read: *Partir, c'est mourir un peu.*

After that people assumed Beaupré had stolen the picture, though of course he might simply have co-opted the incident for his own ends. Either way, his death gave the affair a certain poetic completeness. André Breton's subsequent essay on the beauty of violent death became one of Surrealism's classic writings, and Beaupré took his place in the Surrealist suicides' pantheon. As for the booklet, it soon became a collector's item. Only one hundred were printed, of which most soon vanished, as such things do. The copy I had found at the fête was one of the few that remained.

At the auction house, that would have been the point: rarity equals cash. But I'd got tired of the money bit. Surely there had to be more to art than what it was worth? From where I presently stood, in a dingy office with a view of rooftops and drainpipes and unimpeded aural access to the soundstage that is now Trafalgar Square, my pamphlet possessed ramifications and possibilities. If one were to bring the three versions of the Caravaggio together, they might make the core of a good small exhibition. They had never been seen together, and the Surrealist link offered rich possibilities for associated exhibits. When I got back

16

from Caroline's, I spent the morning concocting a proposal. Then I forgot about it, and took on enough work to drown thought.

I found the Director lurking by a window – one of three, he could take his pick. Sir Anthony Malahide, no less, though no one called him that – he was either Tony or TM. The younger staff members tied themselves in knots to avoid addressing him by name. I, however, had no difficulty in this respect. He'd been a graduate student when I was in my first year at university. We'd even had a mild flirtation, though it never came to anything. Sex wasn't his bag, or not of any variety I could offer. Anyhow, he wasn't my age-group. Even in his twenties he was middle-aged. Now he really was middle-aged, it suited him beautifully. 'Oh, Reggie,' he said, his rising intonation suggesting, as always, that this wholly expected and pre-arranged visit was in fact a delightful surprise. 'Thanks for coming. I'm afraid I don't seem to see very much of you – you know how it is . . . I hope you're enjoying life here?'

'Absolutely,' I said politely, which as far as professional life went was perfectly true. 'Glad you liked my idea.' That was when we had the conversation about my grandmother.

He emerged from his window and sat down behind his desk, a vast mahogany number. On it there was a copy of my proposal, something that looked like, and almost certainly was, a Roubiliac bust, and a phone. Nothing else. He tapped the proposal. 'What do you think?'

I sat down myself, in a large leather armchair. He knew what I thought. That was why I was there. But it was always like that with Tony. Before you could start the actual minuet there were necessary flourishes to be got through, bows and curtseys and ornamental figures. 'I think it could be rather good,' I said, after due consideration.

'The Louvre,' he went on, as if I hadn't spoken. 'You'll need to talk to Antoine Rigaut. He's in charge of their Italian collection. Do you know him?'

'I know the name, obviously. I don't think we've actually met.'

'Oh well, I can help you there. And the Getty should be fairly straightforward. About this other one, though. Private hands, I think you say.' He pulled the proposal towards him and put on his spectacles. Another dance move: he knew perfectly well what was in it.

'Yes.'

'Any idea where?'

You had to hand it to old Tony. He might seem vague, but of course that was just a front – vagueness doesn't get you the top job. And true to form he'd unerringly fingered the weak point in my apparently seamless proposal. There certainly *were* three versions of the picture. The commission for the Santa Cecilia altarpiece was documented, as was its removal by Berenson three hundred years later. We know Del Monte had one because the Barberini family paid 900 scudos for it when the Del Monte collection was sold after the Cardinal's death in 1655. And when the Getty bought theirs, that was the first time it had left the Doria palazzo since its well-attested delivery there by the painter himself. Two of these pictures were shown in a Caravaggio exhibition at an independent gallery in 1952, soon after his return to fashion: the one now in the Louvre and the Del Monte/Barberini version. The exhibition's catalogue, however, listed only a 'private collection', with no further details. Since this was in Paris, it seemed possible the collection might be in France. But the gallery's owner had died in 1990, and I hadn't yet been able to locate anyone else who had had anything to do with the show. There were no auction records for such a picture, and it had made no further appearances. Nor was it on any registers. Finding it would be just the kind of coup that draws the public: long-lost picture identified, the newspapers would be all over us. But without it, my exhibition didn't really exist.

I looked him in the eye. 'I think I may be on its track.'

'Good. Excellent. Let me know how it goes. As soon as you find it, we can set a date.'

'Should I pursue the others in the meantime?'

'Why don't you? Then when the time comes we'll be ready to go.'

Now that the business part of the interview was over he actually looked at me (rather than my feet, or the view of Trafalgar Square) for the first time since I'd entered the room. 'I gather you split up with Joe.'

'Yes – in September.'

'I'm sorry to hear that. I always thought you two seemed rather well suited. Ah well.' He grinned, and for a second became once more the young man I'd known. 'Perhaps this'll help take your mind off it. Best of luck. And don't forget to keep me up to date.'

The Surrealists were great believers in chance and co-incidence. And that was how I saw the pamphlet: a sort of rainbow, a sign of hope from heaven. Something to cling on to. Even if it didn't lead me back to Joe, it might be a way to get over him. All I need do was follow its trail – with any luck to the third Caravaggio, or we were sunk. 'You're not still on about that exhibition of yours?' people would say later. They clearly thought I was slightly un-balanced, and they were probably right. What pushed me on during those months had very little to do with rationality.

I assured the Director that I'd keep him abreast of every development, and left his office feeling better than for weeks.

3

Paris, June

Joe and I had agreed not to contact each other 'until things
simmered down,' as he put it. I bit my lip and held out,
though his by-line was a constant painful reminder that
somewhere in the city he continued to flourish. Six months
passed, then nine, and still he didn't phone. Finally I grew
tired of waiting and called him at work. It was so easy. Just
press a few buttons, and there he was, as though we'd
never parted. He sounded surprised and not particularly
pleased to hear me.

'Oh, Reg – I thought we'd agreed we wouldn't do this?'

'We said we'd wait. It's been nine months.'

'Did we? Christ, is it really that long? I suppose it is . . .
Well, how are you doing? OK?'

Restraining myself from emotional outbursts, I told him
about the exhibition. Things were not going smoothly. I'd
put in my requests to the Louvre and the Getty – in principle would they loan their versions – and in principle
they'd agreed. But the missing picture was still missing.
And just last week, halfway through June, my opposite
number at the Louvre had indicated that some mysterious
difficulty had arisen. I hadn't been able to sort it out by
phone or email, or even make out what it was. All anyone
would say was that there was *'un petit problème'*. But
though small, it seemed distressingly obstinate. I was

going to have to go over and deal with it in person. Confront their top man.

'Anyone I should know?' Joe asked politely. I knew that tone of voice – just filling in time till he could decently hang up.

'I don't expect so. Antoine Rigaut. He's a friend of Tony Malahide's.'

'Rigaut?' He suddenly sounded interested. 'Is he related to the Interior Minister?'

'The Interior Minister?'

'The one that's been mouthing off about the riots. You must have noticed.'

Naturally I'd noticed. The French banlieues were ablaze, and the rioters, feeling their strength, had begun to move their protests to city centres. Some minister – presumably the one Joe had in mind – had been making inflammatory remarks. I was due in Paris the following Tuesday, and had been wondering whether I'd have to postpone my trip.

'His name's Rigaut,' Joe said. 'Jean-Jacques Rigaut. A right bastard. He's aiming for the presidency, of course. Well, they all are. But he obviously thinks this is his big moment. He's as crooked as they come, but no one will say anything. They're all watching their backs in case he actually comes to power.'

'I didn't know you were interested in French politics.'

'I'm interested in politics. You can see the same sort of thing happening here. It's a sort of low-level civil war.'

'I don't imagine they're related. There are probably thousands of Rigauts in Paris.'

'You never know,' said Joe. 'They may be. See what you can find out, anyhow.'

It wasn't exactly a declaration of love. But at least it was an excuse to speak to him again.

As it happened, Jean-Jacques Rigaut was on the news that night – and of course, this time I noticed his name. Otherwise he was unmemorable, a suave figure in expensive casuals uttering reassuring platitudes against some

21

neutral background. It was the usual kind of interview – the kind that tells you absolutely nothing.

Tuesday's early morning news said nothing about riots, so I assumed Paris was open for business as usual. London was dull and muggy with promises of rain: the nation's television screens would soon be filled with pictures of plastic-covered tennis courts. But in Paris the sun shone. I took the metro from Gare du Nord to Châtelet, had a pizza and a bock on a café terrace, then strolled along the river towards the Louvre and my meeting.

The person I'd been dealing with was called Marie-France Dachy. We were due to meet at two thirty. But before that, I thought I'd pay St Cecilia a quick visit to check she was still safely in place. However, when I arrived at the spot she wasn't there.

Surely this was the room?

Was this the problem they wanted to discuss – that she'd been stolen, again?

A second later, through the doorway opposite, I glimpsed a corner of the familiar composition – violin, music, harp, the saint's red dress. There must have been a general rehanging of that section. I breathed again.

When I arrived in front of the picture, it was oddly disappointing. Compared with its neighbours – the Card-Sharps and the Gipsy Fortune-Teller, both so brilliantly observed and executed – the St Cecilia seemed rather un-interesting: a touch wooden, lacking drama and fluidity. If I hadn't known it was impossible – the picture came via Berenson, for God's sake, and he'd taken it from the church it had been commissioned for – I'd almost have thought it was by another artist.

Well, even Caravaggio had his off days – or perhaps it was just me getting older. I'd recently experienced similar letdowns rereading novels that had entranced me in my teens. But it didn't matter. This wasn't an exhibition about a painter's best works. It was about all sorts of quite other things – repetition, resonances, contrasting aims and tradi-tions. I moved on, into a room of Dutch interiors, sat on a

22

bench and called Marie-France. I told her where I was, and she said she'd be with me in five minutes.

I'd never actually met Marie-France – all our dealings had been via email or telephone. She had one of those quick, clear French voices, and I'd expected a person to match – neat, compact, sharply dressed. But she was quite unlike my imaginings. Far from being trim and brisk, the person who now approached was plump, bespectacled, and artistically clothed in a sort of reddish-brown surplice, with a matching bandanna and an African-looking necklace of large dark-brown seeds – cocoa-beans, they looked like – and gold wire. When she saw me she smiled, but no smile could disguise the look of alarm that crossed her face. Evidently she too was the victim of disappointed expectations. 'Régine!' she exclaimed, shaking my hand. 'How delightful to meet you at last. Somehow I'd imagined you younger.'

What did she mean, that such a slight exhibition as mine could only be the work of some junior person? I smiled stonily, and followed her down through labyrinthine basement corridors to her office, a small, airless, white-painted box with just enough room for a desk and two chairs: the usual behind-the-scenes squalor. 'Welcome to my palace,' she said, indicating one of the chairs. 'Coffee?'

The coffee came from a machine, and was terrible. I took a sip, put it down, and said, 'So tell me about this problem. What is it, exactly?'

Marie-France looked flustered and began telling her seeds, perhaps invoking the help of some voodoo goddess. 'Normally this kind of thing is quite straightforward,' she said unhappily.

'So I thought.' The words came out sounding rather stern. But stern was what I felt. What Marie-France needed was a swift injection of backbone.

'We lend pictures all the time. It was all going ahead. And then last month there was a departmental meeting.' She paused, as though wondering how to put whatever it was she had to say next. 'And he said no. We couldn't lend

23

it after all, out of the question. Just like that, wouldn't discuss it.'

'*Who* said this?' For God's sake.

'Monsieur Rigaut.'

I couldn't believe it. 'He said *no*? But he's only just said yes. What's going on?'

'He didn't say.'

'Didn't you ask?'

She shook her head, and the seeds clattered menacingly. 'He wasn't in that sort of mood. He's been very touchy lately. He just moved the meeting on.'

I couldn't believe this. It was crazy. I told her so, and she raised her hands in a gesture of helplessness. 'I thought, a week, I'll go and see him, he'll be in a better mood, I can find out what's going on. There must be a mistake. There's no reason – we've lent Caravaggios before – we've lent *this* one. It's unheard of. *Tout à fait inouï.*'

'But he must have given you some reason.'

'He didn't, that's what I'm telling you. He just announced it. And now he's gone off somewhere.'

'Gone off? Where to?'

She shrugged miserably. 'No one seems to know. I kept thinking, tomorrow he'll be back, I'll speak to him before Régine comes. But he's still away.' She shook her head complicitly, inviting me to share a sigh at the wicked ways of this evil old world, in which impossible men put blameless underlings in untenable positions. But I didn't feel inclined to sympathize. I was trying to take in the full extent of this disaster. If we couldn't borrow the Louvre's picture, then my exhibition was done for. Of course Rigaut's unreasonable behaviour wasn't Marie-France's fault. But I didn't feel sympathetic. In fact it was all I could do not to kick her. I'd feel better, and she might even stop sighing and go on to kick someone else. Kick and kick again, until the kick finally reached its rightful destination. That way, eventually, something might get done. Or not. Probably not.

'Is he often like this?'

'Not really. He's unpredictable, everyone knows that, but not unreasonable. You can work with him. *Normalement*. But this – *c'est tout à fait anormale*,' Marie-France said. Beneath that arty exterior, she was clearly hot on normality.

'Has anyone tried to find him?' I asked.

'Of course. His secretary rang him at home, nothing. And his mobile is turned off.'

'How about his wife?'

'He isn't married.'

'His partner, then?'

'Obviously, I don't know him that well. But just at present, I believe there's nobody. He lives alone.'

'Where, as a matter of interest?'

'I'm not sure,' Marie France said. It was obviously a lie: her face had turned beetroot-red.

'His secretary must know,' I insisted.

She shook her head firmly. 'It's no good. He's not there.'

'Has anyone been round to see?'

'I'm sure they have.' She fingered her seeds again. Perhaps she was saying a little prayer that I'd go away. I couldn't understand why she hadn't tried to stop me coming in the first place. Nor, now, could she – that was pretty apparent.

I stood up. 'Well then, that seems to be that.'

Marie-France looked relieved. 'I'm terribly sorry.'

'Oh, so am I,' I assured her in my crispest voice. 'Is there anyone else I could talk to? Who's his deputy?'

'It's Charles Rey, but –'

'Charlie Rey – of course, I heard he'd got a job here.'

'You know him?' She sounded alarmed.

'For years,' I assured her.

In fact that was a little misleading: we'd met once or twice at conferences years ago – during one particular meeting in Ghent, I recalled being puzzled, and rather put out, that he hadn't made a pass. I still remembered my first sight of the great Van Eyck altarpiece, with Charlie in full excited explicatory flow.

She shook her head firmly. 'He won't be able to do anything about this. It's a matter for the head of department.'

'But he's a colleague. He might know where Monsieur Rigaut lives.'

Marie-France's round face reddened once again. She looked as though she might be about to burst into tears. 'Really, I'm sure there's no way he could help.'

I could have sworn she knew more than she was telling me. Perhaps Rigaut had confided in her – 'Now, Marie-France, I'm trusting you to deal with this – get rid of the woman, there's a good girl' – something like that, and she was afraid that if it emerged she *hadn't* dealt with me, that I'd persisted in asking awkward questions, she'd be marked down as a loser, her promotion prospects blocked . . .

'I'll take a chance. Why don't you tell me where his office is? Is he on this floor?'

If we had to work together again I'd be sorry I'd been so brutal. But she could hardly pretend she didn't know where her colleague's office was. After a minute she gave in. 'If you go down the corridor and turn left it's on your right. His name's on the door. Shall I come with you?'

And muddy the waters? I'd met people like Marie-France before. You have some perfectly straightforward request, some clear line of thought, and then they come along and throw grey mists over everything. 'No, thanks, I'll be fine.'

It was by now three o'clock: not exactly early in the day. Even so, some people might still be out at lunch. But perhaps today was a sandwich-at-the-desk day. I walked down the corridor as instructed, and passed a door whose nameplate read *Dr Antoine Rigaut* and below that *Dr Charles Rey*. I knocked, a little surprised. Surely Rigaut would have an office to himself?

'*Entrez*,' called a female voice.

Inside, a smartly dressed middle-aged woman looked at me inquiringly from behind a crowded desk. To her right and left were two doors, one, presumably, leading into

Rigaut's office, one into Charlie's. So only the secretary was shared.

'*Bonjour, madame*. Is Dr Rey around?'

'Do you have an appointment?'

'I'm afraid I don't. I came from London today to see Monsieur Rigaut about a loan for an exhibition. There's been some sort of misunderstanding, and I hoped he and I could sort it out, but I understand he's not around just now. Charlie and I are old friends and I thought it might be a good idea to speak to him. If he's available, obviously.'

'Unfortunately he isn't. He's out this afternoon. He may pop back at the end of the day. You could try again around five thirty.'

'Thanks. Perhaps I will. I don't suppose you know where Monsieur Rigaut is?'

She shook her head. 'I'm afraid not.'

'I hope nothing's wrong,' I said politely.

'I expect he'll turn up. He's gone away somewhere and forgotten to tell us, that's all. It happens ... Shall I tell Charlie you called?'

I pulled out a business card and put it on the desk. 'Perhaps you could give him this?'

'Of course.' The secretary read out, 'Dr Regina Lee.'

'That's me. I'm afraid I don't know your name.'

'Desvergnes. Janine Desvergnes. I look after ...' She gestured all-embracingly. Clearly this was, in all but name, *her* department.

What now? The afternoon, which should have been so satisfyingly and enjoyably filled with detailed discussions, stretched ahead. I wondered whether to ask Madame Desvergnes for Rigaut's address – she must certainly know it. But she might not want to divulge the information, and then indirect methods might be more difficult to implement. I said, diffidently, 'I don't suppose you have a Paris telephone directory I could look at?'

'Business or private?'

'Private.'

She fished it out from a shelf somewhere near her knees. 'You can use the table over there.'

I sat down with the fat volume and opened it at R. There might be a good many Rigauts, but it was worth a try. However, I was out of luck. The first name on the list was a Rigaut, Bernard. No Antoine Rigaut was listed, nor any Rigaut, A. Perhaps he had chosen to be ex-directory. However, as I scanned down the list for any initial A – Antoine might, after all, be my quarry's second name – something else caught my eye. A Rigaut, J., was listed as living at 72 rue d'Assas.

72 rue d'Assas – it rang a bell. Wasn't that where Robert de Beaupré had lived – or at least, died? 'Yesterday, at 72 rue d'Assas, a body was found hanging . . .'

I looked again at the directory. Maybe my imagination was playing tricks, over-eager to compensate for a frustrating day. Not that I'd been thinking about rue d'Assas at that particular moment. But no – there it still was.

There was probably no connection with the absent Head of Paintings, still less the Surrealist suicide. But here at last was a small stroke of Surrealist chance. And as such, not to be ignored. Here was a possible entrée to the building. I might even get to see the room where the fabled suicide had actually occurred. If so, I would at least have salvaged something from my trip to Paris. I noted down the number, and handed back the book. 'Thanks.'

'Find what you wanted?' Madame Desvergnes inquired politely.

'Yes, thank you.'

I was about to take my leave when I remembered Joe's request. What with one thing and another – general dismay, irritation with Marie-France – it had slipped my mind. 'I was wondering – a stupid thing, really, I was looking at the papers this morning and it struck me Monsieur Rigaut had the same name as the Minister. Are they related?'

'Yes, they're brothers. But better not mention it to

Antoine. They don't see eye to eye politically – he prefers not to be reminded of it, especially now.'

'Thanks, I'll remember.'

'Shall I tell Charlie you'll be back?'

'Perhaps I'll ring first to see if he's here.'

'That would probably be sensible,' Madame Desvergnes agreed, and we bade each other *au revoir*.

When I left the room, Marie-France was lurking in the corridor on the pretence of filling her glass at the water-cooler. 'Was he there?' she asked anxiously.

'No, he's out this afternoon.'

She looked relieved. 'He wouldn't have been able to tell you anything.'

I said coolly, 'Probably not. I'll be in touch.' She wanted absolution, to be told it wasn't her fault, that it didn't matter, that everything would come out in the wash. But I did not feel forgiving.

'I'm so sorry . . .'

The words followed me windily down the corridor. If I saw much more of Marie-France and her seeds I was going to lose my temper properly. And that would never do.

4

Rue d'Assas, June

I bought an ice-cream from a kiosk, and sat on a bench in the Tuileries garden to consider my next move. Should I call Joe and tell him what I'd just found out? The fact that his Rigaut and mine were not just brothers, but political adversaries, might well interest him. But until Antoine Rigaut reappeared, it was hard to see quite how the information might be used. So, on to the rue d'Assas.

It was now three forty; if I started at once I ought to arrive just after four. J. Rigaut would almost certainly be out at work. But I preferred not to know this for certain before arriving on the spot, and in any case, I wanted to see the house where the suicide had taken place.

I'd never been to the rue d'Assas, but number 72 was extremely unlikely to be a private house. It would almost certainly be an *immeuble*, an apartment block built around a courtyard. Even if my man (or woman) wasn't actually there, I might be able to get into the block on the pretext of visiting him or her, and talk to the concierge. That was the person I really needed to see – the one who would know where the premises' suicides had taken place. I checked the route on my street map: it really wasn't far, just across the Pont des Arts and down rue Bonaparte. And what could be more delightful than a leisurely stroll through Paris in the June sun?

Rue d'Assas turned out to be narrow and oppressive, hedged in by walls of tall buildings. Mostly, as I'd anticipated, they were apartment blocks, with small shops on the street frontage. Number 72 was a cliff-like structure of blackened post-Haussmann stone. It had the usual big black porte cochère with a smaller door inset. Once all you had to do to get into these buildings was press a buzzer, and the door unlatched. Now, though, the doors are mostly controlled by a keypad, whose combination only the residents know.

I hate phoning people I don't know. Still, now I was here it would be ridiculous not to try. Students from nearby university buildings eddied around me as though I was a lamp standard. I took out the sheet of paper with J. Rigaut's number and dialled.

I didn't expect an answer. But to my surprise, after two rings the phone was picked up. *'Oui, allo?'* said a bored male voice.

Absurdly, this unexpected development left me somewhat at a loss. I had my approach to the concierge all prepared, but I'd been so certain my immediate quarry would be out that I hadn't really thought how I was going to explain myself to him or her.

'Monsieur Rigaut?' I said, feebly.

'Oui.' He sounded impatient – as though he might ring off at any moment. He probably thought I was a double-glazing salesperson.

I said, very quickly before he could cut me off, 'You don't know me – my name's Regina Lee, I work for the National Gallery in London. It's a bit complicated – would it be possible to come and see you? Or I could buy you a cup of coffee, if you prefer.'

'The National Gallery in London?' He sounded startled, which was hardly surprising.

'Yes. I know it sounds strange.'

'Why the devil does the National Gallery want to see me?'

'It's a bit of a long story. That's why I thought it would be easier to tell you face-to-face.'

31

There was a moment's silence on the other end of the line. Then he said, 'All right, why not? When did you have in mind?'

'Now, if you're not too busy.'

'Now? Where are you, exactly? Not in London, I assume.'

I said, 'No, I'm in Paris. Right outside, actually. In the rue d'Assas.'

Monsieur Rigaut gave a snort of laughter. 'You'd better come in, then. I'll give you the number – no, I'll come out and find you, that'll be easier.'

He rang off, and three minutes later the door opened to reveal one of the tallest, thinnest young men I'd ever seen. He had floppy brown hair, matching olive skin, and bright grey eyes, and his jeans and T-shirt made a perfectly straight line from head to toe.

Whatever I'd been expecting, it wasn't this. My assumption, for some reason – perhaps because I associated the name with Antoine Rigaut, whom I'd never met, but who was certainly not young – had been of middle age. He glanced around, spotted me, noted (I suppose) the phone in my hand and said, 'Regina Lee?'

'Monsieur Rigaut?'

'Manu,' he said, holding out a hand for me to shake. I wondered who the J. was. His father, perhaps. With the other hand he held the door open. 'Come in. I assume this isn't a joke?'

'No, it isn't a joke.' I dug a business card from my bag. He glanced at it, stuffed it into a pocket, and motioned me through.

Inside was the usual dark foyer, with its staircase and lift cage and concierge's window. But my thin young man strode straight through into the court beyond, in which stood a row of tiny houses, each with its own patch of garden, as if a village street had been set down in the middle of the city. I followed him past trim gates and billowing greenery to a perfect, double-fronted miniature villa of pale stone, trim and sprucely painted, with a shiny black iron gate and mansard windows in a grey slate roof. Big bushes of strongly scented magenta roses grew on either side of a neat gravel path, and tubs of pink geraniums flanked the front door, which was approached by a flight of three steps and painted black to match the gate. Manu bounded up the path, and pushed the door open; evidently he had left it on the latch. It was taller than him, but only just.

The door led directly into a small, white-carpeted salon, whose manicured perfection exactly matched that of the villa's exterior. It was panelled in two shades of blue-grey, pale and paler; under the window stood two small armchairs and a two-seater sofa upholstered in cream and blue stripes; further back there was a round glass table and two chairs of tubular steel and white leather. Three plates depicting explicitly drawn lovers in various permutations hung on the back wall. They looked like Picassos, but of course that was out of the question. What young man has Picasso ceramics on his wall? None I had ever met. Above a small grey marble fireplace, a gilt-framed mirror reflected a somewhat dishevelled and crumpled Reggie. My linen suit, in the annoying way of linen, had acquired deep creases, and my cheeks were distressingly pink.

Manu disappeared behind a sort of breakfast bar, which divided the salon from a small kitchen area, opened a large fridge and burrowed inside it. That, at least, showed the young man's touch, being quite empty except for several bottles of beer. *'Eh bien*, Dr Regina Lee from the National Gallery in London. Why don't we have a beer while you tell me what this is all about?'

'That would be wonderful,' I said gratefully. The walk had been longer and hotter than I had imagined.

On the table – apart from the beer, the only sign of independent life in this almost over-perfect space – lay two letters addressed to M. Emmanuel Rigaut, and bearing the logo of INSEAD, the European business school at Fontainebleau. He must be a student there – or a member of staff, of course, but that seemed unlikely. I couldn't imagine this languid young man teaching people about flowcharts and branding opportunities.

Emmanuel Rigaut – didn't I know that name? But before I could identify it my host reappeared with two open beers. He handed one over, and flopped back into one of the armchairs. '*Alors?*'

I dropped into the other chair and took a pull. After the hot, dusty walk the icy beer tasted wonderful. 'I'm trying to think where to begin.'

'Unfortunately, there I can't help you. You speak excellent French for an Englishwoman,' he observed. 'Mostly they're hopeless. I take it you are English?'

'I had a French grandmother. She was called Régine, I'm named after her. But everyone calls me Reggie.'

'Reggie.' He tried it round the tongue, pronouncing it in the French manner, with equal emphasis on both syllables. 'Like me. That's to say, I'm named after my grandfather. Emmanuel Rigaut.'

This time I remembered where I'd heard the name. 'The Surrealist photographer?'

'Exactly.' He nodded.

That would explain the Picassos. Emmanuel Rigaut must have known Picasso – all the Surrealists did. Including Robert de Beaupré.

I waited for some further remark, but none came. If there was explaining to be done, Manu evidently felt I was the one to do it – not unreasonably, in the circumstances. 'So, you were going to tell me what all this is about,' he finally said.

What, indeed. Where, in all this complex saga, was I to begin? At the rue d'Assas, perhaps, since here we were. I took a deep breath and plunged in.

'It's to do with an exhibition I'm trying to organize. It's about a painting by Caravaggio. There's more than one version, and one's in the Louvre, and in 1937 it was stolen. It was returned after a few weeks, and a famous pamphlet was printed about it, showing it photographed in all sorts of places around Paris. It was called *Partir, c'est mourir un*

34

peu. And a little while after that a young man named Robert de Beaupré was found hanging at 72 rue d'Assas, with a copy of the pamphlet beside him. If your grandfather was Emmanuel Rigaut you must know all this.'

Manu nodded.

I couldn't believe my luck. Chance, or my Angel, had led me to the very person I needed. What luck he wasn't ex-directory! Nearly everyone seemed to be, these days. I hurried on with my explanation. 'They never found out officially who stole the picture, but it was almost certainly Beaupré. I've always thought the whole thing was a sort of Surrealist artwork, with the suicide as the climax ... That's it, really. That's why I'm here. I was hoping I might be able to see the room where he – where he –'

At this point I stopped. The whole thing suddenly seemed so crass. I wondered if Robert de Beaupré had lived in this very house. It seemed quite probable, given the Surrealist connection. If so, which had been the fatal room? This one? This neat and overfinished bourgeois space? The very notion seemed unthinkable. Though doubtless it hadn't looked like this, then. And anywhere will do to hang yourself, so long as there's something to hang from and it's taller than you are.

Manu considered his beer, then said, after a while and without looking at me, 'And you thought I might know something about it?'

'It seemed possible.'

'But why? There are lots of people in this building. Why did you call me?'

I took another pull at my beer. After all that talking my mouth felt dry, and I needed to sort out my thoughts. 'Well. You know I told you I was organizing this exhibition.'

He nodded.

'OK, I'd arranged to borrow the picture that's in the Louvre, or I thought I had. That's why I'm here in Paris – to talk to the people there about the details. But when I got here, it turns out they won't lend it after all. The person in charge just said no. No reason – just no. That happened a week ago, and he hasn't been in the office since. So I thought I might try and find him at home. But no one would give me his home address. Perhaps it's policy – that wouldn't be surprising. Anyhow, he's called Rigaut – Antoine Rigaut. So I was looking through the Rigauts in the phone book, and I saw that one lived here. And I'd been meaning to come here anyway, because of Robert de Beaupré. So I called.'

He nodded absently, but gave no other sign that he'd heard a word of what I'd just said. He had finished his beer and was lying back in the little armchair, long legs stretched out in front of him, pale brown hair flopping over his pale brown forehead, fixing me somewhat unnervingly with those bright grey eyes. Above his head the lovers on the Picasso plate beatifically fondled each other's private parts. It felt as though we were engaged in a sort of game: I had to ask the questions, and if they were the right questions, he might give me the answers. I wondered if he was like that all the time – in bed, for instance. Not much fun for his partner, if so.

'Was this Robert de Beaupré's house?'

The fruit machine whirred: ker-ching, three in a row. Manu nodded. 'Yes.'

'And was this – the room?'

'No.'

'But it did happen here?'

'Yes, upstairs.' He nodded towards an open-tread staircase at the back of the room. 'He had his studio there.' He paused, then (perhaps wanting to move the discussion along a little) volunteered a piece of information. 'My grandmother found him. She was his sister.'

'His sister!'

He nodded. I tried to imagine what it must have been like – to walk into your house and find your brother ... 'God! How awful.'

'Yes.'

'Your grandmother – then Robert de Beaupré's sister married Emmanuel Rigaut?'

'Bravo!'

I opened my mouth to make some sharp reply, but caught myself in time. He was doing me a favour, after all. If he wanted to play games, then I'd just have to play along.

'Did she know – I mean, presumably he *was* the thief?'

'*Naturellement.* Everyone knew who was involved. Everyone's always known.'

'Except the police,' I said, glancing surreptitiously at my watch. It was after five: soon it would be too late to catch Charles Rey. But this was more important. I could phone Rey any time, from London.

'Oh, the police knew. It's their job, *non?*'

'But no one was arrested.'

'You can't exactly arrest a corpse. The picture was returned. No harm was done. What would have been the point of making a fuss? Perhaps they thought the family had suffered enough.'

'I'm amazed the police were so tactful,' I said. 'In England they aren't.'

'They probably are, simply you don't hear. That's the point, isn't it?' He raised his eyebrows and waved towards the staircase. 'So, you want to look at the fatal spot? I believe it was just in front of the window. You can photograph it if you like. Perhaps if I put a hook in we could take parties round. The original hook ... The tourism of death. What d'you think? If the photo's good enough you could make it part of your exhibition.'

I let that pass: what could one say? Instead I tried another question. 'Did the house look like this then?'

'I don't expect so. My grandmother had it all done up a few years ago.'

'It belongs to her?'

Manu nodded.

So she was still alive: perhaps she was the J. Rigaut of the phone book. 'I'd love to see her. Do you think that might be possible?'

'Why not? She doesn't come to Paris much, though.'

I opened my mouth to ask where, in that case, his grandmother *did* live, but before I could do so he moved the conversation on. 'Did you want to look upstairs?'

Once again he'd sidestepped me. But I could hardly let the opportunity slip. 'Of course.'

With an exaggerated, courtly gesture, he indicated the staircase.

The upstairs room – it was the middle floor of the house: the staircase, zigzagging back on itself, continued upwards – was as charming and impersonal as the salon. It was a bedroom, also white-carpeted, with wainscoting and built-in panelled cupboards in shades of pale blue-grey. There was a large bed with a bright green cover, over which hung a picture that might have been a small Chirico, of the early period. To the right a door opened into a bathroom; to the left, a window, curtained in the same green fabric as the bedcover, looked on to the little front garden. The ceiling was blandly white and smoothly plastered. Like everything about Robert de Beaupré's fatal exploit, it had been efficiently covered over.

Manu's voice floated up from below. 'Are you going to take a photo?'

I always carry a little camera in my bag, but what would be the point? This might be the same space, but it certainly wasn't the same room. 'I don't think so.'

'Fine, whatever you want.'

I tried to picture the room as it had been, with the swinging body. I wondered how tall Robert de Beaupré had been. Manu would have a job hanging himself in here.

Downstairs, the phone began to ring. I heard him answer it – '*Oui, allo?*' Then, in the first display I'd heard of anything approaching emotion, he said, '*Quoi?*' This was followed by a series of questions – 'Where?' 'You're quite sure?' and a series of Yeses and Of courses. After a while he said, '*A bientôt, alors,*' and I heard him replace the phone. Only then did I venture downstairs.

Manu was striding about the room, as though trying to gather his thoughts from its various corners and crevices.

He looked stunned, thunderstruck. I said, 'Perhaps I'd better go.'

He started – whatever the phone call had been about, it had completely overlaid all memory of my presence. 'Yes. I'm sorry. Yes, there are some things I must do now.'

'Bad news?'

He shook his head like a dog in the rain, as if to slough off what he had just heard. 'My uncle's died.'

'I'm so sorry. Was he ill?'

'No, not at all. It was an accident.'

'God! Who found him – not your aunt, I hope?'

'No, no, he wasn't married ... You knew him,' Manu said, finally answering one of the questions I had failed to put. 'He was head of the Italian department at the Louvre.'

'Antoine Rigaut?' I felt the hairs on my neck stand up. 'Your uncle? When was this?'

'When?' Manu looked surprised. 'I've no idea. Yesterday, today? They just found him. Why?'

I shook my head. 'I'm so sorry. You've been very kind. If there's anything I can do for you ...'

'What could you do?' He held out his hand. '*Au revoir.*'

My head buzzed with questions I'd have liked to ask. *Who was that on the phone? What sort of accident? When did you last see him? What was he like?* But I had to choke them back. Manu had joined the ranks of the bereaved, who operate in a space and time that prohibits these worldly intrusions. We shook hands, and the door shut behind me.

Before I'd reached the garden gate, however, it opened again and I heard him call out. 'I didn't give you my grandmother's address, did I?' And he came running after me, a sheet of paper in his hand. 'Here.'

I opened my mouth to thank him, but he was already back inside the house, and had shut the door.

So that impenetrable façade had been just that – a façade. It wasn't my imagination – he had been hiding something. Before that call, he had not only shown no interest in giving me his grandmother's address – he had actively avoided doing so. Nor had he told me Antoine Rigaut was his uncle. Then he had heard of his uncle's death, and all that had changed.

To do with his father? That was something else I hadn't asked. But unless there was another brother, he must be the Minister's son. Of course there might be any number of reasons – privacy, shame – why he might not want to advertise that just now. I tried to remember what Jean-Jacques Rigaut had looked like on that television interview. I had an impression of elongation – but that might easily be post hoc, a consequence of meeting Manu. He had mostly been a huge talking head.

As the Eurostar sped northwards across the flat fields of the Pas de Calais, I took out Manu's slip of paper and laid it on the table in front of me. It was torn from a telephone pad, and contained a scribbled name, a phone number, and an address with a 24 postcode. Madame Juliette Rigaut, Château de la Jaubertie, St Front d'Argentat, 24700 Meyrignac. Where could that be? Somewhere in the south-west, most likely, where all the towns end in –ac.

Now that I had the information I'd wanted, I felt suddenly unsure what to do with it. This was hardly the moment to suggest a visit – the poor woman must be distraught. On the other hand, Manu clearly thought I should call her. And urgently. Why else had he come rushing out like that?

But perhaps I was reading too much into all this. Perhaps he'd been meaning to give me the address all along, and just thought there was no time to lose. Juliette Rigaut must be getting on. In her late eighties, perhaps even older. She might die at any moment, especially after a nasty shock like this.

Well, at any rate I'd have plenty to tell Joe. I thought how pleased he'd be, and wondered what he was doing. And realized with astonishment that I hadn't thought of him – not really *thought* of him – all afternoon.

5

Meyrignac, July

I phoned Joe as soon as I got back to London. He wasn't in the office, but I left a message saying I had news for him from Paris.

He called me that evening. 'Reg? So, what's this detective work you've been doing?'

I told him, losing confidence with every word I spoke. When it came down to it, it didn't amount to much. Antoine Rigaut had indeed been the Minister's brother, but he had died. I'd spoken to a boy who might be the Minister's son.

'Might be?'

'Well, Antoine Rigaut was his uncle. So unless there's another brother . . .'

'Didn't you ask him?'

'It wasn't like that.'

'But you feel the death's significant.'

'I think it might be. Though I've no idea why, other than what I've told you.'

'Will you go and see the old lady?'

'I suppose so.'

'You suppose so! Where's the spirit of the chase?'

'She's just lost her son. It hardly seems the moment to say I want to talk to her about the Surrealists.'

'The Surrealists?' Joe sounded mystified.

'The Surrealists,' I assured him. 'She was married to one. Her brother was one. It's to do with my exhibition. Remember?'

'Yeah, of course, your exhibition. Well, if you do go, don't forget to keep your eyes open. I kind of feel we may be on to something rather interesting.'

He didn't suggest we met. But at least we were on terms again.

Next morning, when I opened the paper, there was Rigaut's obituary.

Antoine Rigaut, who has died aged 58, was a fixture of Parisian cultural life. His father, the Surrealist photographer Emmanuel Rigaut, made his living after the war as a picture dealer, so that Antoine grew up surrounded by art and artists. He himself would have liked to be a painter, but although he had some facility, it quickly became clear that he was not talented enough to make his living in this way. Although it would have been easy for him to enter the family firm, Antoine preferred instead to devote himself to scholarship. He soon established himself as an expert on the baroque, and by his mid-forties had become head of Italian paintings at the Louvre, a post he held until his death.

Rigaut showed a particular facility for spotting masterpieces in improbable settings, and although some aspects of his career were controversial, leading to occasional fallings-out amongst his colleagues, all would agree that he left the collection distinctly stronger than when he arrived.

Rigaut never married. His mother and a younger brother survive him.

I tore the page out. Naturally, it didn't say how he'd died. For some reason, obituaries never do. You have to translate: 'suddenly' probably means an accident, 'after a long illness' equals cancer or alcoholism. But this one was giving even less away than usual. An accident, Manu had said. But what kind of accident? Perhaps the French press would be more forthcoming.

When I got to my computer at the office, I googled Rigaut's name. There were a number of other obituaries, longer, but almost as uninformative. The French style is less direct than the English, oblique, allusive, given to tailing off in suggestive ellipsis ... Both *Le Monde* and *Le Figaro* hinted at an edgy attraction to rough trade. But they didn't imply that this was related to Rigaut's death. In any case, why would a quarrel with a boyfriend have prompted Manu to give me his grandmother's address? There was also a short paragraph from the news pages of *Le Figaro*, stating that the body had been found at Rigaut's home, and that foul play was not suspected – a phrase which probably meant suicide.

Despite this frustrating lack of direct information, I did manage to glean a few references to old scandals – presumably, the 'controversial' career aspects mentioned in the English obit. There was a dubious provenance regarding a Titian – Rigaut had insisted the painting was genuine, a view which had eventually prevailed, to the extent of its being bought by the Louvre, but which was still, it seemed, strongly contested in some quarters. Also, there had been a string of lucky finds in Switzerland, apparently an improbable venue for such serendipities. Why, I could not quite make out. If you were rich and wanted to conceal the extent of your wealth, wasn't Switzerland the place to go, or at any rate to send the excess, knowing that no awkward questions would be asked? And why, in that case, should the odd escaped picture not find itself floating around Zurich, waiting to be identified by a knowledgeable eye? But these were hardly more than hints – a sense that all was not what it might have seemed. Whatever the story (and maybe there was no story) I would not find it here. The obliterating hand of *nil nisi bonum* saw to that.

The necessary phone call to Madame Rigaut loomed ineluctably. But if I didn't make it, my new line to Joe – that tender shoot – would wither irretrievably. Manu's bit of paper seemed for one horrendous moment to have vanished, but proved, after a short panic, merely to have slipped inside a file. However, when I rang the number, the woman who answered told me, in an accent so broad I could only just make out what she said, that Madame Rigaut was not at home.

I said I'd been very much hoping to speak to her, and wondered when she'd be back.

In a week, said the woman. She was staying with her son.

I thought: her son's dead. But of course she had another son – Manu's father. 'The Minister?'

'The Minister.'

That, at least, was one question answered. I said, 'I'm going to be in Meyrignac in a couple of weeks. Do you think she'd be able to see me then?'

The woman, who must have been a housekeeper – no secretary would speak so broadly, she pronounced 'madame' as three distinct syllables – said, 'You can try, madame.' And we left it at that.

Meyrignac's nearest airport was Bergerac. Joe offered to stand me the ticket, but I was interested in art, not politics. If any interesting facts turned up – interesting, that is, to him – then fine. But this was my trip, not his. In any case, the fare was so cheap that even my exhibition's tiny budget would probably stand the strain.

The day before my departure I called Madame Rigaut again. This time she answered the phone herself. In a dry little voice thin with age she agreed that yes, she would be home the day after tomorrow, and that yes, I could, if I wanted, come and talk to her then about the Surrealists.

'It's kind of you to see me, madame. I know it's not a good time for you.'

'Frankly, at my age it all feels much the same,' she said. 'Bad, mostly. I don't have a great deal to tell you. I hope you realize that.'

I assured her I was happy to take my chances, and we agreed that I would call on her at 10 a.m. the day follow- ing my arrival.

The south-west was a part of France I'd never been to,

but airports are airports – the same wherever you go. Bergerac's was smaller than most, a tin shed and a tent set amid flat fields of maize and sunflowers. But it possessed a car hire shack, at which in theory I'd made a reservation. Although Meyrignac had a train station, and was only fifty kilometres distant, there was no direct line from Bergerac. I'd have to change at Libourne, then wait three hours for a stopping train. We arrived just after ten; taking the train I'd arrive in Meyrignac at three, an average of ten kilometres an hour. It would almost be quicker to walk – far quicker to cycle. But there was no bike hire counter, so a car it had to be. I signed for the smallest vehicle on offer – a Fiat Panda – checked the route on the map, and set off into the shining countryside.

Unlike England's permanent traffic jam, the roads seemed almost empty, and on the back lanes into which I soon turned there was no traffic at all, give or take the odd tractor. A perfumed waft blew in the open window from a field where new-mown hay lay in neat green rows. I stopped the car, got out and luxuriously inhaled the fragrant, fume-free breath of summer. High in the sky two big hawks rode the updraughts, calling to each other like lost souls. An oak wood at the field's edge photosynthesized in the sunshine. I was filled with an unfamiliar feeling that I couldn't at once name, but which I eventually identified as calm.

A little less than an hour later, I arrived at Meyrignac. When I got there, I could see why there'd been no cars on the road. They were all here. Tuesday was market day, and the only free parking space almost on the town's edge, beside the station – not that that placed it very far out. The station itself was standard ministry issue: three arched and glazed double doors placed symmetrically in a flat cream façade, neat seats and shelters, planked pedestrian gangway leading across the rails, stationmaster's vegetable garden. At my grandmother's there had been a model town set with a station just like this, and as soon as I saw it I knew exactly what the rest of the place would be like.

There'd be a grey-shuttered Hôtel de la Poste, a Café du Commerce with brown plastic tables outside, a gravelled champ de Mars where they played pétanque under the plane trees, a church, a mairie with a tricolour and *Liberté Egalité Fraternité* over the grand front entrance, a square with a fountain. There they would all be, and there, as I made my way into town, they were, so that this place, which I'd never seen before, felt oddly familiar, as though it was already part of my life.

My route brought me into the main square, today filled with market stalls. Beneath a plaque marking the spot where twelve *meyrignacois* had been executed by the Germans in 1944, an ancient man in faded denims and a beret stood beside crates of farmyard fauna, cheeping chicks and ducklings, round brown quails, baby rabbits, fluffy grey goslings, all oddly interspersed with ropes of garlic, possibly a serving suggestion. Further on a row of stalls sold monstrous bras and girdles, violently coloured tops, low-cut dresses in deeply artificial fabrics, and arrays of curiously unfashionable shoes.

It was hard making headway through the throng. Judging by their faces everyone in Meyrignac was related to everyone else, and market day a big family party devoted primarily to gossip, with buying a poor second. The summer's invading foreigners stood out like light-houses. Meaty, lobster-pink sweating men and straw-hatted, pastel-bloused women towered blondly above the indigenous gnarled ancients and orange-frizzed house-wives. Dodging a wall of slow-moving baby-pushers, I made for the church tower, which could be glimpsed at the end of a winding street beyond an ancient stone archway flanked by cheese-stalls. Here was another small square, filled today by a farmers' market. Wandering in a sort of daze, I found myself at a stall announcing its produce as '*biologique*'. I was beginning to feel hungry: perhaps this would be the place to buy a picnic. Cherries, for example. Though the cherries here weren't as big and black as on one or two of the doubtless less wholesome heaps I'd noticed elsewhere. Still, size isn't everything. At least you could eat this stuff without worrying about washing off the chemicals.

By the time I reached the tourist office it was almost midday, and the girl at the counter, like everyone else in the market, was looking at her watch preparatory to closing up. She nodded when I mentioned La Jaubertie, and marked its position for me on a map: it was just south-west of the town, near a hamlet called St Front d'Argentat. She gave me the map, along with a list of local bed and breakfasts. 'This one's near St Front,' she said, pointing to the list. It was called Les Pruniers – The Plum Trees. 'Try it, it's very nice. Madame Peytoureau.'

By now I was famished, though it was only just past midday. That was only eleven o'clock, London time, but I'd made a ludicrously early start – up at four thirty to get a seven thirty plane. I found a street that ran sharply downhill to a river between ancient half-timbered houses. To the left, stone steps descended to a low embankment with a pair of benches shaded by a large willow tree. A fisherman sat immobile, cradling his rod, while the fish, ignoring his bait, drifted sideways on the current through glittering green flags of weed. Overhead, leaves twinkled hypnotically in a light breeze. I ate my lunch, lay back, and dozed.

When I awoke it was nearly two. The fisherman had disappeared, and the sun had shifted, leaving me in deep shade. Moving out into the sunshine, I called the bed and breakfast recommended by the tourist office. After five rings a woman answered. Yes, she had a room free; yes, I could come round now. She gave some complicated directions, but I knew, even as I heard them, that I was not taking them in. I'd just have to go to St Front and see what I found.

My map did not show the smaller country roads I'd now be using. For that I'd need one of the large-scale IGN maps, where even individual houses are drawn. Unfortunately, the *papeterie* where I might have bought it would not reopen till three. Still, the general direction was clear enough. Setting out, I followed a series of increasingly improbable signposts and at last found myself driving along a green-lit single-track road between thick chestnut woods. Even smaller tracks led off on either side, each with a crop of signposts bearing names that might indicate a house or a hamlet.

Eventually, to the left, a sign read *St Front d'A*. The road sloped steeply downhill, leading, after numerous twists and turns, to a scattering of more or less dilapidated houses grouped around an ancient fortified church, buttressed and blank-walled, a relic of the religious wars that once raged across this region. A volley of barks greeted the arrival of an alien car. However, not a soul moved – even the bar looked shut. Reasoning that bars never shut, I parked, got out and tried the door, but it was locked; a sign announced that Tuesday was its half-day.

Les Pruniers must be somewhere nearby, but where? I hadn't passed it on the way in, and only one road led out of the village. I drove up it, and a little way along, at a left turn, found a number of signs nailed crookedly to a tree. One read: *Les Pruniers 2 km*. Three minutes later another signpost pointed down a gravelled track that led between tall horse chestnuts to a stone arch set in a high wall.

I aimed the car through it into a square court. It was bounded on one side by the wall with the arch; the house, which was U-shaped and painted a faded apricot, formed most of the square's other three sides. An enormous magnolia grandiflora dominated the courtyard, its huge white flowers, scattered like moons amid the dark, leathery leaves, filling the air with lemony sweetness. To one side stood a dented silver people carrier. No one was in sight.

I parked beside the people carrier and got out. Immediately ahead, in the centre of the façade, was a hefty planked door. There was no sign of a bell, just a knocker in the shape of a brass hand. I knocked: from somewhere to the back of the house the inevitable dog barked. I knocked again, and stood back to wait.

The dog stopped barking, and I heard footsteps approach. Then the door swung open, to reveal a dishevelled-looking young woman wearing cut-off jeans and a blue T-shirt. She was perhaps thirty years old, with a mop of dark, curly hair tied back in a rough pony-tail, a thin-lipped, smiling mouth, and bright dark eyes. A fat black labrador, its muzzle grey with age and breathless with the effort of locomotion, followed some distance behind her, its tail furiously wagging.

'Madame Peytoureau? I'm Reggie Lee – I phoned earlier.'

'Of course – come in.' She held out a hand. 'I'm Delphine.'

The door opened on to a big farmhouse kitchen, dim and cool, with a floor of unglazed pink terracotta tiles. The dog sniffed me comprehensively, then turned and trotted wheezily through a door in the opposite wall. We followed it into a small, elegant room, half-panelled in chestnut, its floor a pattern of thick oak cross-boards and thin lengthways strips. An open french window gave on to a garden, where the dog took its place beneath a hammock slung between two plum trees, closed its eyes, and began to snore loudly.

'Do excuse him,' Delphine said. 'He's getting old.'

The plum trees were part of an orchard, from which, presumably, the house took its name. The hot air, perfumed with bursts of fragrance from the magnolia in the courtyard, echoed with the rasp of cicadas. Delphine rubbed her eyes, a juicy sound that was mildly alarming. She said, 'Sorry, I was asleep. You know how it is, the children are out with friends, I sat down for a minute and I must have dropped off. What time is it?'

I looked at my watch. 'Nearly three. What a beautiful place.'

'Isn't it? We used to live in Paris, and our Parisian friends wonder how we can bear it, stuck out here. But we love it. Olivier, my husband, is from round here . . . He still has to be in Paris during the week. But I wouldn't go back there. Do you want to see your room?'

We walked back through the kitchen to one of the side wings. The room was clean and bare, with twin beds, whitewashed walls, and white curtains. A small shower-room opened off it. Delphine threw back the shutters, letting in a shaft of sunlight and the scent of magnolia. 'OK?'

'It's lovely. Am I the only guest?'

Delphine nodded. 'It's midweek. And the season hasn't really started properly yet. It'll fill up next week, after 14th July. Would you like something to drink? I'm always thirsty when I wake up.'

We wandered back into the garden, picking up a bottle of cold mineral water en route, and sat down at a rough wooden table set under one of the trees. 'Are you here on holiday?' she asked.

'No, I've come to see someone.'

'Really? Who? Or perhaps it's a private matter.'

'Not particularly. It's a Madame Rigaut. It's in connection with an exhibition. I work for the National Gallery in London.'

'The National Gallery, how interesting! I used to think I'd have a career. But then the children came along and somehow it never happened . . .'

'It's just a job,' I said. 'One must live.'

What a lie! Without my job, where – *who* – would I be? I could never live out here, even with children, even in a place as beautiful as this. Whenever I'd felt tempted by Caroline's life all I had to do was try and imagine actually living out there in Gloucestershire. Trees, fields, sheep. Or in this case, geese. Meyrignac's byroads were bespattered with notices inviting tourists to come in and watch geese being force-fed – a curious entertainment, and not (one would have thought) calculated to sell more foie-gras. I doubt whether many butchers would think a glimpse of the slaughterhouse the best advert for prime fillet. But that's the country for you: people so desperate for something to do that they will even pay to watch geese eat.

'Is that Madame Rigaut at La Jaubertie?' Delphine inquired.

'Yes – do you know her?'

'She's a friend of yours?' The drawing-back was un-mistakable.

'No, I've never met her before. Why?'

'Nothing, really.' She fidgeted with her glass. 'It's just – there are some strange stories about her. About the family . . .'

'The family?' I said. Something for Joe, perhaps. 'What kind of thing?'

Perhaps I sounded too eager. Delphine shook her head and looked awkward, evidently regretting her indiscretion. 'Nothing, really. Just gossip.'

Suddenly, all my motivation seemed to have evaporated. Perhaps it was the air. If you breathed enough of it, the outside world would simply fade away, leaving this shim-mery orchard as the only reality. Maybe that was what had happened to Delphine – she'd fallen under the spell, and couldn't break out. I felt about in my brain for the rem-nants of urban edge. 'Is she a murderess or something?' I inquired, carefully simulating casual disinterest.

Delphine laughed. 'No, nothing like that. It's just that – her son's the Minister of the Interior, and not too popular with some people. Though I suppose quite a lot of them must have voted for him. And – oh, well.' She lifted her empty glass, then put it down again. 'More water?'

I shook my head. The anaesthetic hadn't taken long to wear off. 'And?'

Delphine shook her head. 'Oh, it's nothing. Really.' But the mask of virtue was unmistakably slipping. One more push should do it.

'*Allez*, you can't leave it there!' I said persuasively.

'Well – they say – she was shaved. *Tondue.*'

'*Tondue?*'

Delphine put her hand up to her head. Of course. This was the punishment reserved, after the war, for women who had slept with Germans: to have their heads publicly shaved as the crowd jeered. There was a famous photo-graph – the weeping girl, the grinning barber, the crowd shouting obscenities, savage with hatred and relief, happy to pile the communal guilt on to a convenient scapegoat.

'But that's impossible! She was married to a Communist!'

'Who knows. It's just gossip.' She gave an awkward little shrug.

Once more the gauze dropped, the light dimmed. 'Do people still remember that kind of thing?'

'Apparently . . . Of course it doesn't affect people's daily lives any more. But everybody knows. When we arrived, it was almost the first thing I heard about her. The Resistance was very strong round here. Did you see the memorial to the men that were shot in Meyrignac? Most of the people who live round here were probably related to one or another of them. They don't forget who was on what side.'

'Even so. It was a long time ago.'

Delphine blushed. 'I know, it's shameful. Blackening people's names . . . I don't know why I mentioned it. Olivier would say it's because I don't have enough to think about, I'm becoming a local, that's all they do round here, yap yap yap. I've nothing against Madame Rigaut, I hardly know her. She's very old now, she doesn't go out much. The few times we've met she's been charming.'

'Olivier doesn't gossip?'

'Oh, yes, but about politics, not local things.'

'What does he do?'

'He's a journalist.'

'Like my old boyfriend.'

We laughed. 'Why old?'

'We split up.'

'I sometimes think I might just as well have split up with *mine*,' Delphine said. 'We enjoy different things, that's the problem. He likes city life and I really can't stand it.'

'So why don't you divorce?'

She shook her head. 'It's not so easy. There are Fabien and Magali. And when he's here, I love him. He just isn't here very often.'

'What's he like?' I said idly.

Delphine laughed. 'Oh – normal. Charming. You'd like him. Everyone does.'

'Perhaps I'll meet him.'

'Not if you stay here,' she commented, glancing at her watch. 'Heavens, is that the time? I'll have to go and get the children in a moment, they're at a friend's.'

I said, 'How far's La Jaubertie from here? Can you walk there?'

'Absolutely. It's a lovely walk. If you want I can show you the way on the map.'

We went into the kitchen. She picked a map off a heap on a chair, spread it on the table and traced the route in red biro. 'We're here – you want to go out the back, then turn down here – and here. If you feel energetic you can do a circle, or else you can just come back the same way. Do you like walking?'

I said I did, though I hadn't done very much of it recently, apart from the odd few days in Gloucestershire. Of course one does walk in the city, but it's mostly to the tube station and back: not something you could really call walking, even if it does involve putting one foot in front of another in a rhythmic way. Still, the basic technique was there. 'Will I be all right in trainers?'

'Of course. It's not exactly mountaineering.' Delphine pointed to a gate in the wall at the back of the orchard. 'You go out there.'

I took the map and set off into the hot, green afternoon. The gate had box bushes on either side of it, once clipped into neat balls, but now overgrown into enormous mopheads. On the other side, a path of trodden grass led down a gentle slope to a wood.

The way at first was along old green roads, some recently cleared, some almost overgrown, through copses and between fields of still-furled sunflowers and drying hay. Then the path plunged into thick woodland, emerging on to a bare hillside scattered with moon daisies. From here there was a wide view across a river valley to blue hills beyond; in the garden of a villa slightly below and to the left, children played around a bright cobalt swimming pool. The path led away from them; according to the map, La Jaubertie should be quite near, on the next ridge.

By now it was getting on for five o'clock. The hillside was almost colourless in the heat, and by the time I reached the valley floor, my nose was dripping with sweat. But the path up the opposite slope led through a pinewood, scented and shady, and when I reached the crest of the ridge a breeze had begun to blow. La Jaubertie ought to be directly ahead, on the other side of a stand of tall lime trees. I thought I could just make out the pointed top of a conical roof.

I plunged into the shade of the limes, then out into a clearing with a small building. It looked like a private chapel, not particularly graceful – built perhaps in the nineteenth century – and now in a state of some disrepair. A gravestone could just be made out half-buried in the long grass beside it. I pulled the grass away and read: *Robert de Beaupré, 1915–1937, fils bien-aimé d'Etienne et Véronique. RIP.*

So this was where he'd ended up. Back in the ancestral home. There must be a family vault somewhere – all families of this sort had one, a house of the dead where they awaited eternity stacked up in stone drawers – but if he'd committed suicide they wouldn't have been able to bury him in consecrated ground.

I continued walking, and emerged on to a long lawn. There, before me, stood La Jaubertie: a fantastical, four-square castle in pale limestone with a round tower at each corner. I'd arrived by a back route, and the two towers nearest me were comparatively small, but the two furthest away, flanking the building's front façade, were massive. All had steep conical roofs, their fairytale quality intensifying my recurrent sense, on this hot July day, of having moved temporarily into some parallel life.

Keeping just inside the covering woods, I skirted around the back of the château. Beneath its main roof – the most enormous roof I had ever seen, tall, red and steeply pitched – ran a corbelled walkway, lit by widely spaced small openings half-hidden beneath deep eaves. About two-thirds of the way along, the façade was pierced by a low, half-open round-arched door.

By now I was level with one of the big main towers. Here, in front of the house, the gardens, hitherto little more than grass surrounded by woodland, became more formal. A carved stone fountain played in the centre of a mown lawn; on one side a sunken avenue, culminating in a statue, was lined by a double row of box bushes carved, as they receded, into ever-smaller lozenges to create a three-dimensional *trompe l'oeil*. A gravelled drive, emerging from the surrounding woods, skirted the lawn on the side furthest from where I stood, terminating in a sweep in front of the far tower, where a red BMW and a shabby blue Renault 4 stood parked. On the side nearest me two figures sat at a wrought-iron table beneath a cedar tree, while a dog – it looked like an alsatian – lay torpidly in the shade nearby.

The sight of the dog sent me back hurriedly into the shelter of the trees. My walk had been punctuated by frenzied barking every time I passed within sight of a farmhouse, and I had no wish to be found out ignominiously spying. That would hardly be the best of introductions. Fortunately, however, the dog seemed not to have noticed me. Perhaps it was asleep.

One of the figures rose, a man, tall and unnaturally thin. Manu! Why had I not anticipated that he might be here? Somehow all my imaginings had pictured a one-to-one conversation between myself and the old woman. But that, of course, was absurd: at a time like this, Juliette would naturally be surrounded by her family. Perhaps she had told him I was coming – not that he'd be surprised, it was his doing, after all.

The figure turned. It was not, after all, Manu. This man's hair was grey, and cut *en brosse*. It was the Minister, the man I'd seen on television. He was slightly thicker-set than his son, but they had the same attenuated build, the same way of standing and moving. Had he seen me? He seemed to be looking directly at me, but no – the trees were too thick, and he was too preoccupied with something else. He and the old woman were having some sort of argument – he was gesticulating, turned towards her now, while she sat back in her chair, apparently unmoved, certainly unmoving. Finally he flung up his hands in a gesture of supreme impatience, turned on his heel and made for the BMW. Its door slammed and it drove off at speed, leaving her alone with the dog.

There was a flurry of barks: the car's departure had woken the dog, who sensed the presence of a stranger. The old woman shouted at it to be quiet and sit down, but although it subsided somewhat, it soon began barking again, and looked longingly in my direction. I shrank back into the screening woodland and, as noiselessly as I knew how, edged back the way I had come until, with deep relief, I found myself once again on the public path.

6

La Jaubertie, July

When I awoke next morning the weather had changed. Rain had fallen in the night: the magnolia leaves outside my window were covered with drops of moisture. I let the curtain fall and checked my watch. Half past seven. Before time began. Why on earth was I up so early?

The answer came next minute in the form of high-pitched voices raised in argument. Delphine's children had evidently finished their breakfast and were now having an early-morning quarrel in the court. Their voices cut the still morning like scalpels. I cursed them and fell back on to the pillows.

My appointment was not until ten, and it wouldn't take more than a few minutes to drive to La Jaubertie. On the other hand, I knew I'd never fall asleep again. I reached for my book – a biography of Emmanuel Rigaut, brought to remind myself of essential background – propped myself up on the pillows, and thought about what Delphine had told me.

Tondue. Surely it couldn't be true? Not just because it was horrifying – horrifying things happen. But this was incomprehensible. *Tondue* was about collaboration, and Emmanuel Rigaut had been not just a Communist, but a Resistance hero. The book's frontispiece was a photo of him taken at that time – the same tall, thin figure as his son and grandson, no mistaking the line of paternity there. He stared expressionlessly out at the photographer from beneath a flat cap, a cigarette dangling from the corner of his mouth. Under his code name of Bizouleur he had led a network that sabotaged railways and bridges, provided safe houses for those who needed them, and helped with the underground railroad that smuggled Jews and grounded fighter and bomber crews out of occupied France and across the border into Spain. How could such a man possibly remain married to a woman who slept with the occupiers? Although the marriage had ended in the 1950s, Antoine had been born in 1942, and Jean-Jacques in 1947: living proof that while the war was on, and for some time after that, it must have existed in more than name.

At ten precisely, I parked my car on the gravel sweep outside La Jaubertie's front door. Today the garden was empty of both cars and people, and the great studded door was closed. This was the first time I'd seen the château as it should officially be approached, from the front. It loomed greyly over me, its vast roof (which was, I now saw, in a state of some disrepair) rising steeply between the towers like an enormous upturned ark. The original house, with its turrets, arrow-slits and high-level sentry-go, had clearly been built with military defence in mind. But now it was a country manor, a *gentilhommière*. Large stone-mullioned windows had been cut in the massive ashlar walls, four on the ground floor, four on the floor above and two in each tower, and the last remnants of military sternness had been obliterated by climbing roses and wisteria.

The door had a heavy circular wrought-iron handle, but no knocker; the only visible means of announcing one's arrival was a large bell, attached to a dangling rope. I pulled it, and a violent peal echoed round the lawn, soon followed by a rapid crescendo of barking from inside the house. A dog – perhaps the alsatian I'd seen yesterday – rushed up to the other side of the door and made a frenzied attempt to claw its way through. Nothing else happened, however. I continued to wait; the dog continued to bark and scratch. I rang again, rousing the dog to fresh levels of vehemence, but still producing no human reaction.

I pulled out a copy of the confirming letter I'd sent Madame Rigaut. Ten o'clock, Wednesday, 3rd July. And now – this. Was it a deliberate snub, or mere absent-mindedness? Perhaps the letter had never arrived. What a fool I'd been not to phone the previous day to confirm the appointment.

I looked at my watch again. Ten past ten. Obviously no one was in. The question was, how long would they be out? Was this absence merely a shopping expedition, or a definitive departure? Shopping, I guessed: you don't just abandon a dog, and the one I'd seen yesterday had been unmistakably part of the household. Perhaps I ought to go away and come back later. But how much later? Lunchtime? This afternoon?

The one certain thing was that I couldn't stand out here indefinitely. The sky had darkened and a gusty wind was beginning to blow. A heavy drop fell on my head, then another. I ran to the car, and as I got into it the heavens opened. Sheets of water blurred the windscreen. I, too, felt as though I was about to burst into tears. So much effort – so much anticipation – so much *expense*. Neither I nor my exhibition's minuscule budget could afford to throw money away. But the real blow was psychological, the dis-missal, the anticlimax – the insult.

The rain began to ease a little: it should be possible to drive now, though where to, I wasn't sure. I'd checked out of Les Pruniers, and even if I hadn't, the children would be in full cry. Bergerac? But my plane didn't leave till late in the evening. What would I do when I got there? Sit in the shed? Besides, I couldn't just abandon this interview. If I gave up now, what would I tell Joe?

I decided to drive to Meyrignac and find a café where I could sit and collect my thoughts. At least I'd be in the dry. But as I put my key in the ignition headlights approached down the lime avenue, and the Renault 4 I'd seen yester-day puttered round the gravel drive and crunched to a halt beside me. The driver's door opened and an umbrella appeared, followed, as it unfurled, by an elderly woman – a rotund, solid figure, with grey hair in a bun and wearing a short-sleeved cotton print dress-cum-overall. The house-keeper I'd spoken to when I first rang? She certainly fitted the voice.

Whoever she was, she took no notice of my car, but stumped round to the other side of the Renault, extracted a number of plastic bags and a full shopping basket from the passenger seat, and made for the front door. I leapt out and ran to intercept her before she should disappear inside the fastness. 'Madame?'

The woman started: either she had been so intent on the weather and the business of getting herself and her shopping to the door without drowning that she had not noticed my car, or else she had assumed that its occupant was already inside the house.

'I had an appointment for ten o'clock with Madame Rigaut,' I gabbled, falling over my words in an effort to get them out before my listener could abandon me. 'But when I rang the bell no one answered.'

The woman put down her basket, opened the door by simply turning the handle – so it hadn't even been locked! – and motioned me to enter. The alsatian bounded out and rushed towards me, barking furiously. The woman shouted, '*Amos, viens là! Couché!*' and it subsided. 'You'd better come in,' she said. 'It's too wet to talk outside. Don't worry about him, he won't touch you.'

Hesitantly, I followed her. Inside was a room perhaps four metres high, with white limestone walls and a floor of round pebbles, some white, some different shades of pink-ish and bluish grey, laid in a pattern of concentric circles. Orange and lemon trees in tubs lined the walls, in the middle stood a large white dining table made of cast iron in a chinoiserie pattern with six elegant matching chairs, and around the room were scattered a number of cush-ioned armchairs and sofas in white wicker. The woman dumped her shopping on the table, where the alsatian avidly sniffed it. '*Amos, arrète!* You were saying, madame?'

I held out my letter. 'This was the arrangement I made.'

The woman took it and scrutinized it. 'Did you telephone?' It was definitely the person I'd spoken to. I recognized the voice.

'Yes, before I sent this. I believe I spoke to you once. And then I phoned again and spoke to Madame Rigaut. The letter was just to confirm the arrangement we'd made.'

The woman nodded. 'I remember now. She did say something about it. But what with all that's happened . . . But of course you weren't to know about that.'

I didn't contradict her. 'Is she here?'

'As far as I know. She was here this morning when I went out.'

'But surely she'd have heard the doorbell?'

'Even if she did she's arthritic, it's hard for her to get downstairs without someone to help her. But she probably didn't. She's very deaf. Doesn't hear a thing unless she has her hearing aid. And she never puts it on unless there's someone there she wants to listen to.'

'Will she see me, do you think?'

'I'll go and tell her you're here.' And she clumped out of the room, followed, to my relief, by the dog Amos. A few minutes later her heavy footsteps could be heard approaching again. 'She'll see you now. Follow me.'

She led the way to a vestibule from which ascended a grand staircase in white stone. Only one picture adorned the walls here – bizarrely, an inscribed photo of Queen Elizabeth the Queen Mother. We swept past it without comment, to the floor above. Here the rooms were less cavernous, and the walls, though still white, of painted plaster rather than bare stone, while the floor was parquet, laid in an elaborate pattern of hexagons. We turned left into a salon, perhaps eight metres long, furnished with a mixture of old and modern pieces, including a walnut-cased grand piano and, on either side of a great stone fireplace, the pillar-like wooden screws of two ancient wine-presses, each topped with a great bowl of cascading pale-blue plumbago. Walking briskly to a door set directly opposite the one by which we had entered, the woman opened it, said, '*Madame, voilà la dame qui est venue vous voir,*' and left, shutting the door behind her.

This room, a study-cum-sitting room, was much smaller – almost cosy. The walls were covered with bookshelves and pictures, the floor with faded Persian rugs; there was a sofa and a television, and to one side of the window, a writing table. In an upright armchair on the other side of the window sat a tiny, ancient lady, frail but elegant even in mourning, a lifetime's habit of chic surmounting all circumstance. She wore a black cotton blazer over a straight black dress, and her gaze was fixed on the rain-soaked garden. Her white hair (*tondue, tondue,* but thick now even in extreme old age) was cut in a neck-length bob and held back with a black velvet band; her hazel eyes, bright and searching, were sunk deep above wide, high cheekbones in a lined, nut-brown face. She produced a hearing aid from a bag at her feet, and adjusted it; when it was modulated to her satisfaction she said, '*Bonjour, madame.* I'm sorry if I forgot our appointment. I hope you didn't have to wait too long. The truth is, I can't hear the bell unless I'm wearing this, and when Babette's out I might as well not be here as far as visitors are concerned. Why don't you bring a chair over and we can talk?'

I found a small chair and brought it over to the window. 'It's kind of you to see me, madame, especially at a time like this.'

'Oh, I like to be distracted. It passes the time. So, what did you want? I know you probably said in your letter, but . . .'

In fact I hadn't really said anything in my letter, other than that Manu had given me the address, and I wanted to talk about Emmanuel Rigaut and Robert de Beaupré. I opened my mouth to start out on the usual explanation. But no words came out. For as I was fetching the chair I'd noticed a picture hanging on the wall opposite the window, and the sight was so astonishing that I found myself quite unable to do anything but stare.

'Is something wrong?'

'Not at all,' I stuttered. 'It's just – that picture – I couldn't help noticing –'

It was an oil painting containing two figures, a woman and an angel, together with a number of musical instruments. A beam of light shone down from the top left-hand corner, where the angel hovered, brilliantly illuminating the two figures and picking out the instruments in its yellow-gold glow. Unless it was a very good copy indeed, I'd not only found the missing version of Caravaggio's *St Cecilia and the Angel* but also the answer to another puzzle: why Beaupré (for here, surely, was proof that he had indeed been the thief) had picked out, from all the Louvre's treasures, this particular picture.

The old lady gave me a keen look, as though this was something she had been expecting. 'What about it?'

'It's a Caravaggio, isn't it?'

'Yes.' The bright hazel eyes held mine.

'Is it an original?'

'I believe so. That's what we've always understood.'

When he made this version of his picture, Caravaggio had evidently been back on form. Unlike the painting in the Louvre, this one rippled with life. The Angel's wings and the saint's velvet dress were executed with virtuosic lightness of touch and exquisite attention to detail – each wing-feather darkly iridescent, the sheen on the red fabric full of heavy softness.

'Has it always been in your family?'

'Always? Not exactly. My father bought it. That was before I was born, so for me it's always been here. But in fact only since about 1912.'

'And was it exhibited in Paris after the war?'

'You seem to know a lot about my picture,' Juliette Rigaut remarked. 'I thought you said you wanted to talk about my husband?' (So she *had* seen my letter.) 'But perhaps I got that wrong. My memory's so bad these days.

I can remember things that happened a long time ago, but the present, no. It comes, it goes ... Don't get old, that's my advice. There's absolutely nothing to be said for it.'

I tried to calm myself. Too much, all at once, and I might lose everything. 'Do you mind if I record our conversation?'

'No. Why should I?'

She watched impassively as I performed the usual tape-recorder rites, checking for level, making sure it was working. This was one interview I couldn't afford to lose.

'Actually, the picture is what I wanted to talk about, in a way. You know there's a version in the Louvre that was stolen?'

'Borrowed, not stolen,' the old woman corrected me.

'I believe your brother was involved, wasn't he?'

'Unfortunately, yes. My poor Bobo.'

'Did you know anything about it at the time?'

'Of course. It was my idea.'

'*Your* idea?' Whatever I'd been expecting, it was not this. 'Why not?'

'No reason,' I assured her, feeling foolish. How old would she have been then? Eighteen, at the very most. But why should an eighteen-year-old not mastermind an art robbery? 'It's just that your name was never mentioned in connection with it, as far as I know.'

'Mentioned by whom?'

'The press. The literature. What I mean is, I've never seen it mentioned.'

'Probably not. The Surrealists were strange about women. They liked to fuck them, of course,' (how strange that word sounded, coming from those fissured lips) 'but that was about it. That and typing. If some act took place, and two men were involved, it was inconceivable a girl could have thought of it.'

'What made you think of it?'

She looked at the tape recorder. 'It's a long story. But why not? I'd rather think about the past than the present, any day.'

7

La Jaubertie, July

All that morning I listened while Juliette told her story. How outraged she felt when her parents forbade her to see any more of Arnaud Peytoureau ('Peytoureau?' I interrupted. 'I'm staying with a family called Peytoureau at Les Pruniers – would they be related?'

'Les Pruniers?' Juliette thought a minute. 'That must be Olivier. Arnaud would have been, let's see, his great-uncle.')

Would have been. So Arnaud was dead.

Juliette resumed her tale. After the break with Arnaud, she felt she could never live the life her parents had mapped out for her. When they drove her to Libourne to catch the train, as usual, to the convent school in Bordeaux after the 1936 Christmas holidays, she noticed the Paris train waiting on the next platform. Her mother had a dentist's appointment, so her parents, having put her on the Bordeaux train, did not wait to see her off. As soon as they were safely departed, she jumped off and boarded the one for Paris, as she was in her school uniform and wrapped up in her mother's old beaver coat, which she used as a coverlet in the icy convent dormitory. She would join her brother Robert who was supposedly studying law but in fact (as she knew) spent his life among the Surrealists, devising puns and producing trance-writings. His horror when she arrived at the little house his godfather had left him, his fury when she refused to leave, even when her parents came to Paris especially to fetch her, her beloved father taking her part against her outraged *dévote* mother. By then Robert's friend and fellow Surrealist Emmanuel Rigaut had fallen in love with her – convent girls, after all, being the embodiment of every Surrealist fantasy – and had persuaded her to let him share her bed. Robert, meanwhile, was sunk in misery because André Breton, the charismatic Surrealist leader, was no longer interested in him, but had moved on, as he always did, to new favourites and obsessions. Juliette, mazed in the enchantment of first love, had felt for him – had wanted to help him, to devise a way of reawakening Breton's interest. And had devised a plan: they would steal Caravaggio's St Cecilia from the Louvre.

Why that particular plan, I asked her.

She explained that she had found a job as secretary to a relative – one of the ubiquitous Beaupré cousinhood – who was Head of Pictures at the Louvre, had seen and of course recognized the St Cecilia and at once felt the Surrealist push of chance and coincidence. She remembered, from a book of Robert's that she'd read at La Jaubertie, a trick of the great Houdini's: when he wanted to vanish onstage from behind some piece of apparatus, he would slip on a stagehand's white overall and become instantly, to all intents, invisible. In the same way, if Emmanuel and Robert became brown-coated porters, they could (she reasoned) remove any picture unquestioned. If anyone asked, it was off to be cleaned, or on loan. She identified a time when the guard was invariably absent from the Caravaggio room, stood by, looking official, while Robert and Emmanuel, in their brown coats, took the picture down and replaced it with the *On Loan* sign, then ran back up to her office while they hurried down to the basement to remove it from its frame and stretcher in an unfrequented storeroom.

Could it really be that simple, I asked, remembering the layers upon layers of security at the Gallery. It really could, she replied: things were more haphazard then, pictures weren't quite the compact lumps of money they are now. And of course no electronics. Just humans, and humans can't be everywhere all at once.

All the photographs were taken that day and the next, before anyone noticed the picture's absence. But when Robert turned up with the picture at the Surrealists' café gathering (the Cyrano, place Blanche, each evening), Breton ignored him and Dali, Breton's current idol, made fun of him. Even when they produced the pamphlet, Breton remained indifferent.

That summer she and Emmanuel were invited to spend a week with Picasso, near Cannes (I remembered Rigaut's famous photographs of that interlude, of topless beauties and their laughing lovers picnicking on the sand). Juliette had worried about leaving Robert alone in his despair, but let herself be persuaded – it was just a week, how could she resist, why should she resist?

When they got back she'd found unwashed dishes in the sink, old food on the table. She ran upstairs to Robert's studio, and tripped over a chair that for some reason was lying on the floor. As she got up something tapped her on the shoulder: the body of her brother, suspended from a hook in the ceiling, and swaying gently in the breeze from the open window. On the table, the pamphlet. And upon it a note that read: *Partir, c'est mourir un peu.*

She stopped talking and leaned forward in her chair, clutching the arms. Veins seamed her hands. It was well past midday. We sat for some minutes in a silence broken only by the hearing aid's soft whistle. Then she said, 'It was a love story. Can you understand that? My brother loved Breton, who no longer loved him. I loved my brother and hoped the picture might change that. Emmanuel loved me, so he wanted to be part of it. And I loved him. The whole thing was a dance of love. But then, of course, it didn't work.' She sighed. 'Breton was pitiless. He moved on, and that was that. Art before persons, always.'

'Is that really why your brother killed himself? Because of Breton?'

'I've always assumed so. Suicide was the ultimate Surrealist act. His final act of love. And it worked – Breton was caught, he wrote a famous essay about his death, about all the Surrealist suicides. But by then of course it was too late for my poor brother.'

The clouds were parting in earnest now, the sky almost wholly blue. Juliette said, 'I wonder if you would open the window? I only shut it because of the rain.'

I opened it, filling the room with a chorus of birds triumphantly celebrating the return of the sun.

'Children should die after you, not before,' the old woman said, thoughts of her brother perhaps bringing her dead son to mind – as indeed most things must these days. Perhaps that was why she had been happy to make this excursion back into the past – because it got her away from the present. 'It's not natural. Even when they're middle-aged, even when you never see them. Even when you don't much like them. They're still your children.'

That must have been a reference to the Minister. If the scene I'd witnessed was anything to go by, there was little love lost there, on either side. I wondered if she'd always disliked him – always preferred his brother.

'Are you all alone here?'

'There's Babette.'

Babette, who must be making lunch – that immovable French institution. I wondered how I could politely bring the conversation back to the topic of the picture before I had to go. I didn't want to upset Juliette, and to mention it suddenly, at the point we had reached, would seem intrusive – almost rude. 'My grandmother must have been living in Paris when you first went there,' I said. 'She was about your age. Her family lived near the Etoile. She came to London to visit a cousin and married an English businessman she met there. Her parents were furious.'

'Our parents always seemed to be furious. I don't remember ever being furious with my children, not in that

68

way. But of course they were boys so they had more free-dom. When I ran off to Paris I felt I was living for the first time in my life, and when we took the picture it was like a wonderful dream. So vivid. Nothing I've done since has been as vivid as that. Later, of course, it became a night-mare. But it was still vivid. That was the important thing. Perhaps that was what your grandmother felt.'

'We never talked about it – she died when I was twelve.'

'And your grandfather?'

'I never knew him. My grandparents got divorced when my mother was quite young, and she moved back to France. He was quite a lot older than her, and he died before I was born.'

Somewhere, far off, a bell tinkled. Juliette said, 'That means lunch is ready. I'm afraid I can't invite you. But you must come and talk to me another time.'

'I'd love to.' I stowed the tape recorder back in my bag. 'It was kind of you to see me.'

'Not at all. It does me good to remember a time when I was still alive.'

As I stood to leave, the sun reached the back wall where the picture hung, and the Angel's torso and the saint's face and shoulders suddenly shone out. Caught in the double beam of natural sunlight and Caravaggio's ineffable incan-descence, the Angel seemed on the very point of move-ment. Most angels are androgynous creatures, but this one was unmistakably male and unequivocally sexy, with his beautiful black wings, shining brown curls, bruised lips and hooded brown eyes. 'What a beautiful young man,' I said. 'You know the painting of Bacchus? The one with the boy holding the glass of wine? I think this may be the same boy, a few years further on.'

Juliette levered herself out of her chair and, leaning on her stick, limped across the floor towards the picture. She barely came up to my shoulder, so insubstantial you'd have thought that at any moment she might break. Of course people shrink as they get older, but she must always have been slender: her wrists and ankles were tiny, her legs still elegant in their sensible shoes. Standing beside her I felt overgrown and fleshbound, my cheeks too red, my nose too shiny, my hair too springily thick. We studied the picture. 'Perhaps it was his lover,' she said.

'Perhaps they both were. Wasn't he involved in some brawl over a fashionable whore?'

'Probably.' Somewhat to my surprise – I'd been expecting her to move to wherever lunch was served – she turned and limped back effortfully in the direction of her chair. The temptation to scoop her up and deposit her in it was almost overwhelming, but that of course was out of the question. Finally achieving her goal, she sat back with obvious relief. 'At one time I tried to find out about his life, though it's years ago now. But I seem to remember a great many brawls.'

Trying to sound as casual as I could, as though the words had not been hovering in my throat for the past two hours, I said, 'The reason I was so interested in the picture is that I'm organizing an exhibition around it. There are several versions – well, of course you know two of them, and there's another in America. That's why I wanted to find out about your brother – because of the pamphlet, the Surrealist connection. Do you think it might be possible for us to borrow this one for our exhibition? We'd deal with everything – the insurance, the travel.'

'You mean you didn't know it was here?'

'How could I?'

She shrugged imperceptibly. 'Boh – it's possible Manu might have mentioned it, I suppose.' She gave a small, dry laugh. 'No wonder you were surprised.'

'So, do you think it might be possible?' I persisted.

She didn't reply at once, but looked at me consideringly, as though she was weighing something up, conducting an argument inside her head. With herself? Or if not herself, whom? The Minister? *They* had certainly been having an argument. Was that what they'd been quarrelling about?

No, that was ridiculous. At a time like this, a loan request from an obscure curator was not likely to be at the forefront of either of their minds. Not the Interior Minister's, and not his bereaved mother's.

Eventually she made up her mind. 'Yes, why not? I can't see any reason why not.'

I felt exultant – indeed, could barely restrain myself from kissing her. 'But that's wonderful! Of course we'll need a written agreement. Here, let me give you my card. '

'Let's do it now,' she said firmly, taking the card. 'Then it's done. At my age, I prefer to do things at once.' She rose, moved over to the writing table, adjusted the spectacles that hung on a chain around her neck, pulled some headed paper out of a drawer, and began to write, peering now and then at my card. The letters formed slowly and effortfully under her stiff fingers, but eventually she put down her pen. With an air of finality she handed me the result: the argument was over. I read: *I hereby authorize the loan of my picture, 'St Cecilia and the Angel' by Caravaggio, to Dr Regina Lee and the National Gallery in London for the purposes of an exhibition.* It was carefully signed and dated.

I folded it and stowed it in my bag, in the zip pocket alongside my passport. 'I'll write to you to confirm this, as soon as I get back.'

'As you wish.' She held out her hand. 'Goodbye, madame. Excuse me if I don't show you out.'

Making my way back through the grand enfilade, which I was now able to observe more calmly and in greater detail, I saw that the Caravaggio was by no means the only valuable picture in Juliette's collection. The others, however, reflected a very different sensibility – her husband's, perhaps. In the salon, above an ornate gilded commode, an early Chirico – much like the one at the rue d'Assas – sounded a disquieting note. In another corner, a tiny Vuillard interior hung above a Second Empire oval-backed canapé in yellow silk. I made a mental note of them and thought of all the lost gems scattered around Europe in places like this.

As I approached the staircase there was a burst of barking, and the alsatian Amos bounded towards me. I jumped backwards: the dog, sensing my fear, growled and snapped. At length, from some distant place, Babette shouted: *'Amos, arrète!'* The dog paused, and finally Babette herself appeared, carrying a cloth-covered tray.

'No need to be frightened, madame,' she said. 'He won't do anything to you, he's a big softy really, all voice and no teeth. *Amos! Couché!'* She nodded severely towards the ground at her feet; reluctantly, the dog padded over and sat down. 'So. You're off? You've been talking a long time, I hope Madame's not too tired. Did you get what you wanted?'

'Yes, thank you.'

'Lucky I came back in time,' she said, but she did not sound as though she thought it lucky.

Driving towards Bergerac through steamy trees almost blindingly green in the sunlight, I thought about those two exchanges. Had Juliette really forgotten our meeting? Once or twice, when she had thought me occupied elsewhere – with the tape recorder, with the picture – I'd caught her looking at me, a cool, detached glance in which elderly vagueness and memory loss had no place. And what about Babette? Was Amos's appearance on the staircase really a mistake? Or had there been some intention to intimidate? And why had she decided to go so extensively shopping just this morning? She had known I was coming, and that no one would answer the door if she was absent. Market day, when most people laid in their supplies, had been only yesterday. Perhaps she'd calculated that by the time she got back I'd have given up and left. But if she was playing games, whose games were they? Her own? That seemed unlikely. Juliette's? That, too, was hard to believe. So someone else's? Something was going on – and I guessed it was connected with the dilemma Juliette had so clearly been confronting before she agreed to lend the picture. That was why she'd insisted on writing the letter then and there – so that no second thoughts could intervene.

Or perhaps no second person.

When I got to the airport, the plane was late: there would be a delay of two hours. I wandered into a primitive bar that occupied a section of the shed. With any luck they'd sell magazines as well as drinks – I'd finished my biography, and the wordless hours loomed drearily ahead. The only reading matter on sale, however, was the local paper. *Too many people on the beaches this year*, ran its front page. It reinforced my sense of having crossed some unseen border into another world – some parallel universe in which normal twenty-first-century preoccupations played no part.

Leafing through, I suddenly came upon a picture of the Minister. In his persona as the local senator, he had been opening a local sports hall. The photograph showed him standing on a dais, caught in mid-speech: the caption read, *Minister of the Interior Jean-Jacques Rigaut inaugurates Meyrignac's new stadium.*

I glanced at the accompanying article. It mostly consisted of a transcript of the speech: the usual platitudes – thanks to those who had raised the money for this excellent new sports facility, thanks to the regional council for its contribution, pious hopes that the stadium would be well used. A paragraph at the end, though, caught my eye. Monsieur Rigaut thought the stadium would be particularly useful for the local youth, for whom regrettably few facilities were available after they left school. *'Anything is welcome that may staunch the flow of our youth to the cities. We need them here – a place without young people is a place with no future. But what incentive have they to remain? A new sports arena may help, and we hope it does. But we all know the real problem: jobs. We need to build up the economy of our region, and indeed are starting to do so. But it is a gradual process. In the meantime we must make sure that what jobs there are go to our own sons and daughters.'*

73

The meaning, though veiled, was unmistakable. It was a barely coded invitation to racism. That must be what Delphine meant when she said he was unpopular. With some, no doubt; with others, very popular indeed.

I shivered, and hoped the plane to raucous, multi-coloured London would not be too long delayed.

8

Olivier: Paris, July

The letter came three weeks later, dropping like a messenger from another world into the daily round of meetings, research and policy planning that chiefly occupied my working days. The envelope contained a single small sheet of thick cream paper, folded once. I extracted it, unfolded it, and read:

La Jaubertie, 26th July

Madame,
I understand my mother agreed to loan you a picture owned by our family. Unfortunately she is not the sole owner, and the other owners cannot see their way to satisfying your request.

It concluded with the most formal and distant form of words – *Veuillez, Madame, agréer mes sentiments distingués* – and was signed: *Jean-Jacques Rigaut.*

He must have got my name and address from the business card I'd left with Juliette.

I felt winded, as though someone had punched me in the stomach.

Like all public institutions, the Gallery existed in a continuous state of funding crisis. But this gnawing normality contained gradations of seriousness. In the past few days some lurking bubble of severity had risen to the surface and burst: we were in financial crisis – enough even to warrant a mention in one or two newspapers. Everyone had been asked to identify possible savings in their particular area; there were rumours of redundancies. Quite how these would be effected no one seemed to know, but if they proposed to operate the principle of last in, first out, my own position would be distinctly shaky. So that what had begun as an absorbing project of great personal interest but relatively little importance had suddenly acquired disproportionate political significance.

However, it wasn't just the professional implications that worried me. It was the letter itself. A letter from a minister was not to be lightly dismissed. But Juliette hadn't said anything about any co-owners. On the contrary, her letter – I looked at it again, and it hadn't changed – clearly implied that she alone owned the picture and was entitled to make decisions about it. Who was I to believe?

The answer seemed obvious: Juliette. Jean-Jacques Rigaut was a politician and a bully: on both counts, lying to get his own way came as naturally to him as speaking. It seemed clear there had been an argument about me and my request. That would explain the difficulty Juliette had had in coming to a decision. She'd known that for some reason he was against loaning the picture, and had assumed I was visiting her to ask for exactly that. Now he was determined that whatever his mother said, the loan would not take place.

In that case, what the letter said was untrue. So we could disregard it.

Whether that would be wise was another matter. I could not see Tony Malahide agreeing to it. Jean-Jacques Rigaut was a powerful man, and no one in TM's position wants to antagonize powerful men. The Gallery had constant dealings with France, on matters far more significant than this. And what about the consequences for Juliette? At her time of life she could do without yet more trouble.

The sensible thing would be to speak to her – to ring La

Jaubertie and put the matter before her. Then at least we'd know where we stood. But that might be problematic. Babette was the phone-answerer in that house. And Babette, I was pretty sure, was not my friend. I had a feeling that if I rang, and she answered, the news would pretty soon get back to Rigaut. And not just the fact that I'd called, but an account of any conversation between Juliette and myself. Nothing would be easier than for her to listen in on an extension.

It was eleven in the morning. In half an hour I was due to meet curators from other publicly funded collections to prepare for an upcoming discussion with the Arts and Culture Minister; after that, an introductory essay I'd written for a catalogue needed a final proof-reading. But how could I concentrate on proof-reading with that letter burning a hole in my brain?

I reached for the file box into which I dropped everything connected with Caravaggio and rummaged for the piece of paper with Manu's number. At the other end, the phone shrilled – once, twice, three times, four times. No answerphone today, apparently. I was about to replace the receiver when he answered. He'd probably been sitting by it all the time, trying to make up his mind whether or not to ignore the call.

'*Allo, oui?*'

As on that other occasion, I'd so taken it for granted he wouldn't be there that the sound of his voice threw me momentarily into confusion.

'*Allo?*' said the voice again, sounding impatient.

'Manu? It's Reggie Lee. You remember – I came to see you.'

'Ah, Régine, of course. How are you? Are you making progress?'

'On some fronts. That was what I wanted to talk to you about. I went to see your grandmother.'

'Yes, she told me. And was it interesting?'

'Of course. You know perfectly well it was.'

'Good.'

77

'She agreed to lend the picture.'

'Yes, she told me that, too.'

'But now I've just had a letter from your father saying it's impossible. He says she doesn't own it, and the other owners won't agree to lend.'

'Ah.' He didn't sound particularly surprised.

'Is it true?'

'It's possible. You never know, with my father.'

'Would it be worth trying to talk to him?'

There was a silence at the other end. Then Manu said, 'No. I don't think that would be a good idea.'

'Really? Why not?'

'You could say he's not naturally co-operative.'

'Do you think perhaps I ought to wheel in the Director of the Gallery?'

'No. That wouldn't be a good idea either.'

'Why not?'

'Fortunately for you, you don't know my father. My advice is, keep it that way. Think what's already happened,' he muttered, his voice so low I could hardly make out the words.

'What?'

But once again he evaded me. 'What's so important about this exhibition anyway?'

That of course was unanswerable. Once you start asking questions like that, all action becomes impossible. What's so important about anything at all apart from eating, keeping dry and warm and helping others do the same? 'Nothing, really,' I had to admit. 'It's my job, that's all. It's what I do.'

'Then take my advice. Drop it. Exhibit something else. He'll never agree.'

'But –'

'Forget it,' Manu said. 'Just forget it. And forget him. OK?' And he put the phone down.

Think what's already happened – what was *that* supposed to mean?

I stared at the phone for a minute, then dialled Joe's

78

mobile. If I didn't talk to someone sensible about all this I'd go mad, and who else was there? Besides, it was an excuse to get in touch. I hadn't spoken to him on my return from Meyrignac – from his point of view there hadn't been much to report. But this was different. This might be interesting.

'You think he's lying?' Joe said. 'But why would he do that?'

As usual the sound of his voice made me long to see him. But he'd made it clear he didn't want to meet. I'd heard rumours he'd taken up with someone else – someone in television. 'I suppose because he doesn't want to lend the picture.'

'That's obvious. The question is, why . . . You'd think it might be a feather in his cap – look, I'm not just an oik, I actually own Art. In any case, if he's lying he must realize you'll find out. It could be damaging if it got out. I'm surprised he'd take the risk for – well . . .'

'For something so insignificant.' I finished his sentence for him. 'He doesn't care, presumably.'

'So if he is lying, there's something bigger behind it. Well, well . . . Have you seen today's papers?'

I had. Rioting had broken out again, this time in the suburbs around Lyons, and the Interior Minister had made a speech denouncing the rioters. If they didn't like it where they were, why not try life elsewhere? He'd hinted there might be funds to meet the expenses of anyone planning to leave.

'He's trying to set himself up as the new strong man,' Joe said. 'Perhaps you're messing up his arrangements. Though I can't imagine how. Were you thinking of going back?'

'To Meyrignac? I can't think quite what I'd do there. I don't want to put the old lady in a difficult position.'

'Sounds to me as though she's already in one. Well, if you change your mind, let me know. We might be able to help with the expenses. It's all background.'

Later that day, riffling through the back pages of my diary to find a name, I noticed a phone number in the section covering my stay in Meyrignac. It was Delphine's: Delphine, whose husband was also a journalist, and who came from those parts.

'Delphine? It's Reggie Lee – you remember, I stayed with you a while ago. To go to La Jaubertie?'

'Régine – of course . . . Are you coming back?'

'It's possible. I'm looking for someone who can tell me about the Rigauts.'

'What did you want to know?'

'That's the problem, I'm not quite sure. I wondered – you said your husband comes from St Front?'

'Olivier? Yes, but I'm afraid he's not here just now.'

'Still in Paris? Surely these are the holidays?'

'He comes and goes.' Judging by her tone of voice, these comings and goings were arranged to suit Olivier's convenience rather than Delphine's. 'He's due back at the weekend. If you want to speak to him I can give you his Paris number.'

I dialled. The phone was picked up almost immediately. '*Oui?*'

'Olivier Peytoureau?'

'*Oui.*'

I launched into the usual explanation – name, place of work, the exhibition. Delphine. 'One of the pictures I'm interested in is in St Front, at La Jaubertie. But they don't want to lend it, or rather Monsieur Rigaut doesn't. The old lady agreed, but he's just written to say it's all off, she can't lend it unless he goes along with it, and he doesn't.'

'You could ask him why not,' said the voice at the other end reasonably.

'Apparently it's not as easy as that . . .'

'No, that figures.'

'It seems to be part of some sort of family quarrel. Delphine said your family's from Meyrignac – the old lady seems to have been involved with your great-uncle, is that right? So I wondered if you might have any idea what might be going on. Or know anyone who could help me find out. Then I might be able to do something about it.'

'It's possible,' he said slowly. 'Perhaps we should meet. Will you be coming over sometime soon?'

The budget wouldn't really stand endless trips to France. On the other hand, I felt reluctant to ask Joe for money unless I really had to. 'All right,' I agreed. 'I could come to Paris. That would be easier than St Front.'

'Okay, but I'm leaving Friday. Shan't be back for a couple of weeks after that.'

Today was Tuesday. Tomorrow was impossible, filled with commitments of various sorts. So was Thursday, but I could put those off. 'Thursday?'

'You really want to know this stuff!' Peytoureau sounded amused.

'I really do.'

'Lunch?'

'That would be good.'

'I'll see you at the Voltaire, then. Quai Voltaire. Twelve thirty.'

The Voltaire's frontage, slipped in amongst a group of high-class antique shops, was so discreet that you had to look twice: yes, it really was a restaurant. The interior was dim and old-fashioned, with red plush banquettes and white tablecloths. The maître d'hôtel pointed out a table at the back of the room where a youngish man, perhaps in his early thirties, was reading a newspaper. As I approached he stood up and held out his hand. He had black curly hair, cut short, and very bright black eyes, slightly slanted, like a faun. Also in the faun tradition, he was thick-set and not particularly tall: a rugby player's figure.

Neither the place nor the man before me fitted the slightly alternative character I had for some reason – perhaps because his wife ran a country b. and b. – ascribed to Olivier Peytoureau. He wore a well-cut cream suit with a black T-shirt, and was clearly at home in this distinctly bourgeois restaurant, most of whose tables were occupied by business lunchers. The Voltaire had been his choice, not mine, but he was doing me the favour, so this one was on me. And this was an expensive place – far beyond my tiny Caravaggio budget. I'd just have to foot the bill myself, and pretend I was back at the auction house.

'An *apéro*?' He grinned cheerfully across the table, clearly enjoying (as who does not?) the prospect of an excellent lunch at someone else's expense. 'A kir? A *coupe de champagne*?' He held up his glass. 'The champagne's excellent here. Let me order you one.'

I glanced at the list of drinks. A glass of kir cost four euros, champagne, ten. 'I don't think so, thanks. I'm hot, I'll have a mineral water.'

'You're probably right, one really shouldn't drink too much at lunchtime. Especially in this weather.' He studied the menu. 'Let's order, then you can tell me what this is all about. I can recommend the oysters here, they're excellent. Direct from Normandy. Do you like oysters?'

'It's years since I had any,' I prevaricated truthfully.

'Now's the time to try again, then. Unless you'd prefer something else?'

I looked at the menu. Oysters did not figure on any of the *prix fixe* possibilities. 'I think perhaps I'll just have one thing. I'm not very hungry. But you have oysters, if you want. I'm quite happy to watch.'

'Well, then, I think I will. Sure I can't persuade you?' He looked at me with one eyebrow raised – a trick that as a child I thought particularly stylish, and tried endlessly, and fruitlessly, to master. In fact you can't: it's like waggling your ears, something you're born with, or not. It gave him a rather consciously charming expression of amused inquiry that I found illogically annoying. 'This is on me, by the way,' he added. 'Or rather, my employers. I can smell a story in here somewhere. I'm a journalist – did Delphine tell you?'

I nodded. 'But she didn't tell me who for.'

'It's a scandal she\t, you almost certainly won't have heard of it. Very sensationalist and downmarket, very successful. I want to move, but the pay's too good. I'm looking for a golden way out that will buy me a good job somewhere a bit more reputable.'

I said, to make conversation and because it might raise my stock, 'I've a friend who's a journalist – Joe Grissom. He does political stuff. Do you read the English press?'

'A bit. Joe Grissom?' He looked at me with new interest. 'I know the name. D'you know him well?'

I nodded. 'Very. Is that the kind of job you're after?'

'That kind of thing. In French, obviously.'

'And you think this may help you into it?'

'You never know. If Rigaut's mixed up in it. He's such a bastard – the idea that he's Interior Minister and can tell all the rest of us what we can and can't do is, well, absurd isn't quite the word. I'd really love to get something on him. Especially with this election coming up. He may even end up as premier – perhaps even President. It doesn't bear thinking about.' He raised his glass. '*A bas les salauds.*' Then he waved to the waiter. 'Some champagne for Madame.'

We raised our glasses: I remembered, too late, that I don't actually much like champagne. 'Here's to your story,' I said. 'Though I have to say, I don't quite see how my problem could have anything to do with politics.'

He shook his head. 'In this country everything connects to politics. Especially money.' He laughed again, so infectiously that I started laughing too, though what he had said was not particularly, indeed at all, funny. I suddenly found him sharply attractive – the first time I'd really fancied anyone since the break with Joe. But of course there could be no question of any of that. Whatever Olivier Peytoureau saw when he looked across the table I felt fairly sure it wasn't a potential bedmate. A potential colleague, perhaps, a well-connected contact . . . In any case, he was married, with a family I both knew and liked. 'Why don't we start with six oysters?' he said, while I was thinking all this. 'Then if you like them we can order six more. Or a dozen ... And a bottle of Sancerre? Or how about this Mâcon Blanc Villages?'

We placed our orders, and the wine arrived, along with the oysters. I'd forgotten how refreshing they were, concentrated mouthfuls of ocean. The six we'd ordered vanished almost instantly. Olivier called the waiter and ordered twelve more; while we were waiting, I explained about the exhibition – about the three pictures and the various stories associated with them.

'A very small exhibition, then.'

'Oh, very. Though of course there'll be other stuff too – some drawings, and some other paintings. But I can't afford to lose any of the central stuff. And the Rigaut brothers seem – seemed – determined to make sure it won't happen.'

Olivier swallowed his last oyster. He was silent for a moment, seemingly lost in thought. 'I wonder if there's a connection?'

'Between what? Them both saying no?'

'Did you hear anything about how Antoine died?'

'Not really. I was with his nephew when he heard about it' – Olivier looked up abruptly: I enjoyed his astonished expression – 'but all he knew was that his uncle had been found dead. The papers said they don't suspect foul play.'

'That doesn't mean anything,' he said dismissively. 'You can kill people without actually murdering them.'

'What are you saying, that Jean-Jacques murdered his brother?' That seemed to me to be taking obsession to the point of fantasy.

'I'm not saying anything ... You say you were with Manu?'

'You know him?'

'A place like St Front, everyone knows everyone. Everyone's related to everyone, pretty much. He's a little younger than me, but we kind of grew up together ... How did you meet him?'

'You remember, I was telling you about that strange affair with the Surrealist who committed suicide. It's become a sort of legend and I wanted to see the place where it happened. It turned out Manu lived there. The house belongs to his grandmother now.'

'You say you went to see her?'

'Yes, Manu gave me her address. The idea was we were going to talk about her husband. And then – there was the picture. I couldn't believe my eyes.'

'He didn't tell you it was there?'

'No. I knew it existed – it appeared in an exhibition fifty years ago – but it seemed to have vanished.'

'Strange that Manu didn't say anything about it.'

'Isn't it? When I first got there he wouldn't tell me a thing – not even where his grandmother lived. I managed to drag out that she'd been married to Emmanuel Rigaut, and that Robert de Beaupré was her brother. But every time I asked him about her he changed the subject. Then just when I was on the point of leaving he heard about his uncle's death, and for some reason that changed everything . . . Did you know about it? The picture?'

'I think I vaguely remember it. A great big thing. But it's years since I went there.' Olivier tapped his teeth thoughtfully. They were unnaturally white, like a toothpaste ad or an American college girl. Untrustworthy teeth, I always feel, at any rate in a man. 'So what next?'

'That's where I hoped you might help,' I said pointedly. You had to admire his interview technique. So far, I'd learned almost nothing, while he now knew almost as much about the Caravaggio affair as I did. 'I want to find out about the Rigaut family. See if I can find some clue to what's going on.'

He raised his eyebrows. 'For instance?'

He was doing it again! But this time, he might be able to supply some information. 'For instance, I gather Juliette had a romance with an uncle of yours.'

'My great-uncle Arnaud,' he agreed. 'But her family weren't having it. Not rich enough. I remember her mother – a dried-up stick of a thing, always hanging round the curé. A *collabo*, naturally. They all were, that family.'

'But Emmanuel Rigaut was a Resistance hero. He was a Communist. They all were, the Surrealists. That was part of being one.'

'So? People don't necessarily agree, even if they're married. It was a civil war. Brother against brother ...'

And it hadn't necessarily ended, I reflected. Hadn't Joe been talking about just that – a low-level civil war?

'Even if they agreed to start with, people change. Marriages end,' Olivier said, and looked suddenly sad and absent, as though his thoughts had decamped to some other place.

'But that one didn't end. Not then. Jean-Jacques was born *after* that.'

'Yes, it's true, Rigaut stayed with her. After the war she went back to live in Paris with him. People were scandalized.'

'Scandalized?'

'That he took her back, I suppose – who knows what they thought? People weren't entirely rational then.'

'Perhaps it wasn't true, what everyone thought,' I suggested. 'Perhaps it was just gossip.'

Olivier didn't reply at once, busying himself with his plate – he had ordered a skewer of grilled giant prawns, and they were proving conveniently hard to excavate. Without looking up he said, 'Perhaps.'

'And?' I said after a bit.

'I'm trying to think where to begin ... A place like St Front,' he said again. 'You've got to realize. The Revolution isn't so distant, down there. When the war broke out my great-grandfather was mayor. He was a Communist, doctrinally secular. And his political opponent since forever was Etienne de Beaupré, Juliette's father, who of course was an aristocrat and a Catholic.'

'I'm amazed such a tiny place has a mayor.'

'In France *everywhere* has a mayor. It's how you get into politics. Look at Rigaut.'

'He's the mayor of St Front?'

Olivier laughed at the disbelief in my voice. 'Not any

more. But he was, for years. That's how he got into the regional assembly. And onwards and upwards ... And before that it was my grandfather. And before *that*, Etienne de Beaupré. Turn and turn about. Look, I'll tell you what I'll do,' he said, as if coming to a decision. 'I'll help you find out what you want to know. If there really is anything. But if there turns out to be a story it's mine, and I'm free to publish it. *D'accord*?'

'*D'accord*.' I thought about Joe, and felt relieved I'd decided to pay for this trip myself. Though it wasn't as if Olivier wrote for the English papers ... 'Is there anyone in your family who might have met Emmanuel Rigaut, or knew Juliette at that time?'

He nodded. 'My grandmother's still alive. Arnaud's sister. I'll ask her.' He checked his watch and signalled for the bill. 'I'd better go.'

Outside, the sun reflected hotly off the pavement. But the stream of cars that had choked the quai when I arrived had vanished, replaced now by a placard-waving procession. The placards seemed to emanate from some central distribution point: they had slogans like *LA FRANCE POUR LES FRANÇAIS* and *FRONTIERES OUVERTES= CHOMEURS FRANÇAIS*.

Olivier swore under his breath. 'It's the Front National,' he said. 'I'd forgotten, they're having an anti-immigration rally in an hour. Le Pen's due to speak.'

I had imagined Le Pen's FN followers, on the rare occasions I thought of them, as thugs and hoodlums. But few of these marchers fell into that category. There were some, of course – muscular louts with shaved heads and shades, grim-faced men in black T-shirts – but many, most even, seemed to be just ordinary people, the kind you might meet anywhere, at work, in a café, in a bar; many of them distinctly well dressed. They swung along in grim silence, unrelieved by chants and songs, separated from the few spectators by thick hedges of police.

Quite suddenly, a kind of roar broke out fifty metres further along, where the quai met the rue du Bac. Here a rival march, or mob, seemed to be advancing, with the evident intention of having a fight. Soon, despite the police, a full-blown mêlée was in progress between the marchers and the protesters, who were largely North African but also included a fair proportion of young whites, students by the look of them.

'Look at the police,' Olivier yelled in my ear. 'See who they're hitting?'

Indeed, there seemed to be no question of police impartiality. The people who were being dragged away to the vans that (I now saw) lined every side street were the protesters, not the FN. Almost as he spoke a pair of burly police brushed past us, dragging a protester by the feet, his head bumping against the cobbles. They elbowed us out of the way: I almost lost my balance, but Olivier caught me and pulled me back against a wall. My bag, though, had fallen from my shoulder to the ground, where it burst open, spilling its contents – purse, notebook, passport, and my tiny digital camera. One of the cops, in passing, and clearly not accidentally, trod on the camera, hard enough to break it apart.

For a moment I was so shocked that I just stood there. Then I began to shout in fury. He turned, advanced towards us, and with great deliberation trod on my note-book too, grinding it into the dust, before, without a word, continuing on his way to the police van, into which the protester was now being tossed. Olivier, who had retrieved the other objects and stuffed them back into the bag, pulled me away.

'Leave it. You can't do anything. He'll pull you in, too. Come on, let's go.' And he began to walk briskly away from the fighting, pulling me by the hand.

'But that camera cost me over two hundred pounds.'

'So claim it on your insurance. Say it was stolen.'

'But he did it on purpose!'

'Naturally. He didn't want some do-gooding woman taking photographs.'

He was walking fast, and I had to run to keep up. I felt hot and furious, and my ankle hurt where I'd twisted it falling.

'Now you can see the kind of people who support Jean-Jacques Rigaut.'

'You're not saying he's FN?'

'Of course not, he's not interested in the margins. Though they like him fine. But I meant the police. These are CRS, the riot police. His special boys.'

'The FN's armed wing, from what I saw.'

'Not exactly. But you saw what they're like. And believe me, the Minister does not disapprove. So be careful.'

By now we had reached the Gare d'Orsay metro station. Olivier said, 'I must get back to the office. Will you be OK?'

I said I'd probably go straight to the Gare du Nord.

He kissed me on both cheeks, his hands on my shoulders, then disappeared into the metro. It was nothing, the standard greeting between acquaintances. But as I dived underground, I still felt his warm hands on my shoulders. I tried to put the memory out of my mind. But as in so much else, I failed.

9

St Front, August

The following Monday, he phoned me at the Gallery. 'Régine? I spoke to my grandmother. She'd be happy to see you.'

We agreed that I'd return to St Front the following week. The summer season was in full swing, and Les Pruniers had been fully booked, but someone had cancelled at short notice, leaving a room free for me.

I stepped from the air-conditioned train into air like damp flannel. The mere act of breathing made the sweat start. In July the verges with their tapestry of small flowers had been a Pre-Raphaelite vision, almost unnaturally green, but now fields and sky were a uniform non-colour, bleached by heat and drought. The small rental car ('Saxo,' quipped the girl in the rental office, 'like the phone') was oven-like: only after five minutes with all windows and doors wide open was it possible to get inside and start driving.

I reached St Front just after six. Save for the inevitable chorus of dogs it seemed, as on my earlier visit, quite deserted. This time the bar was open, but its only sign of life was an alsatian lying across the threshold – not exactly an invitation to custom. That being mayor of such a place could start anyone on a career in national politics seemed unbelievable.

Five minutes later I arrived at Les Pruniers. The people carrier had now been joined by a grey Peugeot saloon. I slid the Saxo in beside them and knocked on the door. No one answered, but if two cars were here, then someone must be home. I tried the door, which was unlocked, and walked through the kitchen to the orchard. And there they were, clustered at the far end around a freestanding circular blue pool that was being filled from a hosepipe attached to an outside tap. The children, already inside, were happily drenching each other while Delphine, in a swimsuit, and Olivier, in shorts, tried, not very hard, to dodge the drops. They looked like one of those ideal families you see on cereal packets and bags of barbecue charcoal: attractive young mother and father and two beautiful children, one of each sex. Delphine, who was doing something complicated with a towel, waved.

'Come and see our new toy. When the heat gets unbearable we can all sit in it.'

'Even the guests? Where are they all?'

'They come and go. We don't do table d'hôte here, they have to find somewhere else to eat.'

I said to Olivier, 'Still OK for tomorrow?'

'Absolutely. She's looking forward to it.'

That evening I ate in Meyrignac. When I got back an electric storm was flickering on the horizon, spasmodically lighting the far-off hills like a faulty million-watt bulb. But no rain fell, and next morning was as hot and airless as ever.

At breakfast, which took place in the garden room off the kitchen, I met the other guests. There was an English couple whose two children glared suspiciously across at Fabien and Magali, a pair of middle-aged Dutch walkers I'd noticed last night in the restaurant where I'd dined, and who were now tucking into large quantities of cheese, and a couple from the Pas de Calais who had not yet shed their northern pallor. The woman from Calais eyed my dress, a sleeveless blue muslin number from the Liberty summer sale. Eventually she plucked up courage and said, 'Where did you get that, if you don't mind, madame? It's exactly what I've been looking for everywhere, but I can't seem to find it.' I told her; she looked depressed, and conversation flagged.

At a quarter to ten Olivier appeared, spruce in shorts and a blue T-shirt. 'Ready?'

'Is it far?'

'Far enough,' he said, leading the way to the Peugeot. 'The other side of the bourg. It's too hot to walk, and it'll be even hotter by the time we come back.'

Delphine leaned out of a window. 'Will you be back for lunch?'

He shook his head. 'No idea. I'll call you.'

We set out on the Meyrignac road, but after about three kilometres Olivier slowed down, and turned into a narrow gravelled track. At the end of it a cluster of houses formed a small hamlet in the woodland. The one we drew up at was rendered in cream-painted plaster, with a kitchen-garden to one side and a spacious veranda on which stood a table covered with the usual oilcloth. Olivier explained that it belonged to his uncle Francis, a builder, married to his father's sister Anny. 'Doesn't trust wood. He likes to boast that he built his house entirely without wood.'

I noticed that the veranda had iron railings; the gate was also iron. 'Not anywhere?'

'Perhaps just a bit in the roof-beams.'

He ran up the steps on to the terrace, where a wiry, grizzled man in his late fifties had emerged to meet us. Olivier introduced us. 'My friend Régine – my uncle, Francis Laronze. It turns out Francis is doing some work at La Jaubertie.'

Monsieur Laronze had a wide, humorous mouth, small black eyes, and a local accent so strong that I had to listen hard to make out what he was saying. 'I couldn't quite understand, from what Olivier told me. Is it La Jaubertie you're interested in, or the Rigauts?'

'It's really to do with a picture they have there. But the family, too. Everything, really.'

'If you were interested in the house, I could show you some bits you wouldn't see otherwise. I'm just off there this morning.'

This suggestion caught me off-guard. Of course I intended to try and visit La Jaubertie while I was in St Front – I'd brought Rigaut's letter with me, to show Juliette. But the last thing I wanted to do was make her think I was sniffing around behind her back – and what else could she imagine if she or Babette ran into me being given a guided tour by the builder?

'That's most kind,' I said politely. 'But I'm afraid it would be rather awkward, if we suddenly ran into Madame Rigaut.'

'Don't worry, she won't mind,' he assured me. 'I've often done it. It's a historic place, people are interested. And we wouldn't go into the living quarters – just the attics and the cellars. But in any case, no one's there today. I believe Madame's visiting her son. But Mamie's waiting. She's found some things she thought might interest you.'

Francis led us into his wood-free house. It had tiled floors, formica worktops in the kitchen, metal window frames. The result was somewhat echoing, though doubt-less an excellent fire risk. The salon was furnished with a leatherette three-piece suite, a coffee table upon which sat a large, somewhat worn-looking manila envelope, and a flat-screen television. A stout woman with a peasant's muscular arms and legs was seated on the sofa. She must have been well into her seventies, perhaps even eighty, but her thinning hair was still frizzed and coloured: age had not drowned out vanity. Olivier gave her the regulation four kisses, two to each cheek, and introduced us: 'My grandmother – my friend Régine.'

We shook hands. The old woman patted the seat beside her. 'Sit down . . . Francis, why don't you make us all some coffee?'

'Not for me, thanks,' I said. I wanted to concentrate on whatever might emerge without the distraction of juggling a cup.

'Nor me,' said Olivier.

'A glass of wine, then.'

'No thanks, it's too early . . . So what's this you've found, Mamie?'

She nodded towards the envelope. 'Your grandfather's war memories. I found it when he died, and it's been at the back of that armoire ever since. When you said your friend was interested in those days I thought there might be something there.'

I said, 'Can I look?'

She nodded.

I picked up the envelope and gently tipped its contents on to the table. Dust flew up, making my nose run. There was a ration card; a photo of two young men in army uniform, clearly brothers, standing on a street corner somewhere; a few newspaper cuttings recording trains blown up or derailed; a paper dated 5th January 1941 instructing PEYTOUREAU Didier to present himself for war-work in Germany; and, last of all, a photograph of one of the young men who had appeared in the previous pictures, now out of uniform, standing in a garden beside another man, grey-haired and assured-looking, wearing a sweater and plus-fours.

Olivier, looking over my shoulder, said, 'I've never seen any of these.' He picked up the snapshot of the two young men. 'Is that grand-père?'

Mamie took it and held it away from her, squinting. 'Pass my glasses, Francis – that's better. Yes, that's him on the left and that's Arnaud, his elder brother.'

'May I?' I took the photo and studied it. Arnaud was taller than his brother, dark-haired, well set up, his face not unlike Olivier's. A dashing fellow. He and Juliette would have made a fine couple.

'Their father must have taken it in Meyrignac when they were called up, before they got on the train,' Mamie went

94

on. 'Arnaud never came back, of course. After the armistice he was taken prisoner – the whole company were. Didier got away, I don't know how, but he said Arnaud wouldn't come with him – too afraid of getting shot, Didier said. But then the train that was taking them to Germany got bombed, so he died anyway, poor boy. You can see his name on the war memorial . . . So Didier came home alone. On foot, can you imagine? All the way from Soissons. It took him two months. We thought they'd both been killed. And then pouf! he appeared. My mother-in-law was out haymaking and there he was trudging up the hill from Joly's mill. She had hysterics because she thought she'd seen a ghost . . .'

'Where were you?'

'Milking the goats. We made cheese, it was excellent, you don't get anything like that these days . . . Maman came rushing in – she could hardly speak, all she could say was Come, come, you won't believe it. And when we got to the kitchen there was Didier.' She leaned over and picked up the summons to forced labour. 'He'd been back a few months when this arrived. Of course none of them that went came back. Didier didn't go, though. He said he hadn't got away from them once just to give himself up now. He went underground instead. That was the choice, Germany or the maquis.' She nodded at the cuttings. 'Those must have been his work – I can't think why else he cut them out. But mostly he was helping people across the demarcation line. It went just by us – just behind La Jaubertie. The line was the stream in the valley there, the Garaude. We were occupied, and over the other side it was free. That's when Didier's father stopped being mayor. The mayor was the official liaison between the village and the authorities, and how could he do that when his own son was breaking the law? He quarrelled with his wife about it. She said he should carry on, but he said that would mean denouncing his own son. So he went to La Jaubertie and told Monsieur de Beaupré that he couldn't be mayor any more, his health wasn't good enough, and he was handing over. Beaupré was astonished – they'd been political opponents all their lives. But he did it happily enough. I expect he felt it was his turn.'

'Was that why your father-in-law went to prison?' Olivier asked.

'No, that was something else, that happened afterwards. Girardot, the butcher, was going on in the bar about what a great man Pétain was, and in the end Papa couldn't stand it any more and yelled out, *"Pétain n'est qu'un pète et je chie sur lui,"* and stamped out. And Girardot reported it to the Kommandantur, and he was arrested.'

It crossed my mind that if you were going to imprison every pubgoer who called the Prime Minister a shit or a fart, the jails would be pretty crowded. 'He was put in prison just for that?'

'Eight months. He was lucky. It might have been worse. He came back. He was even awarded a silver medal, after the war, for services to the commune. Girardot was so angry he could barely speak.'

I picked up the photograph of Didier with the older man. 'Who was this?'

'That's one I don't understand,' Mamie said. 'It's Monsieur de Beaupré – Etienne de Beaupré. You remember him, Francis? He always used to dress like that. But what Didier was doing with him I don't know.'

'Something to do with the war,' I said. 'If it was in that envelope.'

'I suppose so. But I can't imagine what. They were Pétainists, Catholics. Collaborators, all of them.'

Francis said, 'Mamie, if that's it we'd better get going. I've got work to do. I'll see you there,' he said to Olivier.

She shuffled the papers back into the envelope and held it out to me. 'Take it, if it'll help you. No, go on, I'd like to think it wasn't just lying there. And remember,' she added as we shook hands, holding mine in hers, the palm leathery from a lifetime of milking and haymaking, 'you can't trust the Beauprés. Just because she tells you something doesn't mean it's true.'

Clutching the envelope, I followed Olivier out to the car. He backed us out of the driveway and we started on the road to La Jaubertie. Glancing at me sideways, he said, 'I don't know how useful all this will be. I hope it won't be a wasted trip.'

I was wondering the same thing – it was hard to see quite what Olivier's grandma's wartime memories might have to do with either Rigaut or the Caravaggio. 'Don't worry, it's fascinating,' I told him. 'But I hope your uncle's right about everyone being out at La Jaubertie.'

'You seem to be putting a lot of effort into this exhibition.'

'It's important to me.'

He glanced across at me. 'I didn't imagine it was for the money.'

'Unfortunately not.'

'Something personal, then?'

'Sheer ambition,' I stonewalled.

He nodded: that was something he could understand. 'Ambition gets you everywhere.'

I said, 'At least you don't sound like my ex-boyfriend. He was always complaining I was over-motivated.'

'So you gave him the boot?'

'Something like that.'

'And what does the new one say?' he inquired.

'There isn't a new one. Yet.'

At La Jaubertie, Francis was getting out of his van. He had parked beside a white builder's lorry – the only vehicle there, apart from our own – and was peering up at the vast main roof. 'Look at the state it's in,' he said. 'But the old woman won't spend the money. When I told her what it would cost, if we were going to scaffold it and do it properly, she just said no, too expensive. The money's there, of course – she just doesn't want to spend it. It's that son of hers, if you ask me. He wants all she's got for his precious career. He doesn't care about this place. His wife's got a place of her own down in the Lot, and that's where they spend all their time. There and Paris.' He spoke with proprietorial disgust. This was his place as much as anyone's. Juliette might own it, but without Francis, and all the many Francises before him – he told us that his father and grandfather and great-grandfather, and doubtless an infinity of grandfathers before that, had all worked on this house – it would long since have fallen into ruin.

The roof did indeed look supremely unconvincing. Its tiles, slipped, broken and moss-covered, rippled across it unevenly, as though laid upon a particularly choppy lake. But I could see Juliette's point. Whatever its state, it wasn't going to be her worry for very much longer. Let someone else spend the money.

'Do you know what she thought we should do?' Francis was saying. 'Attach ropes to the top beam and hang off them while we changed the tiles. I told her, that beam's so rotten I wouldn't hang a mouse off it. And that's just one of the things that's got to be renewed.'

'So what are you doing?' Olivier asked.

'Can you believe it, poking the worst tiles out from the inside, then slotting new ones in,' Francis said. 'Michel pushes them out and Jeannot goes round with the barrow picking them up. Here he comes,' he added, as a man appeared round the corner of the house, pushing a barrow piled with broken tiles.

Jeannot gave an almost toothless smile and began decanting his burden into the back of the truck. On cue, at the far end of the house a small shower of tiles crashed to the ground. When I asked whether he wasn't afraid of getting hurt, he just grinned and explained that he knew where Michel was working. If a tile did hit him on the head, it seemed unlikely much damage would be done.

'I told her, it's a waste of money,' Francis grumbled. 'But she insisted . . . Anyhow, come up and see.'

He led the way into the house, and up the stone stairs I remembered from my previous visit. It was true, no one seemed to be around – not even the dog Amos. Perhaps he was shut away because of the builders. We climbed a second, wooden stair, to the floor above. The rooms at this level were smaller and darker, filled with dusty old furniture, and streaked with damp. Here and there, the plaster had fallen from the ceiling. 'You can see how bad the roof is,' Francis said. 'She just sacrifices this floor. Look, I'll show you.'

We followed him along a corridor to one of the small corner towers. It housed a narrow spiral staircase, just wide enough for one person, and lit by arrow-slits. We climbed it, and finally emerged through a stone arch into the roof-space: a vault of enormous beams soaring perhaps eight metres above us like a great upturned boat, with steep, slightly curved ribs and lateral braces. The space was dimly lit by small oeil-de-boeuf windows at the base and slanting rays from an all too visible lacework of sky; dust danced in the sunbeams and rose in clouds with every step. In one corner, up a tall ladder, a fat middle-aged man, his head covered with an old denim flowerpot hat, was poking between the laths. '*Salut*, Michel,' Francis said. 'How's it going?'

'OK, I suppose,' said Michel, not turning his head. 'It's hard to know which ones to leave. They're all rotten.'

'Better leave a few,' Francis said. 'Are you replacing them as you go along?'

'As far as I can. It's hopeless, really.'

We lingered a few minutes, then returned down the spiral stair. 'There, I bet you've never seen anything like that,' said Francis with proprietorial pride.

'Extraordinary,' I agreed

'Now I'll show you the cellars. They're *really* something.'

The cellar entrance was through a low door in the other small tower. A ladder-like stair, lit by a single hanging bulb, led down from a roughly concreted landing to emerge in a cavernous space, dimly lit by high, small openings dug down from ground level. The air here smelt of damp and sawdust, and the floor underfoot was soft. As my eyes grew accustomed to the darkness, I made out an underground chamber perhaps four metres high, from which an almost semicircular arch led into another similar space. The ground was covered with sawdust, and a great pile of logs was stacked against one wall.

Francis flicked a switch, and three twenty-watt bulbs dimly revealed the cellars' full extent. They seemed to be dug into the hill, with uneven walls and rough floors; in places, another storey had been inserted; against one wall, green with damp, some blackened cut stone spoke of an old fireplace. 'This was the original house,' Francis said. 'See those arches? They're eleventh, twelfth century.'

We picked our way across the ancient chambers. At one point a small stream flowed across the floor: the reason, Francis said, that the house had been built here in the first place. Dusty barrels and stone troughs loomed from the darkness; a wooden stair led up to a platform that must once have been a room. At the far end the floor sloped upwards, merging into a heap of stones: some ancient rubbish heap, awaiting its archaeologist.

We turned back, and emerged into the daylight to find that we were no longer alone in the house. A car had parked next to Olivier's Peugeot – the red BMW I'd spied from behind the trees my first afternoon in St Front. Three people were getting out of it: a smart woman in her forties wearing shades and an enviably well-cut red dress, Juliette, and Jean-Jacques Rigaut.

My immediate instinct was to rush back down into the cellars and stay there until the coast was clear, but of course that was impossible. Not only would Olivier and Francis think I was mad, but it would make me seem like some sort of criminal – which was exactly how I felt, sneaking secretly round Juliette's house in her absence. In any case, it was too late: they'd seen us. Francis, who of course knew everyone, greeted them with a jovial '*Bonjour, messieurs-dames,*' and explained that he'd been showing us the roof; Olivier, who also seemed to know them, was shaking hands. Then they turned to me, and Juliette, sounding understandably astonished, said, '*Mais c'est Madame Lee!*'

100

Rigaut, who had been standing to one side looking extremely bored, swung round and stared at me.

I held out my hand to Juliette and explained that I'd returned to Meyrignac because a complication had arisen and it seemed easiest to speak in person rather than on the phone. Would it be possible to come and see her again?

'But of course!' she cried, with unexpected warmth. She would like nothing more – she didn't get so many visitors these days, especially ones who wanted to talk about the old days. Rigaut looked thunderous. I wondered if this effusive greeting was some sort of message to us both. Something to do with his letter, perhaps. Or maybe just another round in their mysterious contest.

Juliette turned to the smart woman and introduced us: Madame Lee from the National Gallery in London, my daughter-in-law Madame Nathalie Rigaut. The one with the place in the Lot. We shook hands and smiled at each other politely. Secure behind her shades, she was unreadable. She muttered something polite and vanished.

'My son, Jean-Jacques,' Juliette said.

I held out my hand. He looked at it, and after a perceptible pause, during which he continued to stare at me, briefly shook it. Close to he didn't really resemble Manu, except in build. His face was broader – more like Juliette's – with dark, intelligent eyes that never really met yours, but seemed rather to be constantly watchful, on the look-out for incoming emergencies. His complexion was weatherbeaten, as though he spent his spare time sailing. Perhaps he did – he was dressed sub-nautically, in a navy and white striped T-shirt and white chinos. His hand, though, felt soft – more used to desks than ropes.

'So you're the one who wants to borrow the picture.' It was a statement, not a question.

I nodded. 'That's right.'

'Unfortunately the answer is no.'

'So I understand.'

His gaze wandered from my head, doubtless sprinkled with cobwebs from our recent explorations, to the shabby espadrilles on my feet. I stared doggedly back. If he hoped to browbeat me that way, he was in for a disappointment. My days at the auction house had inured me to the little tricks chaps use when they want to make themselves felt. '*Et alors?*' he said, after a while.

'I'm afraid I don't quite understand,' I returned sweetly, though of course nothing could have been plainer. I'd had my dismissal – why was I here? He was an important man, he didn't like having to issue orders more than once.

'I'm sure you do,' he said.

I shook my head. 'I've come to see your mother. There were some things I wanted to ask her. *Voilà tout.*'

'It won't get you anywhere, madame. As long as you understand that.'

'It certainly will, monsieur. It will get me another afternoon of conversation with Madame your mother.' And then we'd see.

He shot Juliette an irritated glance, but she was fiddling with her hearing aid, apparently oblivious to our exchange. When she'd settled it she said, 'Are you free tomorrow? Then why not come in the morning. Ten o'clock? *A demain, alors. Au revoir, messieurs-dames.*'

By now it was almost midday. The Rigauts disappeared into the house; Michel and Jeannot drove off in their lorry; Francis took his leave, got into his car and followed them, bound for home and lunch. Olivier and I stood beside the Peugeot, discussing our next move. Did I want to come home to lunch with him? Unwilling to intrude more than necessary into his family holiday, I told him I'd walk back to Les Pruniers – I thought I could remember the way from last time, and I needed to collect myself.

I wandered away from the château in the direction of the trees. As I was crossing the strip of gravel that surrounded the house, I heard a crash, and swung round to see the debris of a tile scattered a few centimetres behind me – doubtless one loosened earlier by Michel. If I'd been walking just a little more slowly, it would have hit me. There was some red tape stretched along the back of the house – I'd noticed it vaguely before, but now realized it must have been put there to warn people away while work was in progress. It didn't stretch to where I was standing, but no doubt if anything had happened the Rigauts would be able to claim they'd done their best, that I'd walked where I shouldn't have. Not that Rigaut would have been tremendously upset. Judging by his parting glance, he would have been not unhappy to see me brained.

I mopped the sweat away and shakily resumed my walk. Rigaut could give me all the black looks he liked: it would take more than that to stop me now.

10

A Walk in the Woods: St Front, August

For all my bravado, I felt distinctly disturbed as I made my way towards the path. I'd met a number of famous and successful men in my time, but none with such a powerful and intimidating presence as Jean-Jacques Rigaut. I'd stood up to him, but the effort had been almost physical. Of course there had been no actual physical threat. But I'd definitely been glad of the company. He wasn't a man I'd care to meet alone.

People have different strategies for calming themselves. One of mine is walking. The rhythmic action, the slowly evolving scene, the real yet not excessive sense of physical effort leading to an equally real and welcome fatigue – these things don't exactly induce tranquillity, but they certainly minimize agitation. And so it was now. By the time I was through the pinewoods and climbing up the opposite ridge, the scented afternoon, the chirrup of the cicadas, and the soft call of wood pigeons were beginning to do their stuff. Above my head swallows wheeled and soared; as I strode along the path, flutters of brown and white fritillaries rose before my feet. Had it not been for a helicopter hovering somewhere overhead, this might have been an unpeopled world.

Five minutes later, the helicopter was still there.

At first I hadn't really noticed it. Aircraft are part of life; unless you're on some busy flight path, they just merge into the background. Of course helicopters are more intrusive. But generally they're passing annoyances – after three minutes they're off and bothering someone else. This one, though, was different. If it hadn't been a nonsense, I could have sworn it was following me.

The path at this point was particularly exposed, over a bare chalk hillside. On one side a field of sunflowers awaited harvest, their enormous brown seedheads rattling ominously in the breeze; on the other a slope thick with gorse and juniper was bounded by woods that, a hundred metres ahead, curved to envelop the path. Above my head, the helicopter continued its infernal din. It was flying very low. Squinting upwards, I tried to make out the letters painted on its side, but the sun kept getting into my eyes. All I could see was that it was painted blue. And then I was in the woods, with their fragrant shade and their concealing canopy of leaves, and it couldn't see me, and I couldn't see it. The path now was wooded all the way down to the next valley bottom, where there was a clearing with a stream, and a field with cows bordered on one side by a small road. Across that, on the other side of a gentle hill and through another small wood, sat Les Pruniers. I hoped the pilot would forget his stupid game and go away to do some proper work.

But although I could no longer see the helicopter, I could still hear it – and the noise of its engines did not recede. On the contrary, it still seemed to be following me. Of course, if that were really its plan – a ludicrous idea, but one that after a certain time couldn't help imposing itself – nothing would be easier. The woods here, however extensive, weren't exactly pathless jungle. On the contrary, they were criss-crossed with tracks, all well marked, and all recorded on maps. Whoever was in the 'copter would know exactly which path I was likely to take, where it led and where it emerged. If I didn't show up where and when it expected, then the large-scale map I'd used when I first came this way showed all the alternatives. I'd have to come out sometime, and when I did, any hovering aircraft would easily spot me.

But that was ridiculous: pure paranoia. Why would some person in a helicopter have the slightest interest in an unknown Englishwoman in the middle of the French countryside?

Other than the alien noise of the helicopter, the silence around me was almost tangible, my footfalls deadened by decades of leaf mould. But of course silence is rarely absolute, and in my nervous state every small noise became a potential source of terror. The snap of a falling chestnut made me jump out of my skin; the intermittent tattoo of a woodpecker transmuted into a coded message. Behind the trees, always just out of sight – a shadow receding into darkness behind that copse of oaks, the crack of a twig in the ditch to my left – I could almost believe that watchers marked my progress.

Ridiculous! But then – that, ahead – surely that *was* a shadow? And that whistle – surely no animal ever sounded quite that shrill, that loud – that mechanical?

The path, which until now had descended steeply downhill, flattened out as the trees began to thin into the remembered clearing. And all at once, paranoia morphed into bizarre reality. I hadn't imagined those whistles, nor those shadows: the helicopter had indeed been tailing me. For the clearing was full of men: on one side, the grim-looking security police I'd last met beating up North Africans near the Voltaire and kicking my camera to bits, on the other a group dressed as protesters, in student gear or what they took to be such. And behind them, talking to one of the police, the umistakable figure of Jean-Jacques Rigaut. For a moment our eyes met. Expressionless, he turned away and resumed his conversation.

Looking neither to left nor to right, I continued on my way. Whatever Rigaut's intentions, and whatever this event might be, it surely hadn't been arranged for my benefit. The police had not picked this spot in order to trap passers-by but because it was unfrequented; the helicopter

106

had merely wanted to make sure I was out of the way before whatever was due to take place – simulated riot? ritual killing? – began.

Walking at a steady pace, I emerged from the wood and crossed the stream. Above me the helicopter finally swung away. In the field, five brown cows chewed obliviously on. In the small road that bordered it three blue buses were parked, and behind them, a red BMW. I crossed the road, and began to climb the hill. Halfway up, I stopped and looked back. The clearing was screened by trees that hid whatever might be happening there. Faintly, on the breeze, I heard whistles and shouts. Whatever it was, was under way.

Logically, that was it. I was through the worst; I hadn't been killed; and as for Rigaut – he was Minister of the Interior, and these were his special troops. If he was in the vicinity, what more natural than for him to review an event such as this? Perhaps that was why he'd decided to visit La Jaubertie today. But my knees knew nothing of logic. Finally and irredeemably, they sank beneath me. At least for the moment, I couldn't go on.

How long that moment would last, I had no way of knowing. Perhaps not too long. But that wasn't the only problem. Before I got back to Les Pruniers I'd have to traverse another wood; and that, in my current state, I knew I could never do. Forward was out.

So, though, was backward. As for sideways, I could take the road – in the end, it would lead somewhere. But it, too, was liable to go through a wood. And in any case, even if I reached the somewhere, it probably wouldn't help much. I only knew four places round here – Meyrignac, St Front, Les Pruniers and La Jaubertie. All were more or less close, but how they all joined up I had no idea. Roads, in this part of the world, meandered from one isolated house to another, and rarely followed the direct route.

I looked at my watch. Almost three o'clock; all I'd eaten since breakfast was a muesli bar. There were blackberries in the hedgerows, but some chocolate would be more to the point. It struck me that there might be some in my bag – I sometimes bought a bar and didn't finish it.

There wasn't; what there was, though, was my mobile phone. And somewhere – with any luck – a bit of paper with the Les Pruniers number on it. Feverishly I scrabbled among the old till receipts and dead handkerchiefs. And yes – there was the card Delphine had given me along with my receipt last time I'd been here.

At the other end the phone sounded shrilly, but no one picked it up, and after eight rings the answering machine clicked on. Naturally. On an afternoon like this they'd all be at the river, or round the new pool.

Hadn't Olivier given me a card? If so it would have his mobile number. I scrabbled again – yes, there it was.

He answered, as I'd hoped he would – no journalist is ever far from his phone. He sounded cross. Probably thought it was the office, after him even on holiday. '*Oui, allo?*'

'Olivier, it's Régine. I'm stuck.'

'Stuck?' Annoyance became surprise. 'How, stuck?'

'Too long to explain. If I told you where I was could you possibly come and find me?' My voice wobbled, and to my horror, I realized I was beginning to cry. Control, control. If he couldn't understand what I was saying, this would be a wholly pointless exercise. I swallowed hard, then described the field, the cows, the stream, the road, the hill.

Olivier said, 'I know exactly. I'll be there in ten minutes.'

I timed it, and in fact it took him seven. The Peugeot approached at speed – from the left, I noticed: lucky I hadn't tried the road, my instinct would have been to turn right – slowed abruptly and parked behind the BMW. Olivier got out and looked around. I shouted and waved; he waved back, and started up towards me.

The relief at his arrival set my tears flowing in unstoppable floods. He sat down beside me, put his arm around me, and waited quietly until I calmed down. Then he said, 'Tell me what happened,' and I did, leaning against his shoulder, while he stroked my hair. After that I burst

108

briefly into tears once more, blew my nose on one of the disgusting old tissues which formed the main contents of my bag, and said, 'I'm so sorry to have brought you out like this.'

'*Ma pauvre* Régine, don't be silly.'

'It wasn't the tile. That was an accident, it could happen to anyone. It was Rigaut. I've never met anyone so scary.'

'Scary? Why, what did he do?'

'Nothing. But then after that helicopter, finding him there in the woods . . .'

'Yes,' he said. 'I can see that. Still, here you are. In spite of everything.' His arm tightened around my shoulders, and he smiled, and then, as though it was the most normal thing in the world, we began kissing, as if the bizarre circumstance had finally freed us to admit that this was what we'd been wanting to do ever since we'd set eyes on each other. Olivier smelt of sweat and soap and Gitanes – I remembered him saying, in the Voltaire, that he smoked them out of solidarity, because so many of his friends and family grew tobacco.

I don't know how long we went on kissing – it felt like an instant, but it might have been hours. Eventually, though, we stopped, and looked at each other. Olivier raised his eyebrow in that annoying way he had and said, 'Régine.'

Who knows what we might have said or done after that? What actually happened was that some of the rioters began emerging from the woods. We abruptly let go of each other (as though any watcher, had he been so inclined, could not have seen us plainly from the cover of the trees). Olivier said sharply, 'What's that?'

'The practice riot I was telling you about. They must have finished.'

'Shit! Come on, let's go.'

We began to make our way down the hill, self-consciously separate, Olivier so concerned to maintain airspace between us that despite my still-wobbly condition he could hardly bring himself to help me over the stile that led to the road.

I could understand that – no one wants to be caught passionately embracing a woman who is not his wife on a hillside five minutes' walk from the family home. What I couldn't understand was why he seemed in such a hurry to reach the car, plunging forward as though it was a matter of life and death, at a pace I found it almost impossible to match. Eventually, however, we made it. Olivier got in the driver's side, and opened the passenger door for me. But before I could shut it, a voice from behind said, 'Well, well. Olivier Peytoureau. What a surprise to see you,' and there was Rigaut.

Olivier said evenly, '*Bonjour*, Monsieur Rigaut.'

'Just taking a walk?' Rigaut glanced at me and gave a perfunctory nod, acknowledging my presence but pointedly not including me in the conversation. 'You two are friends, I see.'

Olivier said, 'And how was the exercise?'

'Impeccable.' Rigaut nodded again, then turned towards the red BMW. One of his aides was waiting there, a great big fellow with a three-day stubble and a crew cut so short you could see the scalp through it, so that the whole of his head, back and front, seemed to be covered with a menacing veil of spiky black hair. He opened the front passenger door for Rigaut, then took the driving seat. I said, 'I wouldn't like to meet him on a dark night.'

Olivier didn't reply. His mind was elsewhere. 'Shit,' he said.

'Do you think he saw us?'

'Probably.' He seemed sunk in gloomy thought.

'Well, why should he care? I'm sure he must have more important things to think about.'

He didn't reply, but started the car. To break the silence I said, 'I still don't know what all that was about, in the woods.'

'Oh, it's the CRS. They have a training centre near here, and it's a good place to practise manoeuvres. Rigaut likes to pay a visit when he's over. I told you, they're his pet boys.'

After that he remained silent until we pulled into the court. Then he said, 'Did you want to tell Delphine?' adding hurriedly, 'About what happened at La Jaubertie.'

'Not particularly,' I said. 'I'm going back there tomorrow.'

'Going back?' His alarm was almost comical.

'To see Juliette.'

'Does Rigaut know?'

'Yes. That's probably why he was so angry.'

'That bastard, he thinks he owns the whole world to do as he likes with.'

I said grimly, 'I'm neurotically counter-suggestible. I'd go back there even if it killed me.'

He shook his head, a small smile on his lips. 'Don't be too sure it won't.'

11

La Jaubertie, August

The day's events, already dreamlike, now took on the differently unreal quality deception adds. I told Delphine I'd twisted my ankle; and although (given that I was clearly able to walk) this couldn't have been very serious, she insisted I take it easy. On no account was I to go out for dinner, as I'd intended: this evening I would eat with the family. In the meantime I pleaded exhaustion, which was real enough, and retired to my room, where I fell into a deep sleep.

By the time I awoke, it was after seven. I lay with my hands behind my head, wishing I didn't have to get up. The last thing I felt like was an edgy evening of pretence. Abstract moral rules have never been my thing, but I do have one or two, and the first is: in a conflict between sex and sisterhood, sisterhood wins. Which, translated, boils down to: keep off your friends' husbands. It seemed a little soon to count Delphine as a friend. But between her and Olivier – no contest. Friendship wasn't his forte – he was too ambitious, too driven, for that. Perhaps that was one of the things that so irresistibly drew us together – like calling to like.

I showered, put on a long-sleeved shirt and trousers to ward off hungry insects, and sallied forth. Delphine was in the kitchen, cutting the small, sweet local melons in half. I asked if I could help, but she shook her head. 'Why don't you sit down and talk to me? Olivier took the kids swimming and they're not back yet. They love it when he's home. We're hoping he won't need to stay in Paris too much longer.'

I couldn't help wondering whether Olivier hoped this as much as Delphine did. 'Would he be able to get the right sort of job near here?'

'He keeps looking. Something's sure to turn up sometime.' She smiled her mischievous, thin-lipped smile and nodded towards the fridge. 'Drink? There's some cold white wine in there. Why don't you pour us a couple and tell me about this project of yours?'

As we sat and chatted in the shady kitchen amid the heavy perfume of ripe melons, I thought again how much I liked Delphine. I should find some excuse to leave – now. Olivier and I would simply have to call off our collaboration, and pursue our stories without each other's help.

I stayed.

At five to eight, the Peugeot drew up in the court and the children, still in their bathing suits, rushed into the kitchen. They'd been to swim in the local river, where the water always stayed cool however hot the weather; tomorrow they planned to take the boat and spend the day there. Delphine sent them away to put some clothes on, and dispatched Olivier to lay the table in the garden. By eight fifteen we were seated around it *en famille*.

After we'd finished eating, the grown-ups sat on drinking a last glass of wine and picking at strawberries while the children rushed off to play. We didn't say much, enjoying the balmy evening while Olivier and I did our best not to catch each other's eyes. At ten, when the children were packed off to bed, I too took my leave. The pretence of normality, with its attendant side-games, was too exhausting. In any case, it had been a long day. With any luck tomorrow should be less exciting; even so, it promised to be effortful in other ways.

I was tired out, but sleep did not come quickly. The day's events replayed endlessly in my head: Juliette and Rigaut, the crash of the tile, the bizarre encounter in the wood. And then those minutes – or hours – on the hillside, the feel of Olivier's arms, his taste, his tongue on mine, the smell of his hair. I told myself it wasn't just wrong, it was ridiculous – he was ten years younger than me, he wasn't an impulsive man, he must have something else in mind. But then I remembered him in the restaurant saying 'Marriages end', and Delphine's evident dissatisfaction with his constant absences. I wondered whether he'd creep round to see me now. He shouldn't – it would be too demeaning, too squalidly deceitful – yet at the same time I wanted him to, so much that my body actually ached. However, he didn't appear. And eventually I fell asleep, awaking only when sunlight on my face told me it was morning, and that last night I'd forgotten to close the shutters.

I'd been alternately dreading and longing for the moment when I'd see Olivier again, but when I went in to breakfast, he was not there. Delphine ran breakfast on a buffet system – a comprehensive array of yoghurts, fruit, cheese, ham, cereals, hardboiled eggs, bread, butter, jam, croissants, thermos jugs of coffee, hot milk, and hot water, and a variety of teabags laid out on a sideboard. By the time I arrived, used cups and plates showed that most of my fellow guests had already been and gone. Only the Dutch couple were visible, eating cheese. They nodded politely and chewed on while I helped myself to cornflakes, greengages, a croissant and milky coffee. After yesterday's experience, I wasn't going to leave without stoking up.

The morning was exquisite. The previous evening there had been another electric storm, and although once again it hadn't rained the air was no longer so heavy, and the sun shone from a clear sky of deepest blue. I could hear the sounds of children playing in the orchard, and eventually went out there myself. The trees were loud with wasps and bowed down with plums, a small, black variety that Delphine had told me were mostly used to make *eau de vie de prune*, the honey-sweet green Reine Claudes I'd sampled at breakfast, and tiny pinkish-yellow mirabelles. The children – Magali, Fabien, and the two English children, who had finally lost their shyness – had left the swing where they'd been playing earlier and were now concentrating hard on something they'd found near the back hedge. How delightful it would be to spend the day in the orchard, to loll in a hammock watching the sky while greengages fell into my mouth! And how deeply I didn't want to set foot in La Jaubertie again!

I was thinking this when Olivier appeared. Despite the untoward ending of our unexpected afternoon, I hadn't been able to stop myself wondering if there might be a sequel, and if so, what it might be. My heart somersaulted; I smiled politely and said, '*Bonjour.*'

He replied equally politely and went straight over to the children. For a minute I felt irrationally hurt. Then he turned and gave me a brilliant, conspiratorial grin, and I was happy again.

Feeling ashamed on many counts, I went into the house. Delphine was in the breakfast room, clearing up. She looked up, smiled, and said, 'Régine, don't think I'm trying to get rid of you or anything, but I was wondering – do you have any idea how long you'll be staying?'

'I've got an appointment at La Jaubertie this morning,' I said. 'I don't know how long it'll go on. Would it be OK to stay tonight? I'll take myself out, obviously.'

She nodded. 'That's fine. Just so I know.'

'Are you full for the rest of the week?'

'Absolutely, and the tourist office just rang with more people. That's why I need to know.'

'That's excellent,' I said politely.

'It is good, though I sometimes think it'd be nice not to work so hard when Olivier's here. Still, I like to be independent. And this was my idea, after all.' She gave a wry little smile. Evidently it wasn't the first time she'd rehearsed this argument.

When I got to La Jaubertie Juliette was sitting out on the lawn under the big cedar tree, in a high-backed wooden chair at a slatted teak table; another chair stood vacant – presumably for me. Apart from the builders, who were still pushing out tiles this Saturday morning, she seemed to be alone in the house – neither the Renault 4 nor the BMW was there. She was reading a paper with the aid of a magnifying glass and, until my shadow fell across the page, had not registered my presence.

'Régine! You gave me a fright.'

'I'm sorry,' I said. 'I didn't mean to.'

'Well. Now you're here, why don't you go in and get us some water? I get so thirsty in this heat. The kitchen's to your right when you go in.'

'What about Amos? Will he let me in?'

'He's not here, he belongs to Babette and she's having a few days off while her son's home.'

The kitchen was cool, small and comparatively modern, with a white ceramic double sink, a small gas stove and a big larder fridge containing several bottles of Perrier and a number of labelled plastic boxes presumably left by Babette: *Déjeuner samedi, Diner samedi, Déjeuner dimanche* ... Armed with a bottle and two glasses I returned to the lawn and poured us each some water.

'You don't mind being all alone?'

'I can manage. Babette leaves me plenty of food, and the bar will send something if I phone. Jean-Jacques wanted to send someone, but I prefer to manage by myself.'

For whose benefit, exactly, the 'someone'? I wondered if her thoughts were the same as mine.

'Did you know your son had written to me about the picture?' I asked her.

'He mentioned something ... What did he say?'

I held out the letter. She took it and read it, again using the magnifying glass, then handed it back, shaking her head. 'He's always so obstinate,' she said irritably, as though we were discussing a problem child. 'He gets an idea into his head ... I told him I'd do what I wanted with my own property, but he's too used to getting his own way, that's the trouble. So when I wouldn't agree with him he

116

tried something else. It's rubbish, take no notice.' I must
have looked sceptical, for she added: 'He's a bully, always
has been. He relies on intimidating people into doing what
he wants. Just ignore him. It's the only way. Do you have
a pen?'

I nodded, mystified, and held it out. Below Rigaut's
signature she wrote: *This is a lie. I alone own the picture and
the loan will go ahead.* She signed and dated it, and handed
it back. 'There.'

I took it gingerly, as one might a stick of dynamite. 'Are
you really sure this will be all right?'

'Why shouldn't it?'

'I don't want to make trouble.'

'With Jean-Jacques,' she said, 'you can't avoid trouble.
He searches it out. Always has. All one can do is ignore it
or stand up to him.'

There didn't seem much point arguing. Presumably she
knew her own son.

I thanked her and stashed the letter safely away in my
bag. I'd brought my little tape machine along, and now I
pulled it out. 'I was wondering, since I'm here, if perhaps
you could tell me a bit more of your story.'

'It's rather long,' she said drily. 'Which bits did you have
in mind?'

'What happened after your brother died. And during the
war.' Perhaps we'd get to the bottom of that rumour. Or
perhaps she wouldn't mention it at all.

She sat back in her chair. For some minutes she said
nothing, and I wondered whether she'd drifted off to sleep.
But then she spoke. 'So long ago,' she said. 'But to me it
seems like yesterday.'

After Robert's death, Juliette said, she collapsed. She
knew it was her fault, and she wanted to die too. She
refused to go home to La Jaubertie but took refuge with an
aunt, her mother's sister, in Passy. Eventually, however, she
began to recover, and the question arose: where would
she go? Her aunt and her parents naturally assumed it
would be La Jaubertie, but that was out of the question. So

was rue d'Assas (which now belonged to her: her parents, on her father's insistence, had made over their share in it). Emmanuel wanted her to live with him – he was making a good living as a photographer, and had a chic new studio in Montparnasse. But she'd put her parents through so much – she couldn't add to their misery after what had happened. So Emmanuel came up with a solution: they would get married.

That was in the spring of 1938. Then in 1939 war was declared, and Emmanuel was conscripted. When France fell he was near St Quentin, and there was no word to say what had become of him. She refused to leave Paris, but continued with her job as a legal secretary. If he had been taken prisoner, or had escaped, she would have heard, so she assumed he must be dead.

One day someone cautiously opened the door and slid into the studio. She cried out in alarm: the intruder swung round: she found herself staring at a pistol. Terrified, she raised her eyes.

Emmanuel.

He wasn't in uniform, and his clothes were different from the civilian clothes he usually wore. He explained that they were English. He'd come from England – from London. Officially, he didn't exist.

'Then how will you eat?' she asked. Everything was rationed, and without papers there were no rations.

'I've got some papers,' he said, but did not tell her whose.

Later, she heard his story – or some of it. The armistice had caught his company near St Quentin. In the confusion of the retreat he and a friend had made off, lain low for a while at a farm near the fortress of Ham, then made their way to the coast at Hardelot-Plage near Boulogne. There, one night, they stole a dinghy and rowed across the Channel. They got across against all the odds, only to have their adventure nearly ended when in theory they had finally reached safety. It was four in the morning, first light, and they were beaching their boat, when a patrol of the

Home Guard came across them, took them for German spies, and almost shot them. Fortunately they managed to persuade their captors that they were French, not German, and were taken to the local schoolmaster, who was also the commanding officer, and who eventually put them on the train for London, where they joined General de Gaulle. Now Emmanuel had been sent back to France, charged with various missions. He wanted to know who Juliette saw, how she spent her days, whether she knew any Germans, whether she ever came across the Resistance.

He didn't live at the studio, though he often appeared there, and sometimes stayed the night. She didn't ask what he was doing, nor where he got the money to live; nor did she mention his presence to any of her friends. She didn't even know what name he operated under, though she did know that it was not his own, and that he had several sets of false papers. She simply did what she was told, without ever asking why, or knowing whether her action had had the desired effect. If there were others – and there must have been others – she never met them. She took instructions only from him, and only directly, by word of mouth, never in writing. Her life became a series of apparently random encounters. In the galleried café of the Samaritaine department store, with its many exits and entrances, she sat at the table he had specified, beside the wrought-iron balcony railing that overlooked the scurrying ground-floor shoppers, and passed an envelope, concealed in the menu, to a waitress who announced herself by tapping the table twice with her pencil. Another day, in the hat department, when she tried on a small red confection with a pheasant-feather after it had been rejected by a chic blonde woman in her thirties, she found a note behind the feather, which she passed on without reading it to a tailor in the rue Christine. In a little bookshop near the Odéon, she left a parcel in the back room, addressed to a Monsieur Denoyau. Taking her friend Arlette's little girl Aurélie to a nursery near the parc Monceau, she exchanged the child for a slip of paper with an address, passed on to her by a girl with black curls in a red and white print dress. On these occasions she felt much as she had that April morning in the Louvre – scared, excited, jubilant, defiant, triumphant.

Then he vanished again; what might have happened to him this time, she had no way of knowing. She thought of going over to the rue d'Assas to check on the house, but decided not to, partly because the place still filled her with revulsion, partly because it was possible she was being followed and she didn't want to risk endangering any of his plans. Grimly, automatically, she went on with her life, but as the months passed, she feared the worst. The hardest thing, she found, was that there was no one she could talk to. Emmanuel's appearances and disappearances were things she had never mentioned: as far as the world was concerned, her husband was dead or in England.

And then, one day, there he was again, waiting for her when she returned from work, sitting in the old armchair by the window. He told her he'd had to vanish, fast. For the moment, however, the danger seemed to have abated. Their old life resumed, though not quite as before. Emmanuel was warier, his appearances even more spasmodic, and he no longer asked her to run errands for him. It seemed that the network had been betrayed by one of the people at the bookshop, and it wasn't safe to use anyone who had been even tenuously connected with it.

Two months after his return, she knew she was pregnant.

Emmanuel was horrified. He would have liked her to have an abortion. When she refused, he suggested she go home to have the baby at La Jaubertie. At first she just laughed. But the more she thought about it, the more appealing the idea seemed. It might thaw her mother, who since Robert's death had retreated into fanatical Catholicism. And (since there could be no question of Emmanuel living with her) it would be better than trying to manage alone in Paris.

She left in May: she was two and a half months gone. The journey took three days in trains that were infrequent, slow, and full to bursting. Her father met her at the station: on their way back to the house, she told him she was pregnant. When she asked if he was pleased he gave her a look she remembered from when she was ten years old, and had said something unexpectedly stupid. 'Of course I'd *like* to be pleased,' he said. 'But whose child is this, exactly? I suppose you do know?' And she remembered that as far as the world was concerned, Emmanuel was dead.

So she told him the whole story – how Emmanuel had escaped, and was working for the Resistance. And he sighed, and said they'd better not mention that to her mother. She wasn't to be trusted – Robert's death had unhinged her slightly, she blamed it on his Communist friends, she was a hardline Pétainist. And there was a German staying in the house – an officer, one of the occupying force, billeted on them. He was living in Robert's old room, and her mother was very friendly with him. So – discretion. They'd think of some story. Meanwhile Juliette should keep quiet.

Unfortunately, pregnancy isn't a secret anyone can keep for long. Their old *bonne à tout faire* Suzanne guessed immediately. She, too, assumed Juliette had been sleeping around – and this time, there could be no explanation. That was when Juliette took in how hard life might become. So she began to do the kind of heavy work that might bring on a miscarriage – like digging the vegetable garden. Which was how she met the German. He offered to help, and she told him to go back to Germany – that would be the best help he could give her. Then, realizing how foolish she had been, she waited for some reprisal. But it never came.

By then she'd confessed about the baby. 'What do you think I am, blind?' Véronique asked bitterly.

The question of paternity naturally arose. Juliette told her mother the child was Emmanuel's. 'Back from the dead?' Véronique mocked. Juliette explained that he was indeed alive, but moving around, and thought she'd be

121

safer at La Jaubertie. Which of course could mean only one thing – the Resistance.

'Why didn't you tell me this before?' her mother asked. She was very angry. 'You thought I'd denounce him, is that it?'

What could Juliette say? It was exactly what she'd thought.

The showdown cleared the air, and things became easier. The atmosphere lightened, and the coming baby was acknowledged, if not joyfully welcomed.

By this time Juliette knew the German better. He was called Kopp – Helmut Kopp. In civilian life he was an architect, and came from Hamburg. He was good-looking – tall, blond, with high cheekbones and grey eyes: a true Aryan. They'd got talking one day when he found her in her father's study. He said he wanted to look at the picture. He'd guessed it was a Caravaggio – one of his favourite painters. And by the end of the conversation, Juliette had to admit that she rather liked him. As her mother had said, he was just another human being. One day he asked her when the baby was due. She told him, December.

He said, 'I like the idea of a baby. Such a normal thing in all this craziness.'

'I wonder if you'll still be here then.'

'Do you hope I won't?'

'Of course,' she replied, but they both knew that things had got too complicated for 'of course'. After that she tried to avoid these encounters: her feelings about him were too confused.

At the beginning of December, most of the German troops moved on, and Helmut with them: military exigencies demanded their presence elsewhere. Juliette's mother mourned his departure – he had been such an addition to the household, so cultured, so delightful – and to her shame, Juliette, too, found herself missing him.

The baby arrived on 31st December, at three in the morning: a boy, called Antoine after Juliette's grandfather. He was a big baby, and wakeful. During the next months, she spent many night hours walking about the house with Antoine suspended in a sling on her hip, trying to lull him to sleep. It was during one of these perambulations that she became aware of her father's hidden life.

It was April, 1943: Antoine was just over three months old. As usual he had begun to cry after his evening feed, and continued inconsolably until midnight. Tired of walking the dim rooms she decided to vary her route, and descended the staircase to the garden room. She paced along the front, then turned towards one of the small towers at the back. She had just reached it when its door began to open.

She opened her mouth to scream, but was so paralysed with horror that as in a nightmare no sound came. The door opened wider – and her father emerged, holding a hurricane lantern in one hand and a shopping basket in the other.

It was hard to say which of them was the more astonished. Juliette, anxious not to wake the baby, whispered in the low croak that for the moment seemed to have replaced her voice, 'Papa! I thought it was burglars! What on earth are you doing?' Her father started as though he had been stung. The hurricane lantern went out, leaving everyone in the dark. And Antoine, roused by the sudden switch from light to dark, or by his mother's transmitted terror, began to bawl. She hugged him close, jiggled and kissed him, but he yelled inconsolably on.

'Shush, *petit*,' Etienne said. 'You'll have the whole household down.'

'What are you talking about?' said Juliette, angry with relief. 'There's only Maman, and she's not going to get up because Antoine's crying. What on earth were you doing?' she asked again.

He shook his head. 'Nothing that need worry you. Go back to bed.'

Two days after the midnight incident, they had a visit. Lunch was over, it was a sunny afternoon, and Madame de Beaupré, who however mixed her feelings regarding her daughter was unequivocally besotted by her new grandson, was walking him round the park in Juliette's old pram. Juliette, as often in these periods of respite, was in her father's study. She was dozing over a novel when a sharp knock on the door brought her to abrupt wakefulness.

Her father, who in his capacity of mayor was used to these interruptions, said, '*Oui*,' and went on writing. The door opened, and in marched three Germans in the uniform of the Gestapo. They must have arrived while Juliette was asleep. Craning out of the window, she could see their car parked by the tower.

Etienne put down his pen. '*Alors, messieurs?*' he said politely.

One of them said something in German. Etienne shook his head. 'I'm sorry, messieurs, I don't speak German.'

The youngest of the three visitors came forward and repeated the request, this time in French. 'Monsieur, we would like to search your house.'

'Search my house? What for?'

'We have information that some people we are looking for were seen in this area. We are searching all the houses in the village. I must remind you, you should tell us if you know anything about this.'

'But of course I'd tell you, I'm the mayor, that's my job,' Etienne said politely. 'By all means search. I'm afraid it's rather a large house. Do you want me to show you round?'

'Thank you, we can do it,' said the officer.

'Will you begin here?' Etienne gestured round the room.

The Germans, clearly somewhat embarrassed, looked around. There was in fact, as Juliette knew, a secret door behind one of the bookshelves, leading to a space in the wall, which at this point was two metres thick. It had been a favourite hiding-place in the games she and Robert used to play with their friends when they were children. No one knew who had made it, or why, though it probably dated from the wars of religion. She watched as the Germans blundered past it and wondered whether anyone was hidden there. It seemed unlikely.

They left the room and moved on. For the next three quarters of an hour they could be heard moving round the house, carefully shifting and replacing furniture, opening cupboard doors. Etienne continued with his interrupted business. Juliette, looking out of the window, saw her mother approaching with the pram, got up and went out to meet her. 'The Germans are searching the house,' she warned, as her mother wheeled the old-fashioned perambulator with its sleeping baby into the garden room.

Leaving Antoine asleep, they mounted the stairs. Overhead, footsteps sounded on bare boards. Then the young French-speaking officer appeared on the stairs, followed by his colleagues. 'Can you show me please how to get to the space under the roof, and the cellar?'

Silently, Juliette indicated the doors in the small towers. 'Please be as quiet as you can,' she said sternly. 'I don't want the baby wakened.'

The Germans disappeared, and they joined Etienne in the study.

'Are they still here?'

'They're in the cellar,' Juliette said, watching him.

Etienne nodded: he seemed unmoved. He continued calmly with his work, while Juliette and Véronique sat in tense silence. Twenty minutes later there was a knock on the door. The Germans had finished, evidently without finding anything. The one who was in charge, a fleshy, burly man with a florid face, clicked his heels. '*Danke, Herr Bürgermeister.*'

Etienne nodded and went on writing.

One sunny day in early July, Emmanuel arrived at La Jaubertie. The Beauprés were away for a couple of days at a cousin's first communion, and Juliette and Antoine were sitting out on the grass, Antoine practising crawling, while Juliette picked wild strawberries to share with him. Intent on her task she didn't hear the footstep – and then, when she looked up, there he was, standing before her. '*Bonjour,*' he said, and dropped down on to the grass beside them. *'Bonjour, mon bébé!'* He picked up Antoine, held him up in the air, pretended to drop him, and caught him in the nick of time. Antoine laughed madly, and Emmanuel did it again.

'I can't believe it,' Juliette said. The whole thing seemed unreal. She half-believed this wasn't the real Emmanuel at all, but an apparition. However, when she put out a hand and touched him, he seemed solid enough – though even thinner than before, and older-looking, his hair receding, and new lines on his face, which was grimy and stubbled. But real.

He told her he'd been moving around – impossible to get in touch. But he was working nearby, at least for a little while. He couldn't stay, for reasons they both knew – he'd waited to come till he knew Juliette would be alone.

'You can stay tonight, at any rate. Papa and Maman won't be back till tomorrow evening, and I told Suzanne I'd look after myself.'

Later, Juliette looked back on those fleeting hours as the nearest she ever really came to happiness. At the time, though, it was almost impossible to enjoy them fully, because the future, in which nothing was certain, was already almost upon them. At five in the afternoon on the second day, Emmanuel said he must be off. Her parents would be back soon, and in any case, he had an appointment to keep.

'Shall we see you again?'

'Of course,' he said, 'it's just a question of where and when. I'll try and drop you a line.'

So life went on, with its absence of young men, its shortages, its bitterness. People heard that their sons had died working as slave labourers in Germany. In Meyrignac the Kommandantur was blown up, and in reprisal twelve local men were shot in the pétanque alley, under the plane trees. There were rumours of refugees – airmen who had been shot down, Jews on the run from deportation – but no one ever admitted having actually seen one. Antoine continued wakeful, but Juliette, on her nocturnal perambulations, avoided the garden room. Occasionally a postcard would arrive for her, unsigned, but proof that Emmanuel was still alive, and still thinking of her.

And then, suddenly, the Germans were in vicious retreat. In St Front, there was panic: troops were rumoured to be burning and raping in the next village, and for a day and a night the entire population (fortunately it was summer) took to the woods. One of Etienne's friends, the owner of a nearby château, rang to say that they had had a looting party. The local Gauleiter had had his officers make a list of all the antiques and artworks they had noticed in the various châteaux where they had been billeted, and the Germans were systematically removing them, to be sent back to Germany ahead of the retreat. 'They'll be round at your place next,' he said. 'You might just have time to hide your best pieces.'

Juliette, Etienne and Véronique stood in the study around the Caravaggio. It was by far the most valuable item in the house, and Helmut, who had been so struck with it, must inevitably have mentioned it. Véronique wanted to hide it in the secret space behind the bookcases. But Etienne wouldn't let her. 'If they know about it they'll know we've hidden it – in any case, imagine the mark it'll leave – and they'll tear the place apart to find it,' he said. 'I'd rather sacrifice one picture than lose the house.' He was adamant. Nothing was to be hidden. If the Germans came, they came. 'What does it matter?' he said. 'It's only things. If that's all we lose, we'll be a good deal luckier than most.'

All that day and all the next they sat and waited to be robbed. But nobody came, and nobody came. The Germans had gone, and La Jaubertie, alone of the local grand houses, had been spared. For some reason (and Juliette thought she knew what that reason might have been) Helmut must have seen to it that they were not on the list.

The next thing anyone heard, Paris had been retaken and France was free once more. And that was when the murmuring began. For of course, now that the Germans were defeated, everyone suddenly discovered that they had supported the Resistance and had never contemplated co-operation with the hated Boche. And as this had clearly not been the case – as everyone knew that there had indeed been collaborators, people who had been more than happy to go along with the new regime – the search for scapegoats was on. Madame de Beaupré's politics were well known; and had not Etienne been only too happy to take over the mayor's job when his old adversary Peytoureau had resigned it? Hadn't that German officer been billeted on the Beauprés at just about the right time . . .? And nothing taken from the house. It didn't take a genius to put two and two together.

Fancy a girl deceiving her husband like that! Poor young man, it was hardly his fault if he wasn't around. For somehow, now, everyone knew about Emmanuel – how he was none other than the famous Bizouleur, whose Resistance network had organized an underground railroad that had saved literally hundreds of unfortunate refugees.

One morning Suzanne arrived looking grim. A mob was gathering on the road, she said. They were saying that Antoine was the German's child, and everyone knew what happened to women who had slept with the occupiers. Obviously it wasn't true, at least about the baby (and here Suzanne, who of course knew Juliette had been pregnant before she arrived at La Jaubertie, gave a sly look that made clear her guilty pleasure in Helmut's company had not gone unnoticed). But delicate questions of when exactly conception had taken place were unlikely to hold much sway in a situation like this.

They all knew what this meant. Juliette would be pulled out into the crowd, and there, in the middle of them all, holding her baby, her head would be shaved. After that, bald and weeping, she would have to run a jeering gauntlet every time she went out, not just once, but for months, until her hair had grown back and the sign of shame had finally vanished. Who could survive something like that? It would kill her. It would kill them all.

'Come on,' said her father. 'There's only one thing to be done. We've got to get you away. Go and pack a few things for you and Antoine, and we'll go.'

She didn't ask what he had in mind – she didn't need to. Hastily she ran to her room and packed a bag – the lightest she could manage: a few of her own things, a few of Antoine's. The rest could be sent on. She ran back down, picked up Antoine, kissed her mother, and followed her father to the cellar door.

He was carrying something – she couldn't quite make out what – but she didn't pause to ask what it was. Shutting and locking the door behind them, she followed him down the winding stair and out into the twilit cellars, with their smell, so familiar from her childhood, of mingled sawdust and mushrooms. She knew where they were going now.

The cellars at La Jaubertie were very ancient, far older than any portion of the above-ground house. The limestone hills in this part of the world were honeycombed with caves, and it was upon one such system that the house had originally been built. The cellars now were lit from shafts at ground level, but although round romanesque arches and huge beams supported the house above, and the walls, half buried under the detritus of centuries – discarded bottles, salt troughs, old logs, broken furniture – were of dressed stone blocks, the floor beneath their feet was earth, while stalactites here and there depended from the ceiling.

Etienne, following the light of a torch, walked swiftly to the far end. Here the wall was hidden behind a stack of old door frames and other assorted woodwork, the relics of some long-past building works. He slid behind the stack – and vanished.

Juliette, following, retraced the steps of a thousand childhood games of hide and seek. For, as every child who had ever lived in the house knew, the caves on which La

Jaubertie was built did not stop at the cellar, but extended much further. She didn't remember this stack of wood – it had obviously been moved since she had last come this way – but she knew what it concealed: a low natural arch that led from the cellars into the caves beyond.

The cellars proper were lofty and spacious, but in the cave the roof was low, and the way littered with stones. Holding Antoine tightly by the hand – fortunately he was now walking – Juliette followed the beam of her father's torch.

For about ten minutes they stumbled along in the cramped semi-dark, and then, suddenly, the passage opened out, as she knew it would, into a large, dry space. Here Etienne put down the torch beside an as yet undifferentiated heap of objects, pulled a box of matches from his pocket, and lit a hurricane lantern.

By this new light, they could see that the heap consisted of a neat pile of bedding, a camp stove, some cans of food, and a few bicycles. Etienne pulled out two bicycles, a man's and a woman's, and picked up the object he had carried here from the house. It was a child's bicycle seat – Juliette's own old bicycle seat, on which she had so often ridden behind her mother or father when the family cycled out into the country for a summer jaunt. With the familiarity of long practice Etienne fixed it to the woman's bike.

'Nearly there now,' he said. 'Not that I need to tell you.'

Handing Juliette her bike to wheel, and holding it while she sat Antoine on the child-seat, he took the other and strapped her bag on to its back carrier. By the light of the hurricane lantern he traced an upwardly sloping path that she knew led to the cave's mouth. She said, 'Was this where you brought them?' It was the first time she'd spoken since they left the house.

'Yes. Mostly they were just passing through, but sometimes someone had to stay for a little while.'

'That's what they were looking for, that time.'

'I suppose so,' he said. 'But I never felt there was much

danger of anyone guessing. What better camouflage could one ask for than your mother?'

'Did she know?'

'Don't be silly,' Etienne said. 'Here we are.'

The cave opened on to a hillside, on the far side of the pinewood through which the Jaubertie path ran. In the valley behind them, beside the stream, was a high barbed-wire fence. Nodding towards it, Etienne said, 'The line of demarcation. Over there it was occupied, but here it was free. In a manner of speaking. At any rate, once they were out here they were safe. Or safer.' He looked at his watch. 'We'll cycle to Meyrignac and you can get the train. With any luck you'll be in time for the twelve twenty, and that should get you to Libourne in time to pick up the one thirty to Paris. Will Emmanuel be there?'

'Even if he's not, I've got the key.'

In fact Juliette had had a letter from Emmanuel. He was getting the studio in order, and when it was ready he'd let her know. When that would be he hadn't said, but if all else failed there was her house. Though she'd rather not go there. What kind of state it would be in, she didn't like to think. Not to speak of the other reasons.

So Juliette and her father cycled off into the summer morning, along the roads of her childhood, her baby riding behind her just as, years before, she had ridden behind her father. But this time the purpose was not pleasure but to escape people who had met her on those very rides, people she had thought her friends, whose children she had played with and grown up with. Perhaps some of those very children were shouting for her now, as she rode.

Half-blinded with tears, she pedalled the steep roads. Meyrignac wasn't far – perhaps seven kilometres – but the ride was taxing: even though most of it was downhill, there were some hefty climbs, especially with Antoine at her back.

Half an hour later, they rolled into Meyrignac station. Her father pressed some money into her hand. 'Good luck, *mon chouchou*,' he said, and waved as the train pulled out.

She never saw him again.

12

La Jaubertie, August

'So,' she said, when eventually the relentless flow of words trickled to a halt. 'Is that what you wanted to know?'

Was it? Or was it what she wanted me to know? If those were two different things. *You can't trust the Beauprés. Just because they tell you something doesn't mean it's true.*

Though of course, Juliette was not the only one here with axes to grind. Quite apart from the families' political differences, there was the still-rankling question of Arnaud. Olivier's Mamie must be much the same age as Juliette. I wondered whether she'd been one of the one-time friends Juliette had dreaded meeting, one of the mob that had gathered outside La Jaubertie that summer day.

Dusk was beginning to fall: little flittering bats swooped busily past our heads amid the black silhouettes of trees; every few seconds a midwife toad emitted its two-tone electronic signal – fa-doh. For a while we sat in silence. A jumble of contradictions and questions jostled inside my head. I wondered about that last flight, trying to work out, from what I could remember of the cellar, where the hidden exit must be – perhaps behind that mound of stones heaped against the end wall? – and where, on the hillside, it came out. But that could be verified. Unlike almost everything else.

In general I thought she'd been telling the truth. Antoine had been born here, the elder Beauprés had behaved as she described, the German officer had lodged at the château and had in some way saved the Caravaggio from the looters. It was the particulars that were troubling. Who was really Antoine Rigaut's father? About Jean-Jacques' parentage there could be no question: I had seen many photographs of Emmanuel Rigaut, and Jean-Jacques looked just like him – there was no mistaking that attenuated build, which he had in turn passed on to his own son. But Antoine had not looked like that. His photos showed someone squarer, blonder, with high cheekbones – unlike either Rigaut or Juliette, but similar to Juliette's description of Helmut Kopp. Whether this meant anything was of course another matter. Likenesses skip generations: failing a detailed timetable of arrivals and departures, or a blood test, there could be no proof either way. Of course, for the mob such questions had been neither here nor there. For people whose sons and husbands were slave labourers or prisoners, or had risked their lives every day with the maquis – or who had guilty secrets of their own to conceal – the Beauprés offered too tempting and convenient a target. Details were beside the point.

And her escape. Had it really happened like that, or had they, as Meyrignac gossip proclaimed, in fact caught her? One side or the other was substituting the desperate wish for the ghastly, or thwarted, reality. But which? And if this was so cloudy, what confidence could be placed in the rest of her tale? What else might she have changed – or simply left out?

Still, as between Juliette and her son, there was no contest in the truth stakes. When it came to the picture's ownership, he was lying. Of that I was certain. Why, that was the question.

After a while I broke the silence. 'What happened to your father? You say you never saw him again. Did he die? He can't have been very old.'

'He was killed that autumn in a hunting accident.' Juliette's tone was scornful and she raised her eyebrows dismissively as she spoke.

That dated the photo in Mamie's envelope: it must have been taken in September or October, 1945. Didier Peytoureau, returned from underground, had evidently known about Etienne de Beaupré's activities. Perhaps that was why he had been photographed with him – Didier's friendship a proof of Etienne's bona fides. If so, that hadn't been enough to save him: word hadn't got around, or if it had, had not been believed. Everyone knew that Juliette's mother, whether or not in technical terms a collaborator, had been sympathetic to the invaders. As for her father, had he not agreed to serve as mayor under the hated regime? – unlike his old political opponent Alban Peytoureau, whose son, now dead, had been considered not good enough for Mademoiselle de Beaupré. Such things were not easily overlooked nor forgotten.

'You don't believe it was an accident?'

She shrugged, a graceful, expressive gesture recalling a time when her neck was not yet concertinaed with wrinkles. 'Who knows? Accidents do happen. Every year the papers are full of them. But there were an awful lot that particular autumn. You couldn't help noticing.'

'But people must have known he wasn't a collaborator by then. Lots of people must have known that.'

'I don't think so. You had to keep those things very, very quiet. And afterwards, why would he talk about it? He wasn't that sort of man. Of course there may have been one or two who knew. But most people had no idea what my father did until your Queen came here, to thank us personally.'

'Was that when the photograph was taken, the one on the stairs?'

Juliette nodded. 'She came in 1954. By then, of course, my father wasn't here any more. But my mother was glad enough to take the credit,' she added drily. 'A visit from the Queen of England was something I don't expect she'd ever imagined.'

1954, I thought. By then the Queen of England was in fact her visitor's daughter. Yet another unimportant detail.

134

A queen was a queen – and in this context, this was the queen that mattered.

'Were you and Emmanuel in Paris then?'

'Yes. He was very surprised to see me and Antoine when we first arrived. Not particularly pleased. During the war he'd led this extraordinary life, very dangerous, always moving about, and I don't think he found it easy to adapt to just everyday existence with a small child. And of course everything was a terrible mess. There'd been Germans living in the studio while we were away, and in my little house. They'd used his papers for kindling, and burned half the furniture. And – well, anyway, we cleaned it all up, and life began again, and I got pregnant again. But in the end we couldn't make it work. We'd married very young. And too much had happened to us separately.'

'What a life you've led.'

She sighed. 'Unfortunately.'

'Fortunate, unfortunate . . . I could never have done all the things you did.'

'With any luck you'll never have to find out. It's not really anything personal. When you look back you realize it's a question of when and where you were born, nothing more.'

'Yes, but going to Paris in the first place. That was brave.'

She shrugged. 'I couldn't bear the alternative, that's all. That, yes, that was a decision. But everything else just – happened. That's how it is, circumstances take over. There was Emmanuel. There was the war. There were the children. That especially. Do you have children, Madame Lee?'

'No,' I said. 'I don't.'

'Why is that, if I may ask? Or perhaps you couldn't.'

'No, I probably could.'

In fact there was no probably about it. Like so many of the women I knew I'd once found myself unexpectedly and inconveniently pregnant, and had a termination. It wasn't a decision I regretted, though inevitably I sometimes wondered how things would have turned out if I'd had the child. 'It just never seemed to be the right

135

moment. So it didn't happen. It's as you were saying. Circumstances.'

'And are you successful in your work?'

Surprised – this was the last question I'd have expected – I said, 'I suppose I am. Quite. Not as much as I'd want. But then, is one ever? Even if I seemed, as you say, successful to other people, I don't expect that's how I'd think of myself. Not in those terms. I mean, is there ever a moment when you say, Yes, I've done it, I've got where I wanted?'

'It's hard to imagine,' she agreed.

'Impossible. And if you're a woman there are always too many choices. If you're not careful you can fall between all the stools.'

'Not when I was a girl,' Juliette replied firmly. 'There were no choices then. I suppose that was one reason I ran away. I'm not a very domestic person, I'd have liked a career, and in the convent that was a sort of blasphemy. In the end, of course, domesticity was what I got. Most women did, in my generation. But what I dreamed of was a life like yours. In your place, though, I'd imagine that's the question I'd always be asking. Am I successful enough to compensate?'

'Put like that . . .' I couldn't help laughing.

'Excuse me – I must seem very impertinent. I was interested, that's all. Isn't that why this exhibition of yours is so important to you?'

'I think it would be important anyway. But you're right, it means a lot to me. Madame, can I ask a favour?'

'You can ask, of course.'

'I'd like to look at the picture again. Perhaps take a photo or two.'

'I don't see why not,' she said after a while. 'And there are some other things I can show you that might interest you.'

Stiffly she rose from her chair and led the way into the château, turning on lights as she went, so that the garden, which had seemed merely twilit, was suddenly plunged in

136

blackness. We passed the Queen Mother, looking as always sweetly regal and pastel-tinted, and made our way through the enfilade to the study.

Juliette lit a lamp, and the Caravaggio sprang into life. I brought my camera out of my bag – I'd taken Olivier's advice about insurance and replaced the one I'd lost in Paris with a superior model, even smaller but technically more advanced. As I took the photos I thought of the young German who had stood in this spot sixty years ago – now, presumably, a very old German, if indeed he was still alive. I wondered what his memories of that time were.

'Did you ever hear from the German after the war? Helmut Kopp?'

She shook her head and said firmly, 'Never.'

'Did you ever wonder about him?'

'I put him out of my mind,' she said, and lowering herself on to a stool in front of one of the bookcases, began searching among the folders and file-boxes that occupied its bottom shelf. Eventually she found what she was looking for and slowly, slowly, declining all offers of help, levered herself upright again.

The object she now held out to me was an old notebook, with board covers and marbled endpapers. On its front was a peeling label upon which could just be made out, in faded round script: *V. de Beaupré, achats 1910–1914.* 'I told you my grandfather was a collector,' she said. 'He kept a record of what he bought and where. He bought the Caravaggio in 1910. I thought you might be interested to see his notes.'

I took the book to the lamp, but its faded writing was not easy to make out. It seemed to be a kind of diary, with records of meetings. Flicking through it I noticed some names – Mascagni, Sangallo – that rang faint art-historical bells. Hadn't they been dealers around the turn of the nineteenth and twentieth centuries? Perhaps one of them had sold Juliette's grandfather the Caravaggio. But whether or not the book was relevant to the exhibition, it was certainly interesting, and full of the kind of detail that needed longer

137

study than I could give it here – tonight, at any rate. I said, 'Could I borrow it? I'd bring it back tomorrow.'

Juliette considered this, then shook her head and said, reasonably enough, 'No, I think I'd prefer you to look at it here.'

'Then perhaps I could come back tomorrow morning? We're both tired, and the light's not very good. What time shall I come? Would nine o'clock be all right?'

She nodded, clearly exhausted now, drained of colour, her skin stretched tightly over her cheekbones. 'Perhaps a little later. I'll call to tell you when I'm ready. Is there a phone where you're staying?'

I gave her the number of my mobile.

It was past nine o'clock by the time I left La Jaubertie. I drove first to Meyrignac, where I ate a pizza in a café, then back to Les Pruniers. By the time I got there it was twenty past ten, and I went straight to my room. Various sounds – banging doors, someone talking on the phone, a child briefly crying – indicated the presence of others. But they didn't disturb me. I fell into bed, and into a profound sleep.

I woke at eight, showered, dressed and went to find some breakfast, wondering if Olivier would be about. To my relief he remained invisible, though I caught a glimpse of Delphine in the depths of the kitchen, and we exchanged cheery bonjours. In the breakfast room the Dutch couple were once again deeply occupied with cheese. I'd decided that the quickest and best way to record the book's contents would be to photograph them, so back in my room I transferred last night's photos to my laptop and stowed the camera in my bag. Then I sat by the window and waited for my phone to ring. Nine o'clock, five past . . . By ten past I was quite sure Juliette had decided not to call after all. She'd had second thoughts, she was too tired – it was all off. Perhaps I'd written the number down wrong – perhaps she'd mislaid the scrap of paper . . .

Five minutes later, the call came.

'Régine? Juliette Rigaut. You can come now, if you want.'

In the now-familiar driveway, I saw with relief that no other car was in evidence. Evidently Babette was still away. I parked in the usual place at the foot of the tower and rang the bell to announce my presence. No one answered, so I tried the door. It was unlocked: I let myself in, closing it behind me. There was no sign of Juliette in the garden room, but I knew she was up and expecting me. I ran up the staircase, but she was still nowhere to be seen. When I reached the salon I called out, 'Madame, it's Régine,' but there was no reply.

What now? She must be somewhere around, but I could hardly comb the house looking for her. I decided to go straight to the study and get on with photographing the notebook. Perhaps I would find her there waiting for me.

Juliette was not in the study, but the notebook lay on the table beside the window, where we'd left it the previous night. The light still wasn't wonderful – a lowering sky promised yet more storms – and I'd have felt more confident if I'd had a tripod to hold the camera steady, but I'd done this sort of work before, and it ought to be all right. Starting with the first page, I photographed spread after spread, without bothering to read what was written there. Time enough for that when the job was done.

I'd got about halfway through when I heard footsteps approaching. They sounded too heavy for Juliette's, but whoever this might be I didn't relish being caught out in what might look like some underhand deceit. I hurriedly closed the book, put it at the bottom of a heap of papers on the desk, stowed the camera in my bag, and looked innocently out of the window.

The newcomer reached the study door, then stopped short, doubtless surprised by my unexpected presence. Turning, I found myself face-to-face with the looming figure of Jean-Jacques Rigaut.

For perhaps half a minute we stared at each other in silence. He was dressed much as when we'd met before, in expensive leisure garments. But his expression was as unleisurely as possible – a mix of astonishment and fury, as though my presence was the last straw in what was clearly already a very bad day. I noticed a vein throbbing in his temple, and his forehead was beaded with perspiration. Had Juliette told him what she'd done to his letter? (Had I left it in my bag or decanted it into my suitcase? I sincerely hoped the latter – Rigaut in this mood would be quite capable of helping himself to anything he felt like possessing.) Or perhaps he had a migraine. Joe got them sometimes, with not dissimilar effects. If so, he'd be even more unpleasant than usual: migraine renders its victims exquisitely irritable. Where on earth had he sprung from? He must have arrived in the past few minutes while I'd been too absorbed to notice – unless his car was parked somewhere out of sight, in which case he could well have been here all the time.

'May I ask what exactly you're doing?' he demanded, not unreasonably.

I felt like asking him the same thing. Instead I said meekly, *'Bonjour*, Monsieur Rigaut. I'm waiting for Madame your mother. We arranged yesterday that I'd come round this morning. I rang the doorbell, but nobody answered, so I came in. I thought I might find her in here.'

'Well, you thought wrong. She's away,' he said.

I felt the blood rise to my face, and knew my ears must be glowing red as traffic lights. 'But that's impossible. She telephoned me not half an hour ago, to tell me to come. She must have been here then.'

'I'm afraid you're mistaken,' he said coldly. 'Do you usually walk unannounced into strange houses?'

'I wasn't unannounced. I told you, Madame your mother asked me to come.'

He glared, then swept the room with that restless gaze of his, glancing first at the picture – still there – and then, or so it seemed to me, checking that all the small, movable objects were in their accustomed places. Just when I thought he was going to ask me to open my handbag for inspection he said, 'And what exactly were you hoping to do when she arrived?'

I felt disinclined to tell him about the notebook, still less that I'd already photographed part of it. In his current mood he'd probably demand my camera and insist on deleting the photos then and there. I'd already lost one camera to him, indirectly – quite enough, in my view. And I wanted to look at what I'd got. Of course there was no way of knowing if I'd photographed the relevant bits, but it was possible: I'd done about half the book, a fifty-fifty chance. I said, 'I wanted to talk to her a bit more about your father.'

'I'd be grateful if you would stop pestering my mother,' he said. 'I've already made it perfectly clear that borrowing the picture is out of the question. She's a very old lady, and I don't want her tired by journalists. Also I think I should remind you that it's not only impolite to break into other people's houses, it's illegal. *Au revoir, madame.*' He looked at his watch. 'Please go,' he said. 'I have things I need to get on with.'

Arrogant pig! I decided to join him on his high horse – there was plenty of room for two, and what did I have to lose? 'I'm not a journalist, Monsieur Rigaut,' I said stiffly, 'but a curator at the National Gallery in London. Forgive my asking, but what is it about this picture? What exactly is the problem about lending it? I'd be genuinely interested to know.'

It was clear my question astonished him – perhaps less for what it asked than the fact that I'd had the nerve to put it. If he gave an order, people didn't question it – and not just because he was Monsieur le Ministre: they never had. Some people charm their way up the ladder, some out-manipulate their rivals, but with Jean-Jacques Rigaut it was clear that, as his mother said, intimidation had always been the weapon of choice. 'I don't think I have to explain my reasons for doing what I like with my own property. Just because you're desperate for something doesn't give you the right to have it.'

'I'm not desperate for it, as you put it, though it's true I'd very much like to borrow it. And I still believe it

141

belongs to your mother, in which case it's up to her to say whether or not that will be possible.'

'Are you saying I've lied? I'd be careful if I were you, madame.'

He looked so angry as he said this – the vein throbbing so violently that I was afraid he was about to have a stroke – that it was almost an admission. For a moment I felt tempted to threaten him with lawyers – then we'd find out the real truth. But that would be stupid: quite apart from the expense (I could just imagine Tony Malahide's expression!) the law was his to play with, and the odds would be stacked against me, whatever the objective situation. Better, and more effective, to try and defuse things. I said 'Monsieur le Ministre, this is all getting rather out of proportion. You keep acting as if I'm trying to steal this picture. The National Gallery of London is probably the most respectable institution in the entire art world. We're mounting an exhibition and we're asking for a loan. That's all.'

He swallowed and breathed deeply, visibly calming himself. 'Please excuse me, madame,' he said. 'I didn't mean to lose my temper.' (Liar! That was *exactly* what he'd meant to do.) 'But things are rather difficult just now. The fact is, it's not possible either to speak to my mother or to borrow the picture. You'll just have to accept it.'

We stood there, looking each other in the eye, and to my horror I caught myself thinking how attractive he was. The sheer furious intelligence in that face was something you don't often meet, and you don't have to like someone to want to go to bed with them. The truth is, powerful men have that effect on me. Rigaut wasn't the first I'd met, but he was my first demagogue, and even when he didn't have a crowd to please you could feel his magnetism, lurking there like some dangerous animal. Caroline always said that whenever she met a magnate the first thing she wondered was what crimes he'd committed en route to the top, and perhaps, shamefully, that was one reason I found power sexy. I was simply less evolved than Caroline. She'd progressed to the point where civilized values outweigh primitive evolutionary urges, whereas I was still unable to resist the sight of the biggest ape pounding his chest. In conventional terms Manu scored over his father in every way – he was young, good-looking, good-natured insofar as he allowed himself to exhibit any nature at all. But in the sex-appeal stakes he didn't begin to compete. Fortunately, or perhaps unfortunately, it seemed unlikely Monsieur le Ministre shared my present fantasy (which though brief was surprisingly detailed). Judging by the way he looked at his wife he wasn't attracted to women of a certain age, and it was hardly probable he'd make an exception for me. Short of undressing on the spot (which might or might not have the desired effect) I'd never find out.

There seemed little more to say, so I nodded with as much dignity as I could dredge up and said, 'I'll speak to Madame Rigaut another time, monsieur. *Au revoir et bonne journée.*'

Have a nice day – that was what everyone said round here. In this case I felt it achieved exactly the level of subtle insult I was aiming for. Unwise, perhaps – but it made me feel better. If there had been anything to lose I'd lost it already. Rigaut didn't respond.

I left the room without looking back, got in my rented Saxo and drove off, resisting the temptation to wave goodbye out of the window. Bastard! There was no other car in sight: where he had sprung from I couldn't imagine.

Despite my nonchalant exterior, I felt extremely agitated. 'You'll just have to accept it,' he'd said. But I couldn't – not without answers to a few questions. In particular, where was Juliette? I *had* spoken to her: it *hadn't* been a hallucination. Had he locked her in her room and forbidden her to see me? It looked very like it – and if so, that could only mean she'd told him what she'd done, and perhaps that I was on my way. In which case they'd have had a shouting match, and he'd gone his usual route and simply bullied her. But that was not just out of order, it was ludicrous, excessive. Why should anyone do such a thing?

If it wasn't absurd – he was the Minister of the Interior, for God's sake, after the President and the Prime Minister the most powerful man in France – I'd have said I had him rattled at some fundamental level. There was something he deeply didn't want found out, and it was something to do with the picture.

I drove back to Les Pruniers and found Delphine in the kitchen drinking a mid-morning coffee. 'Well,' she said. 'How did it go? Have you found what you came for?'

I said I had, more or less, and she asked if I'd be spending another night. I said no, paid my bill and put my bag in the car. She then said she was just off to join Olivier and the children at a lake where they sometimes spent the day: the threatened storm had receded but it was very hot and heavy, and if I felt like a swim, she'd show me where it was on the map. But I declined. I had other plans for the afternoon.

Delphine left, and told me to make myself at home. Wandering through the garden room she used as an office I found the phone directory lying on the floor beside the table. On impulse, I called Juliette's number. But no one replied.

I spent the morning in the orchard, reading and eating the greengages which were falling off the trees all around me, and waiting for time to pass. At two o'clock a combination of boredom and impatience convinced me that the moment had come, and ten minutes later, I pulled up for the second time that day outside La Jaubertie.

There were still no cars in evidence, but judging by the morning's encounter that didn't mean anything. Rigaut must have some other parking place, round the back. I sat in the Saxo for a while, but no one appeared. The chairs beneath the cedar tree, where Juliette and I had spent the previous afternoon, were empty, and the windows all shuttered up – but that was normal in heat such as this.

After ten minutes or so, I got out of the car, softly shut

the door, and began to prowl round the outside of the house, turning first to my right, a side I hadn't examined during my earlier explorations. The lawn here was less extensive, the trees closing in nearer to the château. In amongst them stood a stone outbuilding I hadn't noticed before, a barn, with big double doors. I tried them, but they were locked. The grass in front of them was worn and slightly rutted. You could easily leave a car here. Perhaps it was here still. There was no way of knowing.

Nervously, I walked back to the house, rang the bell and waited. Nothing.

I rang it again. Still nothing.

I tried the door. It was locked. So was the small door at the back. La Jaubertie was closed. Rigaut had gone, and taken his mother with him.

Seething with frustration I got back in the car and drove to Angoulême, where the TGV whirled me towards Paris, the Eurostar, and a sleepless night in Kentish Town.

13

Freddie Angelo: London, August

I got back to find London depopulated. At work all those who had children were absent on holiday duty. My inbox was full of spam offering penis extensions, my voicemail harboured legions of bluff Yorkshire voices urging me to call premium line telephone numbers and be ripped off while I waited to learn if I'd won a holiday in Majorca, no extras included. Outside, the rain rained and the wind howled, driving tides of tourists to shelter in the Gallery's free, dry halls. I loved it all, even Kentish Town High Street, where swirls of old newspapers blew round my ankles as I scudded past the endless estate agents on the way to the tube. It was all so wonderfully normal and ordinary. Although I couldn't help wondering about Juliette, from the familiar perspective of the mundane workaday world the events of the past few days seemed wholly unreal. Jean-Jacques Rigaut was no ogre, just another overblown politician. Even my moment of passion with Olivier, at the time so all-consuming, had begun to fade, a sort of shipboard romance.

Amid the nonsense on my voicemail, one message caught my attention. 'Good morning, Miss Lee,' it began. The speaker was male, cultured, confident, slightly drawling. 'You don't know me, my name's Freddie Angelo. I understand you're working on an exhibition around the Caravaggio St Cecilias. Could you call me? I've got

146

something here you may be interested in.' He left a central London telephone number.

I called him back, but no one was there. On the answering machine the same voice instructed me to 'Please leave messages for Freddie Angelo after the tone,' so I did, telling him I was back in the office and awaiting his pleasure, before immersing myself in a conference paper I was supposed to have finished last April.

Half an hour later, my phone rang. 'Miss Lee,' said the voice. 'Angelo here. So kind to call me back so bright and early.' (Early? I looked at my watch – it was a quarter to eleven.) 'There's something I'd like to show you. I wondered if you might like to come round here and see it?'

'Depends what it is,' I said.

'Ah, that would be telling. When could you manage? Are you free tomorrow?'

'Any time.'

We agreed that I'd visit him at eleven the following morning. Bright and early.

The address he'd given me was in Albemarle Street. It had stopped raining, so I walked there under a fitfully lukewarm August sun. In Leicester Square a mournful Mongolian busker made sad sounds on some ethnic stringed instrument, and was comprehensively ignored by crowds of almost-naked schoolgirls, their whole attention concentrated upon their mobile phones. As I progressed down Piccadilly it was noticeable that the ratio of visible flesh diminished sharply – perhaps in deference to all those tailors in Savile Row, perhaps because the passers-by were older, and less inured to the chill of a British summer.

Freddie Angelo's directions took me to a shiny black panelled door set between two shops, with a highly polished brass knocker. Beside the door was a round brass bell-push, also very shiny, and a brass plate engraved with the name *Angelo*. Unfortunately, when I pressed the bell it didn't seem to be working. That's to say, I couldn't hear anything, and there was no response. I looked at my watch: five past eleven. Surely he must be there? I rang the bell

147

again, but still no one answered. The knocker produced no result either, and nor did anyone answer the phone, whose number I'd noted down. That figured, if it was inside the building outside which I now stood. If Mr Angelo had a mobile, he hadn't given me its number. Perhaps he hadn't wanted to run the risk of being disturbed before time began at 11 a.m.

I looked at my watch again. Ten past. Obviously he wasn't coming. Time to get back to my desk. Doubtless he'd call again sometime. Or not.

I'd almost reached the Royal Arcade when a cyclist passed me, a portly fellow in a white suit with thinning dark hair and a pink complexion, riding an upright black gentleman's model. He stopped outside the door at which I'd been vainly ringing, swung his leg athletically over the back wheel, undid the bicycle clips that tethered his trousers to his legs, settled his jacket, opened the door and wheeled his bike inside. By then I was on the spot. 'Mr Angelo,' I said severely.

He wheeled round, his face a picture of unruffled urbanity. 'Dr Lee? Have you been waiting long? I'm most awfully sorry. I got delayed. When I didn't see you I thought, Thank goodness, I've made it in time. But you'd already been and gone ... Still, here we are after all. Coffee?'

I said I'd love one.

'Excellent. There's a Caffè Nero just over the road – I do have a coffee machine somewhere, but it really can't compete. Let's go and get some and take them up.'

Lattes in hand, he led us up a flight of narrow stairs and into a dark, panelled room looking on to Albemarle Street. There was a sort of dais at one end, in the centre of which stood a painting on an easel, covered with a cloth. The only other items in the room were a couple of chairs facing it, sub-Sheraton or possibly even the real thing, the sort called carver chairs, with wooden arms and padded seats and a narrow padded panel in the back. The effect – the gloom, the panelling, the attention focused on the raised easel – was slightly church-like. To our left an open door led into another, larger, brighter room, with a desk, a sofa, some shelves of reference books, and a large sash window giving on to a flat roof, doubtless the back of one of the shops, from which the sun, which had now come out in earnest, reflected hotly. My host removed his jacket to display a pair of red braces, hung it on the back of the desk chair, pushed up the window's lower sash to its fullest extent and nodded at the sofa. 'Do sit down, Dr Lee.'

'Call me Reggie. Everyone does.'

'Fine, and I'm Freddie. Well now,' and he sat back expansively, sipping his coffee and fanning himself between mouthfuls with a private-view invitation picked off the mantelpiece at random. 'How very nice to have you here. And how's the exhibition going?'

'Coming along,' I said cautiously.

'Good, good. Lots of interesting stuff?'

'Lots.'

'Been talking to everybody, I suppose.'

'Quite a lot of people.'

'Of course you have. That's the wonderful thing about art historians, always something to say, even if it's only to slag off another art historian. How old was Caravaggio when he died? Thirty-nine? I could give you the names of quite a number of people who've been thinking about him far longer than that. They all know *far* more about Caravaggio than Caravaggio ever did.' He chortled with pleasure at the thought.

There didn't seem any very obvious reply to this, so I said nothing.

'I expect you're wondering why I asked you here.'

'I am, rather.'

'All right. Finished?'

He took my empty cardboard cup, threw it with his own into a capacious waste paper bin, and led the way back into the adjoining room, shutting the door behind us. Sitting me on one of the chairs, he switched on a light over the

149

easel, and whipped off the cloth to reveal the picture it supported.

It was the, or a, Caravaggio St Cecilia, similar in every way to the others save for a scatter of luscious fruit heaped in the bottom left-hand corner.

'How about that, eh?' he exclaimed triumphantly.

I stared at it, no doubt stupidly, and heard myself say, 'Is it genuine?'

'Oh, absolutely. Not a shadow of doubt.'

'But it can't be,' I said. 'There were only three. There's no record of a fourth.'

'Indeed. One for the church, one for Del Monte, one for Marcantonio Doria. No records of any more. If there are four,' he said, with the emphasis on the 'if', 'one of them's a fake.'

'How d'you know it's not this one?'

'Easy. I'll show you. How much d'you know about Caravaggio's methods?'

'His methods?'

'Yes. His methods of painting.' He nodded towards the St Cecilia. 'That was made in 1604 or 5, right?'

'If you say so,' I said stiffly.

'Oh, believe me, all the tests have been done, it's the right date, no doubt at all. Original stretcher, right pigments, right canvas. So he was still in Rome, under the protection of Cardinal Del Monte.' I nodded agreement. 'Who of course was a friend of Galileo. Up with all the latest in the world of optics.'

'Optics?'

'Lenses. Mirrors.'

'Well, of course I know Caravaggio used mirrors,' I said. By this time I was feeling thoroughly defensive. I might not have been thinking about Caravaggio for thirty-nine years, but I was not, as Freddie Angelo seemed to imply, proposing to curate an exhibition about an artist of whom I was wholly ignorant. 'The contemporary accounts all say so. His pictures are full of self-portraits. How else could he do that?'

'That's not quite what I meant.' He went back into the office, where he rummaged in a drawer and returned with a powerful magnifying glass. 'Look at this,' he said, walking towards the easel.

I followed him. He was holding the glass over the open music book which lay at the saint's feet. 'Here, take it. Have a look. What can you see?'

I looked, feeling stupid. What I could see were musical notes, a few enormously magnified blobs of black paint on a parchment-coloured ground. 'What am I supposed to be looking for?'

'The brushstrokes. Which way do they go?'

I peered through the lens. The brushstrokes were indeed visible, the impress stronger where the artist had first put brush to canvas, then tailing off as he raised it. 'From bottom to top,' I said.

'That's right,' he agreed, taking the glass and peering at the picture himself. 'What does that tell you?'

I felt like a first-former who hasn't done her homework. What did he expect me to say?

'All right, let's have a look at something else.' Putting the glass down he made for a large cupboard in the panelling, from which he extracted a concave mirror and a photographic tripod. 'Come on!' Handing the tripod to me, he rushed back into the office, where he deposited the mirror on the sofa, picked up a small piecrust table, climbed through the window and placed it on the flat roof. Leaning back in, he asked me to pass him a vase of pink roses that stood on his desk, set this on the table, then climbed back in, pulled down a dark blind over the top portion of the window, and pinned a large sheet of black paper on to it. 'All right?'

'All right,' I agreed, mystified.

'Excellent. Just a couple more things now and we're ready.'

Carefully he set up the tripod facing the window, fixed the mirror to it on a sort of flexible stalk, then waggled it until he had it in the position he wanted, climbing in and

151

out a couple of times to slightly alter the position of the table. Finally all was ready. 'Now. Now what do you see?'

What I saw was an upside-down image of the vase of roses, projected on to the black paper. Although it was quite faint, and blurred around the edges, the glowing colours and heightened shadows gave it a jewel-like brilliance, nearer to painting than nature. The effect was oddly hypnotic. You wanted to play with it, to try out more images – to catch it.

'You see?' said Freddie Angelo. 'The painterliness of it. *That's* what they meant when they said he used mirrors. Of course if the room was darker it would be more distinct. But see how the projection simplifies the highlights and tones? People wonder how he got those photographic effects, those amazing foreshortenings – easy, he was using projections. By 1605 he'd probably moved on to proper lenses. The field of view's much wider, you don't have to set up your painting in so many little bits. But the effect's the same. He used mirrors from very early on. Concave mirrors. And of course, mirrors and lenses both do the same thing.' He swung round, triumphantly twanging his braces. 'Elementary optics. The rays of light cross at the point of focus. So the projection's *upside down!*'

'Yes, I can see that.'

'All right, so where would you start if you were going to make a painting from that projection?'

'I don't know – top left-hand corner?' I caught my breath and laughed. 'I *see* what you mean!'

'Exactly. If you were going to paint a sheet of music, would you paint it from the bottom up? Of course you wouldn't! You'd go from the top down. It's natural. Of course later, when he made copies, he wouldn't have had any need to do that – he'd just have copied them. So you see what all this means?' This time he didn't wait for me to answer. 'This must be the *originario* – the first of the series. That's why it has the fruit. Whoever commissioned it saw one of those gorgeous still-lives he'd done a bit earlier and said, And put me in one of those while you're

152

about it. So he copied it from whatever picture that was –
I could probably find it for you – and stuck it in the corner.
If you look, you can see the highlights are all wrong – the
light source here's from the top left, but the fruit seems
to be reflecting something from the right, that's why it
looks so odd. It wasn't part of his original plan, and he
didn't bother with it for the others. Now. Have I convinced you?'

'You've bemused me,' I said. 'But it certainly seems
convincing.'

'That's because it is.' He began dismantling his set, taking down the mirror, folding the tripod, replacing the roses
on his desk and the table in its spot beside the sofa. 'Have
you seen all the others?'

'Yes.'

'How many? Come on, the truth. I promise I won't tell
tales.'

'Three. Or rather, I haven't actually *seen* the one in the
Getty, just the photo. But both the others.'

I have never seen anyone look so wonderfully astonished. His eyebrows moved up his forehead, his eyes
widened. Then he threw his head back and laughed.
'Really?'

'I promise.'

I could see now why he'd been so patronizing earlier.
He'd thought he'd caught me out – assumed I'd been skat-
ing on thin ice, that I didn't know where all the pictures
were, that I only knew of two and that he'd found the
third. And indeed, as regards the thinness of the ice, he
hadn't been mistaken. Although I had found three pictures,
only one of them was available for loan. It was no thicker
now, either – just differently cracked. I still only had one
picture promised. And one of the ones I'd already found
must be a fake.

'Well,' said Freddie after a while. 'That certainly is a
turn-up for the book!' He counted them off: 'There's the
Louvre's – came from Berenson who stole it from the

153

church in the first place. The Getty got theirs direct from the Doria palazzo, terrible condition, but provenance indisputable – never moved since the family bought it from the chap himself. And the mysterious Other, that appeared in 1952 and then dematerialized. Del Monte's. This one.'

'It wasn't this one, actually,' I said smugly. 'In any case, how could this one be Del Monte's? Wouldn't the *originario* have been the one he did for the church? That was the commission, surely he'd have wanted to do that first and get paid?'

'Del Monte was his patron, they'd been friends for years. Maybe he liked this one best, or persuaded Caravaggio to let him have first pick. You've got to agree it's far better than the one in the Louvre.'

I nodded: there was no disputing that.

'So,' he continued. 'Where's this mysterious other picture you've found? Or aren't you at liberty to say?'

'In France,' I told him, truthfully but unhelpfully. 'It's certainly the one that was in the exhibition. Where did you find yours?'

'Oh, it emerged,' he said airily, 'the way these things sometimes do. You know how it is. Someone decides to sell, they need the money, or someone's left them something they don't like, or haven't the room for. Why they're doing it's no business of mine.'

We grinned at each other: fifteen all.

'Are you a dealer?'

'In a small way. I just handle a few things. I'm sure I don't need to tell *you*,' he added confidentially, 'that it's not just a question of selling, look what I've got. You need to set the scene, build up a buzz, create the right atmosphere. I'm rather good at that, though I say it. Caravaggio's always been a particular favourite of mine, and of course the missing St Cecilia's one of those things everyone always hopes they'll find. When I first saw this I couldn't believe my eyes.'

'Whose is it?'

He shook his head. 'A private collector. I think he'd prefer not to have his name known. But you can imagine how I felt when I heard about this exhibition of yours. I met Tony Malahide at a dinner-party and he mentioned it to me. I said to him, but how can she possibly do it when nobody knows where the third picture is? But he insisted you were on to something. Touching faith, I thought, but frankly I didn't believe him. I knew exactly where it was, and you certainly weren't on to *that*. But there we go, you were telling the truth all the time. I think this deserves a drink, don't you?' – and he opened yet another panelled cupboard to reveal a fridge, from which he extracted a bottle of champagne. 'Whether this mysterious find of yours is *right* is quite another matter, of course,' he added. 'Even so, it's interesting. Very.'

We clinked glasses, and he said, 'So tell me, do you have a photo of your find?'

'I do, actually.'

'Not on you, I don't suppose?'

I was about to say No when I remembered that my camera was still in my bag. I brought it out and checked through its contents. I'd taken several shots of the picture, in case any of them failed to work. One wasn't up to much – I'd been standing too far away – but the other two were not bad. I passed the camera over, and Freddie studied them intently, switching from one to the other. 'Too bad they're so small,' he said.

'We could download them into your computer if you've got the right software. Then you can blow them up as much as you want. Otherwise you'll have to wait till I get back to the office, and I can send them to you.'

He brightened. 'Shall we have a go?'

As every computer-user knows, these things never work. The compatible is never really compatible, PCs won't speak to Macs, the disk is never readable. But this time a miracle occurred, and there was Juliette's St Cecilia up on Freddie Angelo's twenty-inch screen. He studied it intently. 'Interesting,' he said. 'Look.'

155

He pointed to the Angel's left hand, which was held over St Cecilia's head, index and middle fingers extended in a sort of blessing.

Once again he had me maddeningly mystified. I shook my head.

He led the way back into the other room, uncovered the picture, switched on the light and pointed to his Angel's hand. Only the forefinger was extended. 'I thought so,' he said, and twanged his braces again, a habit of his, as I came to realize, whenever he was excited.

Back in the office, he took a big Caravaggio book off the shelf and we looked up St Cecilia. Disappointingly, it showed only one of the pictures – the one in the Louvre. The Angel there, as at La Jaubertie, showed two extended fingers. 'Two!' he pointed out triumphantly. 'Otherwise they're all very similar, aren't they – almost identical, apart from the fruit. I'd say he must have taken a tracing. Of course, with photos like this there's no way of knowing what the treatment's like. The one I've got here's a very finished piece – look at the fruit, and the treatment of the fur – no trouble too great. He knew which side his bread was buttered . . . I'd take bets yours is altogether thinner. More impressionistic.'

'Mine!' I laughed. 'If only! Actually it's rather fine.'

'Well, you know what I mean. As for the Louvre's . . .' But he was deep in his book again, unwilling to waste so much as a word on the Louvre's picture. 'Can't imagine why they haven't got the Getty's here. Perhaps it was still back in Palazzo Doria when this was published.'

I said, 'But the Getty collection's online.'

Not only was it online, but sorted alphabetically: C for Caravaggio. We zoomed in on the Angel's hand. It had three fingers extended.

'Well,' said Freddie. 'I wonder what that can mean.'

'It could just be the order in which they were painted,' I suggested.

He looked downcast. 'It could, I suppose. But wouldn't

that be a pity! Still, if it is, then there's another proof I'm right.'

Freddie poured us two more glasses of bubbly, and we sipped contemplatively. I was already beginning to experience that feeling where you hover just above ground level – possibly a result of all the excitement, but probably not unconnected with the champagne. All those bubbles – fatal. I said, 'I hope you're going to be able to lend this for my exhibition.'

He laughed. 'I wondered when you were going to ask. If I still have it, I don't see any reason why not. Think if you produce four, when there are only supposed to be three. *Won't* that set some cats among the pigeons.'

Four! I should be so lucky. At least, though, now, I could probably count on two.

14

Olivier: London, August

By the time I reeled away from Freddie's place it was nearly half past two, and all capacity for real work had been efficiently removed by the champagne. Instead, when I got back to my desk, I downloaded the photos I'd taken of the notebook, blew them up as large as seemed practical, and printed them out. That was work too. Of a sort.

I'd managed to photograph about twenty pages before being interrupted, and all seemed legible – or at least as legible as the originals allowed.

Juliette's grandfather, Valérien de Beaupré, had evidently been a sort of amateur art-fancier. Well-to-do gents of his generation often were – they had to find some way of occupying their time, and this was at least as good as billiards, or dog-breeding, or sinking into a vinous stupor. But unusually, instead of sticking to French artists, as one might expect from a country squireen – de la Tour, Ingres, Greuze, Fragonard – he had somehow, somewhere, acquired a taste for the Italian baroque. Perhaps it simply reflected his purse: what was fashionable was dear, and in France, fashionable meant French. The less wealthy connoisseur did better to concentrate on the overlooked – a category which at that time included Caravaggio. The notebook was simply a brief record of meetings and transactions, possible and actual, beginning in 1910 and continuing until just before the outbreak of war in 1914. Most were purchases, but he also seemed to have made a few sales, perhaps of objects he'd grown tired of, or which he'd maybe bought because he thought he could sell them on at a profit.

It wasn't exactly a diary, but it did proceed chronologically. And I was in luck. Not very far in – to be precise, on page three – came the first mention of the transaction I was interested in. The dealer in question was called Sangallo – one of the names I'd noted glancing through the notebook at La Jaubertie.

1 May. Sangallo, 67 Botteghe Oscure. Reni, soi-disant. No. St Cecilia –?M. da Caravaggio? – Possible – S swears yes. Asked where from – C copy of St C church altarpiece, apparently.

Botteghe Oscure – that must mean the via delle Botteghe Oscure, in Rome. But he didn't stay in that city long: the following entries showed him in Siena, where he bought an old book from a dealer in piazza Salimbeni and sold it the following evening to an American, a fellow guest at his hotel, and from where he proceeded to Florence, where he bought a painted marriage chest from Giorgio Mascagni, the well-known dealer whose name I'd also noticed when I first glanced at the book. I couldn't remember seeing a marriage chest at La Jaubertie: perhaps that too had been sold on, though no such sale was recorded in the pages I'd photographed. Or maybe it was in a part of the house I hadn't visited. But soon we were back in Rome.

23 May. Sangallo. St C – good but exit problems. S to advise. St C church – altarpiece? None in place.

The exit problems presumably referred to the law then recently passed by the Italian senate in an attempt to stanch the flow of antiquities and artworks out of the country. You had to get an export permit, and if the work was particularly valuable or interesting, no such permit would be forthcoming. In theory. In practice, of course, such obstacles could always be overcome. As, apparently, in this case:

25 May. St C exit extra. Agreed.

Soon after that Valérien left Italy, or at any rate stopped buying. There were no more entries until April the following year, and no more mentions of either Sangallo or the Caravaggio, at least in the pages I'd photographed..

I wondered how I could find out more about Sangallo. The name was vaguely familiar, but no context came immediately to mind, and when I googled it the only references were to a pair of early Renaissance architects. But I knew someone who might know.

Dear Freddie, A little puzzle: you wouldn't happen to know anything about a dealer named Sangallo, working in Rome around 1910, would you? All information gratefully welcomed. Best wishes and thanks for the champagne. Reggie.

Next morning, I found his reply.

Dear Reggie, has this something to do with your mysterious find? Or maybe it's just a passing query. Anyway, Sangallo. I think you must be referring to the so-called Barone Sangallo, who for some years sold antiquities and objets d'art in the via delle Botteghe Oscure. If this was the same person, I'm afraid to say it doesn't bode very well for your picture. Sangallo was an alias of Marcello Cavalletti, a restorer whose main customer was Joe Duveen. Duveen used to visit the Cavalletti workshops in Trastevere when he wanted a few nice shiny pieces for the American market. The Barone's establishment was far more discreet and stocked only pieces that were market-ready. Being a Barone gave him a special appeal for wandering aristos, always happy to be gently guided by someone of the right class. I wouldn't exactly describe Cavalletti/Sangallo as a forger, but he could take an unimportant piece and transform it into something rather special (and expensive . . .). After the war (WW1, that is) he seems to have disappeared, at least from the art scene. Perhaps he was a combatant, though I have a sense that he was a bit old for that. More likely he just retired on his profits.

It was delightful meeting you. Good luck with your project, and don't hesitate to approach me if I can help in any way. With best wishes, Freddie.

That all rang true enough. But somehow Freddie's description of the Barone Sangallo's stock in trade didn't chime with the picture I'd seen at La Jaubertie. That wasn't a shinied-up piece of second-rate stuff, nor did it feel like a fake. One of the lessons I'd really learned when I did my degree was to *look*. If you look hard enough and long enough at a picture, it's surprising what that can tell you about it. Including which bits (if any) seem right, and which don't.

I called my photograph up on to the screen, and studied it. Obviously, a photo can't tell you as much as the object itself. But it reminded me of the picture – and once again, it smelt right. Perhaps just for once, Sangallo had sold someone the real thing. It made sense. Why fake a Caravaggio – something that wouldn't fetch much even if it were an original?

My computer pinged, announcing another email.

Régine – j'ai un tas de choses à te raconter – pas possible de tout écrire, je passe par Londres après-demain, tu seras là? Donne-moi un coup de fil, ou émel – ton Olivier.

I'd been so pleased with myself, I was back in the real world, had put him firmly to the back of my mind, that was that, over, done with. But all it took was a word (*ton Olivier*) and my heart turned over in my chest. Literally. A most uncomfortable experience.

When I'd recovered my breath I considered what I should do. Or rather, what I wanted to do, which of course was a different thing altogether. What I *should* do was email him and arrange to meet for lunch, preferably here at the Gallery, or else in some other suitably public space. What I *wanted* . . .

In the end I simply emailed him my work telephone number. If (when) he called, we'd take it from there.

He called in the morning, just after half past nine. Granted, we're an hour behind – for him it was half past ten. Even so, it was gratifyingly prompt. When I heard his voice, my heart did that thing again.

'Did you take the Eurostar?'

'I just got off. I'm in Waterloo. I tried earlier, but you weren't there. When are you free?'

'Lunch? Dinner? How long are you staying?' So much for my resolve to stay cool. It had lasted just about five seconds.

'Depends how long the story takes. Overnight, perhaps. I've got to interview someone, and we'll take some photos. Lucky, *hein?*'

'I thought you were on your holidays.'

'I was, now I'm back at work. The photographer's got to get back to Paris this evening but I can probably stay till tomorrow. So, dinner?'

I invited him round to my place.

I don't really know how I got through the day. It was just a space, to be negotiated until the evening finally arrived. I passed the time, or some of it, planning dinner. Nothing complicated – this wasn't the evening for complex cookery. Nothing smelly, so no fish. Not steak – I can't face those great solid lumps of meat at the best of times, and this particular evening I knew I'd never get more than a mouthful down, particularly as the weather was hot, not an unknown occurrence in August. In the end I bunked off work early and slid down to Selfridge's food hall, where I bought a jar of lumpfish roe, and the butcher slivered me off some beef for carpaccio, and I knew the tomatoes would be reliably sweet enough for salad. I prepared it when I got home, leaving the tomatoes and mozzarella to soak up all that delicious basil and balsamic vinegar (no garlic today,

162

thanks). Then I put a bottle of Prosecco in the fridge and took a long shower and painted my toenails a fetching shade of dark crimson, after hesitating between that and a silvery green that I finally decided was more a winter colour. And it was still only six o'clock. So I put on my favourite floaty white dress that showed off my tan, then changed it for some green silk trousers with a white silk-knit top, then the dress again, then decided the trousers were better. Then I tried on a few more clothes, but in the end came back to the trousers. Then I hesitated between beaded sandals and bare feet, and looked at my watch, which now said a quarter past seven, and wondered whether Olivier would really manage to find his way to this somewhat outlying part of London. And then, at a moment when I had one shoe off and one on, and the bed was strewn with discarded clothes, the doorbell rang and I heard a taxi drive away.

He looked, for an unexpected second, slightly smaller than I remembered: perhaps because this time the turf was mine rather than his. There were other details I'd forgotten, too – a slight dimple in his left cheek when he smiled, the way he was square and at the same time wiry – but as soon as I saw him I knew that all that palaver about clothes had been a mere device for passing the time. Clothes were neither here nor there. He followed me in, and shut the door. The taste of him, the fit of our bodies – I remembered it all now. I don't think we even spoke – certainly not coherent words. We simply made for the bedroom, where within about a minute our clothes – those carefully selected clothes – joined all the others on the floor as we fell joyfully into each other's arms.

And what, you may wonder, of my liking for Delphine, of all those notions of female solidarity? Did they melt as soon as our clothes hit the floor and our bodies the bed? No, long before. That battle had been won, or lost, as soon as we agreed on dinner at my place. Yet somewhere, in the recesses of conscience, they lingered. At one point during that blissful interlude, as I lay tracing the contours of a cheekbone, I found myself thinking: I shouldn't be doing this. I really shouldn't. And then, as so often before in similar situations, I went on doing it all the same.

At one point I asked him, 'Do you often do this?'

He hesitated, then said, 'I try to resist it, but living so much of the time apart, of course it happens.'

'Did you try to resist me?'

'Yes,' he said simply, and that was the end of that conversation.

Later, I asked him whether he really was over on a story.

'You think I just came to find you?' he said, raising his eyebrow.

'It seems possible.'

He laughed. '*Eh bien, ma petite chérie*, I'm sorry to disappoint. There really is a story. But I must admit it's a very boring story, the sort of thing that normally I'd try quite hard to avoid. The editor was astonished at my insistence. I was surprised myself. But I had to see you. Quite apart from this' – he waved his hand over the tangled heap of sheets – 'there are things I must tell you.'

'Then tell.'

He reached for his cigarettes, extracted one, and offered the packet to me. I shook my head: I don't smoke. Olivier lit a patriotic Gitane, inhaled luxuriously, then turned towards me as I lay beside him, the better to enjoy my astonishment. 'Jean-Jacques Rigaut has announced he's going to run for President.'

'He'd never get elected, surely?'

'He might or might not. The party probably won't support him.'

'Then he can't, can he?'

'He says if they don't, then he'll run anyway.'

'As an independent?'

'Or set up his own party ... He'd stand quite a good chance, I think, all the rest are so discredited. And he has his own following, however much one might wish he didn't. But that's not all. Juliette Rigaut is dead,' he said. 'They found her the day after you left.'

164

15

Bombshell: London, August

At first his words didn't really register. My mind, it must be said, was elsewhere. Propped on one elbow, eyes narrowed, eyebrow raised, Olivier had suddenly reminded me of Joe. Perhaps it was something about the stance, perhaps quite simply the fact that Joe was the last person I'd made love with on this bed, or indeed anywhere. At any rate, for an unnerving moment they merged, and for that moment I was suddenly uncertain exactly who it was, hovering up there. The confusion didn't last long: they were too different, Joe fair, lanky, his chest covered with abundant tawny fur, Olivier dark, sleek, tanned and, given his sedentary occupation, surprisingly muscular (I suspected a regime of morning pushups). And that was just the physiology. Then my vision cleared and sharpened, rather as when one inserts a contact lens, and in the shock of pleasure when the outlines settled themselves definitively into the shape of this improbable new lover I understood that one of the gifts he had brought was closure. Finally, I'd recovered: Joe was in the past. In sheer delight I kissed the nearest part of him, which happened to be his side. Olivier, however, intent on his revelation, did not react to this embrace. Instead he brought his cigarette gracefully to his lips, inhaled, blew a smoke ring (a man who could not only raise one eyebrow but blow smoke rings, how lucky was I!).

Only then did I actually take in the second part of what he'd just said.

'Dead? Madame Rigaut?'

He nodded.

'Where?'

'At La Jaubertie, where else?'

'I can't believe it.'

Suddenly I felt very unsexy indeed. I rolled away from him, got out of bed, pulled on a dressing gown and began to pace about, as I always do when I'm really perturbed. A terrible weary sadness rolled over me. Although we'd spent so little time together Juliette and I had become oddly intimate, in a way that was unusual in my life. My brother and I had hardly anything in common, and, while my parents' yearning for grandchildren made visits there awkward, met rarely. Naturally I had friends, but most, apart from Caroline, were comparatively superficial; and Olivier notwithstanding, the gap Joe left had not been filled. Of course, in the world's eyes I barely knew her – how often had we met? Twice? Three times? Nevertheless, by the end of that last afternoon she and I had become something more than just acquaintances. Perhaps because she was old, and not much time might be left to us, we'd somehow bypassed the preliminaries. Paradoxically, the result had been something quite outside age: the person I'd met that afternoon had been simultaneously the old woman sitting before me and the audacious, resourceful girl whose story she was recounting. And now I'd never see her again.

But the shock I felt was more than grief. There was also a terrible, numbing guilt. I knew, with absolute certainty, that this death and my visit must be connected. How, I could not yet imagine, or perhaps did not care to try. The detail was unimportant. It was the conviction that mattered. It lodged toad-like in my stomach. If I hadn't gone to La Jaubertie, Juliette would be alive today.

It also, of course, meant that Jean-Jacques Rigaut now really was the owner of the St Cecilia.

Olivier was clearly astonished by my reaction to what, for him, was no more than local tittle-tattle concerning an old woman I'd barely known. He'd been expecting *Gosh, lucky I got to her in time*, and what he'd got was full-scale distress. How was he supposed to deal with that?

'You say they found her ... How long had she been dead?'

He shook his head. 'No idea. All I know is, the house-keeper found her.'

'Babette.'

He nodded. 'Yes, I think that's her name. She'd been away, apparently, and when she got back, no more Madame.'

'Do they know how she died?'

'I told you, I don't know any details. If you like I can try and find out.'

'If you could, I'd really like to know.'

Juliette – dead. It made no sense. Or perhaps it made only too much. I kept returning to the same image: Rigaut in the door of the study, dishevelled, unnerved, so completely panicked by my unexpected and unwelcome presence that he'd committed the ultimate blunder – told a lie that the slightest questioning would instantly find out. Anything to get rid of me. And that, surely, could mean only one thing?

I said, 'I need a drink. Let's go downstairs.'

I had a quick shower, then left the bathroom to him and dressed in the first garments that came to hand – as it happened the sexy silk trousers, that now seemed so glaringly inappropriate. I put some food on the table, opened a bottle of wine – not the Prosecco: I'd rarely felt less in the mood for bubbly – poured two glasses, and drank one off.

What, if anything, was I going to tell Olivier? My acquaintance with him was just about the opposite of that with Juliette. In terms of time and physical presence I'd known her hardly at all, and yet I felt I knew everything about her – or almost: now, I reflected, the real truth about Helmut and Antoine would be forever a mystery. And I'd have told her anything. Whereas although I'd been as physically intimate with Olivier as a woman can be with a man, in any real sense of the word I hardly knew him at all.

Of course, her death might well have been entirely natural. She might simply have had a heart attack: felt ill, fallen down and died. Given her age and frailty, that was what everyone would assume. But I wasn't convinced. She hadn't shown any signs of illness the previous evening. She'd been tired, yes – though not too tired to mark up the notebook. Nor to invite me round in the morning. If she'd been feeling ill – *that* ill, on the point of death – she simply wouldn't have called. Or if she had, somehow, dragged herself to the phone, it would have been to summon help, not confirm our rendezvous.

So she must have died just after that. And Rigaut had been there. Only that could explain his behaviour. If she'd simply been taken ill, he'd have said so. You find your mother on the point of death, you look for help. That's the normal, human reaction.

For God's sake, it's the reaction if you find your mother *dead*.

I poured myself another glass of wine and took a deep breath. 'What I'm going to tell you now is a big secret. Nobody else knows about this.'

His eyes widened. 'Something to do with Madame Rigaut?'

I nodded. 'And her son.'

'Jean-Jacques . . .' He could barely conceal his delighted anticipation. His initiative was paying off, in spades.

I suddenly felt overwhelmingly hungry. In the circumstances the celebratory meal I'd prepared seemed somewhat out of place, but it was all there was. I said, 'Let's eat and then I'll tell you. You'll need to take notes.'

He looked at me curiously. 'All right. What a strange woman you are, Régine.'

We ate in silence, each preoccupied with our own thoughts, and finally, over the coffee, I began my tale.

Rigaut's letter. My last afternoon with Juliette, the note-book, our appointment, the phone call, her failure to answer the door when I rang, the house open, the un-expected encounter with Rigaut. Going back later to find the house locked up, apparently empty. In the end we taped it, on my tape machine – the same machine I'd used to record Juliette's tale. I needed to be sure he had the story quite straight.

When I got to the end of my recital, Olivier shook his head. 'I don't understand. To kill your mother? Over a picture?'

'I don't understand, either. But that seems to be what happened. What other explanation can there be?'

He stared into his glass, considering. 'Is that what you thought at the time?'

'Of course not. Though I knew something was wrong.'

'What an idiot, to go back in the afternoon. Imagine if you'd run into him.'

'I had to,' I said. 'I just knew something had happened, and that somehow it was my fault. I still feel that, even though I didn't actually do the deed, whatever it was. How could I leave without trying to find out? You won't believe this, but I even thought about trying to get in there by a secret tunnel she'd told me about, that leads to the cellars.'

'I remember there were stories about a secret tunnel,' Olivier said thoughtfully, pouring himself another glass of wine and lighting another Gitane. I'd have been seriously worried about his smoking habit if I were Delphine. Fortunately I wasn't. As husband material, Olivier really was not convincing. I suspected she might be reaching that conclusion, too.

He inhaled slowly, and blew another smoke ring. I said, 'What are you thinking?'

'About Rigaut . . .' He stubbed out the cigarette half-smoked, perhaps remembering some wifely injunction. 'If he stands, he might really win. He's very clever. He's never been implicated in anything. Lives quietly, doesn't go for great shows of wealth, puts it about that he isn't a rich

169

man. Not that he's poor, you saw his wife, you don't dress like that for nothing, but she has her own money. He lives on his salary, no business connections, all political contributions accounted for. He takes a trip, he pays himself, or at any rate it doesn't come out of the slush-fund all the rest of them use.'

'Sounds too good to be true.'

'It is. But as I said, he's clever.'

'I suppose he'll own La Jaubertie now. Not that that's going to make anyone rich.'

Olivier laughed. 'Quite the contrary, I'd imagine. But if he's really planning to start his own party, he's going to need some funds.'

'The picture.' I thought about the notebook entry and that dodgy Florentine 'barone'. 'If it's genuine.'

He clicked his tongue thoughtfully against his teeth, then gave his sudden brilliant smile – the one I'd dreamt about most of last night. 'You mean it's not? What a fantastic story *that* would be . . . The old mother dies, and for what? I wonder . . .' He ran a finger absently round the rim of his glass, making it ring – a sound that's always set my teeth on edge. 'It might be worth flying a kite. Just to see how he reacted.'

'How d'you mean?'

'State the facts. Just tell the story – you wouldn't have to say anything in so many words. Then see what happened.'

'You'd never get away with it.'

'Not in England, no. Fortunately, things are a bit different in France.'

After that, conversation lapsed. Without sex to oil the wheels and pass the time we had not much to say to each other that had not already been said. I could think of nothing but Juliette, and Olivier was clearly planning his story. Our fling was over – evaporated as suddenly as it had blossomed. I wondered if his motivation had ever been more than what might be termed professional. Not that we hadn't fancied each other – that sort of thing can't be faked – but it seemed fairly apparent that his main reason for

170

coming to London had been to recount his juicy morsel in hopes that it might lead to a story. He was a chancer, as Caroline would doubtless have been the first to point out – yet another in my litany of unsuitable men.

The night before us, to which I had looked forward so eagerly, now promised to be something of an embarrassment. Olivier offered to go to a hotel, but that seemed ridiculous: mine was a large bed, and we could perfectly well spend a civilized night in it together. By the time we'd cleared up it was bedtime: we bade each other goodnight, and turned over to sleep. But although I was exhausted I couldn't stop the churning of my mind, and lay endlessly awake while Olivier snored, gently but insistently.

He was booked on the nine thirty Eurostar, which meant leaving the house at seven forty-five. We rode the Northern Line together: my stop was Charing Cross, he went on to Waterloo. The tube was crowded, but we managed to bag two lean-against semi-seats. As the doors shut and the train began its rattling progress, I remembered something that had occurred to me as I lay awake during the night. 'By the way, have you any idea what's likely to be happening at La Jaubertie just now?'

He looked at me blankly. 'Happening in what sense?'

'I meant, will it be closed up, or will someone be there?'

'I've no idea, but I can easily find out. I expect they're waiting for the will. Though of course everyone knows what's going to happen, it'll all go to Jean-Jacques.'

'So no one can go in or out?'

'Of course they can. They'll put an official seal on the front door, but you can still get in round the back.'

'Is your uncle Francis still working there, do you think?'

'I've no idea. Probably not just now. But I expect he'll still have a key ... Why?'

I explained that I needed someone to go in and take a sample of paint from the picture for testing – a tiny fragment, preferably from behind the frame. 'And if he could get a little piece of canvas as well, that would be wonderful. He'll need to take the picture down, but it's light, it shouldn't be difficult. The canvas is nailed to the stretcher, when he turns it over he'll see. He can take a bit from the back. Just a tiny bit, perhaps where it's come away round a nail.'

'Won't there be an alarm?'

'Not in the house – I'm pretty sure of that. And I don't think there'd be one on the picture. I certainly didn't notice anything when I was there. The insurance would be terrific, and who's going to look for that kind of thing at La Jaubertie? I'd do the job myself, but that might be a bit difficult just now.'

'I'll ask him. I shouldn't think he'd mind.'

Just before the train drew in to Charing Cross he said, 'What are you going to do now?'

'Go in to work,' I replied, slightly surprised.

'No, I meant about the story. What we were discussing last night.'

'Nothing,' I said. 'I'll leave that to you. *Bonne chance.*'

Sometimes work is a distraction, but that day I found it almost impossible to concentrate on anything, however simple. At a quarter to six I gave up, and an hour later was back at the house. It looked as though it had been hit by a hurricane – bed tangled, kitchen filled with dirty dishes, bathroom under water, the whole perfumed with Gitanes.

I'm not one of the world's natural housewives, but *in extremis* cleaning can be quite comforting. It's constructive, and simple, and the results are more or less instantaneous. Grimly I attacked the bathroom.

I wondered what Joe would have to say about it all. Perhaps, now that he was in the past, I'd phone him, to see.

16

Antoine Rigaut: London, August–September

As if to focus our minds, the papers suddenly seemed full of Jean-Jacques Rigaut. As Olivier had predicted, all the many scandals that for years had hovered around the Elysée seemed to be gathering into a great head of pus that threatened to spurt out and drench the various participants in a noisome coating, one of whose effects would be to leave them at least temporarily unelectable. It seemed as though only Rigaut, severe and upright, stood apart from this uncharmed circle. Because of this, and also because he offered those tempted by the Front National a way of indulging their more disreputable instincts without actually voting for fascists, he was now a serious prospect for the Presidency, as part of either the ruling party or the new one he talked of starting.

Unable to concentrate on anything else, I passed the time listening to the tapes of my interview with Juliette. And they in turn led me to think about Jean-Jacques' brother Antoine, whose birth had been so problematic and whose death had propelled me into this strange adventure. His agreeing to lend the picture hadn't been a figment of my imagination – there were letters and emails confirming it. Positively charming – suggesting we meet sometime to discuss the exhibition, he might have some suggestions to offer. And then, suddenly, he had changed his mind. And before anyone could ask him why, died.

Other than the fact of it, however, I knew almost nothing about Antoine Rigaut's death. It was the consequences, not the event, that had concerned me. First the impossibility of contacting him (hardly surprising, since he was already dead), and then the fact that the discovery of his body for some reason changed Manu's mind about putting me in touch with his grandmother. What that reason was I still could not say for certain, though I was beginning to have some inkling. But whatever might have been in Manu's mind that day, I didn't think he would share it with me now. On the contrary – given a choice of everyone in the world, I was probably the person he least wanted to see. I wondered if he had connected his grandmother's death with my visit. If and when he did, it would probably be impossible to get him to speak to me ever again.

On the other hand, this might be the moment to resume contact with the Louvre. Now Rigaut was safely out of the way, might they not rethink his arbitrary refusal to lend the picture? And maybe, incidentally, shed a bit of light on the affair . . .

I picked up the phone, dialled the Louvre, and asked for Charles Rey.

This time, he was in. He answered his phone with a brusque *'Oui?'* – a busy man, annoyingly interrupted in the midst of important concerns. When I introduced myself, he sighed. That seemed a bit uncalled-for, considering the terms on which we'd parted last time we'd met. Not that after twelve years one expects effusiveness, but surely, at the very least, a pleased curiosity? Perhaps the redoubtable Madame Desvergnes had filled him in on my previous visit, and he now connected me with the tangle over Rigaut and the cancelled loan.

'*Eh bien*, Régine. I gather you called round. Sorry I wasn't there . . . What exactly did you want?'

'It's about the Caravaggio St Cecilia. I don't know if you know – you probably weren't concerned – but we were hoping to borrow it for an exhibition here at the National Gallery.'

His worst suspicions confirmed, he dug around in memory's far recesses. 'Yes, I seem to recall something of the sort.'

'It was all agreed, and then Monsieur Rigaut suddenly withdrew permission. Nobody really explained why, so I was hoping perhaps, since he's not around any more, it might be possible to reconsider. I understand you're in charge now, is that right? How are you, by the way?'

'Oh, fine, fine,' he said absently, his mind clearly else-where.

The silence that followed was so long I began to wonder if he'd rung off. Eventually, however, he spoke – but only to say, 'I'm afraid I can't really take that sort of decision. I'm just the acting head. They haven't made a permanent appointment yet.'

I didn't argue, though I could have. If acting heads can't take decisions, what can they do? 'Of course. It's just – I thought you might have some idea what was going on.'

'Why would I?' he asked sharply.

'No particular reason, just that you were colleagues ... I don't suppose you know why he refused? Or know some-one who may know?'

'No,' he said shortly. 'I'm afraid I can't help you there.' He clearly wanted to end this conversation.

However, I wasn't ready to let him off the hook now I'd got him nicely dangling. You never know what little detail may jog someone's memory. 'Or what happened to him? It all seemed very mysterious.'

He sighed. 'I'm afraid not. All I know is what I found.' He stopped abruptly, as though the words had slipped out before he'd realized what he was saying.

So that was where he'd been the afternoon I visited his office at the Louvre! 'What you found?' I said conver-sationally. 'My God, was it you that found him? How terrible for you!'

He didn't deny it. 'I'd rather not talk about it,' was what he said. 'And now if you don't mind, I have to go to a meeting.'

Meetings, meetings, what convenient things they are. Still, I'd made some progress. Not professionally – I somehow had a feeling the Louvre picture had slipped irretrievably out of our grasp. But it was clear now that Charles had known Rigaut not just as a colleague but well enough to call round – to get into his apartment, indeed. Had Rigaut confided in him? I was willing to bet he had. In which case, Charles knew exactly why Rigaut had suddenly changed his mind.

So why wouldn't he tell me?

Well, perhaps he didn't know after all. Nevertheless, here, amid the swirling mists, was a fact: Charlie Rey had found the body. It would be nice to have another fact to join it. Perhaps the press reports of Rigaut's death might yield more, now that I was slightly better informed than when I first read them.

Googling Antoine Rigaut produced 58,802 possible websites. Among the first were the official obits I'd already read, followed by a number of reports, almost identical and evidently syndicated, of his death and the events that had followed it. He had been found 'by a friend' (presumably Rey) at his apartment. He had died of gunshot wounds, and the gun had been found beside the body. The assumption was suicide, though no one could suggest any reason why he should have wanted to take his own life. Emotional problems were hinted at.

I scrolled through the various sites, dipping in here and there when something sounded promising. Only a small proportion were of any interest. Many dealt with Rigaut's brother, and some with his father. One told me about an Antoine Rigaut who had been born at a place called Douchy in the eighteenth century, another concerned a saxophonist with a band called CRIME. There were accounts of auctions at which my man had bid, of paintings he had authenticated, committees he had chaired, news conferences he had given following particularly interesting or prestigious acquisitions. I flicked through the pages, which became increasingly less relevant. And then my eye was caught by the words *Russian Paintings Scandal*.

When I called the page up, it turned out to be an old magazine story, dating from 1995. Someone, or some several people – a picture dealer in Zurich, an employee of Sotheby's, various unattached names I did not recognize – had been running a scam around acquisitions for public galleries. The dealer, it seemed, was in contact with the staffs of various galleries in the ex-Soviet Union, now impoverished and looking for ways to stay alive. From time to time this meant that important artworks suddenly and mysteriously arrived on Western markets. When something potentially interesting was about to come up, the dealer would notify one or more of his contacts and a sort of private auction would take place. Then, some months later, and for considerably more money, the artwork would arrive in some public collection. The author of the story, a journalist named Janet Colquhoun whose name I vaguely recognized from the saleroom pages, had somehow insinuated herself into the confidence of a member of this ring – perhaps the Sotheby's man, whom she must have met in the course of her work; though on second thoughts that seemed unlikely, since surely he would have known she was a journalist? Antoine Rigaut's name featured only tangentially: the Louvre had been one of the paintings' eventual destinations, and he had authorized the purchase in question. Interviewed by Colquhoun, he had expressed his horror at being involved, however indirectly, in a scam that not only deprived the Russian people of its patrimony but at the same time defrauded public collections in the West.

I stared at the screen for a while, then printed the item out. Switzerland. Rigaut, according to one of the obituaries (I scrolled back and found it) had made several lucky finds in Switzerland. The inference was obvious: he must have been far more closely caught up in the scam than this article implied. It was one of those pies everyone had a finger in, though they weren't spelling that out, at least in the obits.

At this point my resolve was further quickened by the arrival of a note from the top man himself: *Dear Reggie, perhaps you would like to give me an update on your Caravaggio project sometime? TM.*

As usual, I found him hovering between his many windows. 'Ah, Reggie,' he said, sounding as always slightly surprised, as though he had half expected me to forget our appointment, or (more likely) had forgotten it himself. 'Come in, come in. Just a bit of an update, you know. How's it going?'

'Quite well, actually,' I said, and told him about Freddie Angelo.

'How very interesting,' he said, in that airy voice of his. 'Quite a character, isn't he, Freddie. I do seem to remember mentioning something about your project, but he never said a word then. Well, well. A positive shower of Caravaggios. If you find any more we'll be overwhelmed. How about the one that was in private hands? Did you ever get anywhere with that?'

Yes, I told him. I'd found that, too, in France, as I'd suspected. Been to see it again only two weeks ago.

'Excellent,' he said approvingly. 'I can't wait to see all this in the catalogue. The lost Caravaggio ... We'll have quite a popular hit on our hands if it keeps on this way. Well. Keep up the good work. We'll have another review soon and perhaps set a definite date. What d'you think?'

I told him terrific, and hurried back to my office. To my relief, he hadn't asked anything about whether or not people were prepared to lend. Perhaps he assumed that in a sane world – the kind of world he inhabited – there would be no problems on that score. Or perhaps he simply wasn't bothered. He was past the point where life is a constant low-level hurdle-race. I, on the other hand, still had to keep jumping. If I jumped high enough often enough I, too, might one day achieve a room with three tall windows. In the meantime, holding on to my job would be an excellent start.

Back at my desk, I surveyed the course ahead. To get any further, I needed help. Specifically, inside information. TM could almost certainly have told me at least some of what I wanted to know. But asking him would have been unwise on a whole raft of levels. For one thing he wasn't a natural gossip. He could do it, I'd seen him, but always with a slight aura of distaste, as though this wasn't something chaps – decent chaps – should really indulge in. For another, my project, as far as he was concerned, was whole, sound and progressing steadily, and that was the way I wanted to keep it. My questions would have introduced a note – more than a note, a whole chord, a virtual orchestra – of uncertainty, not to say a certain flakiness. No. In a situation like this, Freddie Angelo was my man. Something told me that uncertainty and flakiness were no strangers to him.

'Reggie!' he exclaimed when I introduced myself, his delighted tones balm to my hypersensitive ears. 'How clever of you to call, I was just thinking about you. I had the picture out for another little think, and one thought led to another.'

'I need a bit of help,' I said, 'and I wondered if you had a moment.'

'Absolutely. About Caravaggio? Of course, what else. Why not tell me over lunch? How about that? Do you happen to be free?'

I admitted that might just be the case, and we agreed to meet at a winebar he knew, off Bond Street.

He was waiting when I got there, bald head shining, red braces extensively displayed over a blue and white striped shirt, making him look like a living Union Jack, or perhaps a tricolour. He waved and said, 'I've ordered us a bottle of Sancerre. Hope that's all right. Need something to keep you going through the afternoon, that's what I always say.'

I reflected that half a bottle of Sancerre wouldn't so much keep me going as shut me down entirely, but it would have been rude to say so. Besides, I like Sancerre. I ordered some fizzy water on the side, to at least dilute the effect, and some smoked salmon sandwiches to act as blotting paper. Freddie was having the cold beef, which he assured me was excellent here. He tried to persuade me to have some too, but I didn't feel strong enough for anything so unequivocally meaty.

'Well,' he said, filling our glasses. 'Fire away.'

I fired, straight in. 'I was wondering if you happened to know Antoine Rigaut.'

'Rigaut? Yes, I knew him, poor fellow.' He looked at me shrewdly. 'Hadn't seen him for a few years, but at one time we were great mates. What did you want to know, exactly? If it's gossip you want, I'm afraid I'm not current. It must be at least five years since we met.' In other words, if I wanted to know about recent events, Freddie Angelo was making it quite clear he was not my man.

I at once disclaimed all interest in such things. 'No, what I'm interested in is further back than that. Did you ever know anything about some scam based in Switzerland? About ten years ago. Pictures coming out of the old Soviet Union, being bought up cheaply and sold on later for much more.'

'I seem to remember something of that sort,' he agreed vaguely, without, however, specifying exactly what. 'Was Antoine involved? Surely he must have been at the Louvre by then.'

'I've no idea. That's what I wanted to ask you. I came across an article about it that mentioned his name. Not as being involved, but as someone who knew about it.'

'Well, naturally he *knew* about it. Everyone knew about it. Everyone always does, until someone breaks the eleventh commandment and the *Daily Mail* gets hold of the story, and then, dear oh dear, tsk tsk, who would ever have imagined such a thing could happen. It's inevitable, isn't it, when you think about it. Art's hard currency – where would you put *your* cash, pictures or euros? Hardly even a question, is it? – and where there's currency there's speculation. With added uncertainty, of course. You see a fake, I see an original worth millions. Pick your expert and take your choice. Those poor Russians were experts all right. They knew they were sitting on millions, and they hadn't been paid for months – years. What were they expected to do, starve slowly in the name of art? But they could hardly sell the stuff openly, could they? So they sold it under the counter and got peanuts and had to watch other people make the millions. Still, I expect a peanut went quite a long way in Russia then. D'you know how that particular story came to light?' he went on, all vagueness cast aside now in the interests of a good gossip. 'Some journalist fell out with her boyfriend.'

'Janet Colquhoun?'

'Janet, yes,' he agreed, giving an approving nod. 'A *very* ambitious young lady. Not so young any more now, of course,' he added, not without relish.

'Who was the boyfriend?'

'Now what was his name? I did know it . . . No, it's gone. All I can tell you is that he worked for Sotheby's. I believe he left her for another. So she took her revenge by telling all. Consternation all round, *dear* oh dear. Moral,' he concluded, 'steer clear of journalists.'

I felt myself blush, and hid behind my glass of wine, but he spotted it and took it for a comment on himself. 'Take no notice of me, dear girl, I'm an old cynic. But when you've been in the business as long as I have . . .'

Bringing the conversation back to the matter in hand, I asked, 'Are you saying Rigaut may have been involved?'

'Involved, involved . . . If something interesting comes up, it's his duty to acquire it if he can, at the best price he can. That's part of his job. Or was, poor fellow,' he corrected himself. 'Why are you suddenly interested in all this, anyway? As you say, it was years ago.'

'Oh, I happened to be surfing, you know how it is, and I saw something about it and got curious, that's all. And then I remembered one of the obits mentioned he made lots of lucky finds in Switzerland.'

181

Freddie wasn't to be drawn any further. 'I believe one of his boyfriends was Swiss,' he murmured, and beamed as the food arrived, effectively closing the subject.

My sandwiches looked very anaemic and well bred beside Freddie's beef. He ladled on a generous dollop of horseradish and took a capacious bite. 'I hope,' he said through it, 'that Antoine's popping off like that's not going to put too much of a spoke in your wheel.'

'Not more than was there already.'

He looked up: like my previous revelation that I'd found three pictures, not two, this was something he hadn't expected. 'What d'you mean?'

I made him promise he wouldn't mention any of what I was about to say to Tony Malahide, then told him the puzzling story of Antoine Rigaut's veto on lending the Louvre St Cecilia.

'How *very* odd,' he said, wiping his mouth and pouring himself another glass of Sancerre. Instead of taking a sip, however, he sat back and fingered his braces. Not quite twanging yet, but clearly this lunch was proving more interesting than he had anticipated. 'Now why should he have done that?'

'Refuse permission? I've no idea, it's one of the things I'm trying to find out. What's even odder is that he didn't refuse it, at first. It was all going through as normal. But then he suddenly put his foot down.'

Freddie shook his head wonderingly. 'I'd plug on with them, if I were you – if they've changed their mind once they can change it again. Though it's amazing how obstinate people get when they know they're in the wrong ... But I'm afraid all I can do is wish you the best of luck. Now Antoine's gone I'm afraid I don't have any strings to pull at the Louvre.'

'There was just one more thing,' I said hurriedly, before the subject of Antoine Rigaut finally closed. 'I don't suppose you know his address in Paris?'

'It always used to be 14, quai des Grands Augustins. Of

course, he might have moved . . . Why d'you want to know that?'

'No particular reason, I just wondered. When I was at the Louvre everyone seemed determined not to tell me. He wasn't there, and I wanted to find him, and they were being protective. I realized afterwards he must already have been dead.'

For the rest of the lunch we discussed technical matters: optics, faking techniques, the picture he'd shown me, its prospects, various other interesting items that had at one time or another passed through his hands. At the end of the meal he insisted on paying, as I had known he would. I thanked him profusely, but he waved my thanks away. 'My pleasure. I'm afraid I wasn't much use to you this time, though.'

I assured him he was wrong: he looked slightly alarmed. 'Oh well, anything I can do, you know,' he murmured, perhaps not quite as enthusiastic now (what was it he'd inadvertently given away?) as earlier in our meeting. 'Any time.'

Reeling back to the office (of course I hadn't been able to resist a second glass of wine, nor even, to my shame and undoing, half a third) I tried to work out exactly where I stood now, and what I should do next. But my poor fuddled brain was in no state to cope unaided, so I had to wait until I was once more at my desk and could write things down. Getting out a nice clean sheet of paper, I jotted down a few notes and headings.

Pictures
Getty – ex-Doria – promised.
Louvre – ex-Santa Cecilia via Berenson – refused – why?
Jaubertie – ex-Cavalletti – dubious – refused by JJR – why?
Freddie's – the first? – ex-Del Monte if so – probable.

I stared at what I'd written, but it still refused to make sense. I could have sworn that the Jaubertie picture was 'right'. But there were only three versions of the St Cecilia, of that I was pretty sure; and of the four pictures, Juliette's, whatever I might think, had unquestionably the most dubious provenance.

Oh, well. Onwards.

To do
Check sample from La Jaubertie?
Janet Colquhoun?
Retry Louvre.
Olivier re JJ.

Here at least were four solid objectives for instant action. But I didn't feel up to Olivier quite yet (and besides, he was writing his story and mustn't be interrupted). And I needed to have something else under my belt if I was to make any progress with Charles Rey. So, Janet Colquhoun. It was not easy to see quite how she and her Swiss scandal fitted in with all this. But I was convinced that the two Rigaut refusals, from the Louvre and from La Jaubertie, were somehow linked; and whatever that link was, it was not straightforward. I was likelier to stumble upon it by a roundabout route, if at all. And once I'd found it, there might be some way of dealing with it.

I found my printout of her piece, then checked to see if she had a website. Sure enough, she did. The photograph at the top looked about twenty-five – a bit of cheating there: judging by her CV, she had to be getting on for forty. The website listed her publications, and I saw they included a book on the Swiss affair: *Bread, Butter and Canvas – from Russia to Sotheby's*, published in 1996. I'd better check that out before contacting her. I rang the Gallery's library: yes, they had it. If I liked to come down, they'd point me in its direction.

The book, though, told me little more than the article I'd already read. There were too many breathless reconstructions of scenes in hotel rooms and heartrending, though doubtless accurate, descriptions of destitute Russian curators left high and dry by the fall of Communism.

184

However, it included, which the article had not, the name of the dealer concerned, which it seemed was Hegelius, and also of the Sotheby's boyfriend, one Tim Salisbury-Newall. And the interview with Antoine Rigaut was omitted, though I noticed that some of what he'd had to say now appeared as general wisdom, without attribution, and the Louvre was included in the list of collections that had acquired works by this route.

I turned back to the website. It gave an email address: that would probably be the easiest way to get in touch. I wondered how approachable Ms Colquhoun was, and took the opportunity of a tea-break to ask my friend Alice, who had the office next to mine, if she'd ever met her.

Alice stopped compiling a list of possible invitees to a conference she was organizing and swivelled round to face me. 'Janet Colquhoun? The journalist?'

'That's the one.'

'Not actually. Doesn't she write for the *Financial Times*?'

'Mostly. I've got to ask her about something and I wondered what she was like.'

'No idea,' said Alice, shaking her head. 'Just ask, what's your problem?'

But something told me it might not be as straightforward as that. If Freddie Angelo was right about her motivation, then this might be an episode Ms Colquhoun did not much care to recall.

On the other hand, if I didn't ask any questions she most definitely wouldn't answer them.

Dear Janet Colquhoun, I'm at the National Gallery

No. The fact that I was at the National Gallery was neither here nor there in this particular inquiry. Anyway, it would be obvious from my email address.

Dear Janet Colquhoun, I'm trying to find out about Antoine Rigaut, who as you probably know committed suicide earlier this year.

185

No, that wouldn't do either. What I wanted to know was about the scam. After that, we could move gently on to Rigaut. Or not.

Dear Janet Colquhoun, I'm trying to find out one or two details relating to an artworld scam that took place in Switzerland about ten years ago. I read your book and wondered if it might be possible to come and talk to you about it? Yours, Regina Lee.

Next morning, when I checked my email, Janet Colquhoun had not replied. Nor was there anything in the afternoon, nor the following day. Perhaps she was away on a story. Or maybe she didn't check her website mailbox very often. I phoned the *Financial Times*, and they confirmed that yes, Janet Colquhoun did work there, and yes, had an email address there. So I copied my message to that address. Next morning, there was still no reply. Clearly I'd have to phone.

When the switchboard put me through, the phone was picked up almost at once. A cool, brisk Scots voice – an Edinburgh voice, with those little squeezed-up vowels – said, 'Janet Colquhoun.'

She was there, then.

'Oh, Ms Colquhoun, I emailed you – perhaps you didn't get it. My name's Reggie Lee. It was about that art scam in Switzerland in 1995.'

'Yes, I think I did get something.' She sounded bored, blasé: wholly unenthusiastic. Perhaps she really was all those things, but I sensed embarrassment: she'd been intending to ignore my messages, and I'd caught her out.

'I'd really like to talk to you about it. Could we meet for a drink, perhaps?'

'I don't quite know what you expect, ten years after the event,' she drawled. 'People always seem to think if you write a book you must have left out the really juicy bits. I can't imagine why.'

I ploughed on regardless. Eager obtuseness, that was the

tone. 'I'm interested in Antoine Rigaut, that's how I came across this. I notice you mentioned him in your original article, but not in your book, and I couldn't help wondering why not. Was he involved?'

'Antoine? There wasn't much going on he *wasn't* involved with.'

'So he was?'

'That's not quite what I said. Read the book, it's all there. All I know, anyway.' And she rang off.

Not much joy there, then. Still, all was not lost. I could always try and find the boyfriend. With a monicker like that it shouldn't be too hard.

17

London, September

The following Tuesday, I found a small padded envelope postmarked Meyrignac lying on the mat when I got home. Olivier had evidently passed on my message, and Francis had acted upon it, more promptly than I had dared hope. I rushed upstairs and tore the package open. Inside was one of those transparent plastic seal-tight pouches, and inside that, the samples I'd asked for.

The obvious place to test them would be the Gallery – we had a whole department devoted to such things. But I didn't want to do that, just as I hadn't wanted to ask the Director about Antoine Rigaut. People naturally prefer to know what it is they're working on, what they're supposed to be looking for, and word gets around. So I decided to call one of my old university teachers, who specialized in this kind of work. She'd been comparatively young when I knew her – in her early thirties. That would put her in her fifties now. Still around somewhere, even if she'd changed jobs. As I dialled my old college I pictured her in her eyrie there, up at the top of the old house in Bloomsbury.

'I'm trying to contact Dr Lindsay Hillier.'

'Hold on, please. Putting you through,' said the woman at the switchboard.

Still there, then. Whether I'd find her in the office was another matter. It was by now the beginning of September, but term wouldn't begin for a few weeks yet. If it were me

188

I'd take the opportunity to lie on the beach a little while longer, or get on with my own work in blessed peace somewhere. Lindsay's work, though, was inseparable from her workbench. So maybe she'd be around.

She wasn't in college that evening, but the voicemail was taking messages for her, so she must come in from time to time. I didn't leave a message, preferring to try again next morning.

This time she answered. Surprisingly, she remembered me, or said she did. I explained where I was working and said I had something for analysis that might possibly be rather interesting, and would she mind giving me a quick opinion? To which she replied that of course she was, as always, very busy, but that if I wanted to bring it round, she'd try and have a look at it sometime the following week. I said I'd bring it straight over.

It was strange finding myself back among Bloomsbury's tree-shaded Georgian squares, and as I mounted the familiar, shabby stairs and threaded my way through the labyrinth of dingy corridors, the sense of being caught in a time-warp became ever stronger. Or perhaps it was a ghost-train: from time to time, as I navigated some dark, narrow passage, a door would fly open, and there would be a half-remembered face from my student days, peering at me with a puzzled expression. Was I someone they should recognize? Doubtless I seemed vaguely familiar . . . Finally, at the very end of a corridor, and up three flights of increasingly rickety stairs, I arrived at my destination.

The door was shut: in my student days, a sign that Dr Hillier was to be left severely alone. But I wasn't a student any longer. Fortified by an appointment, I knocked and entered. And there she was, exactly where I'd left her last time we'd met, at her bench of samples beside the mansard window, the back wall stacked with canvases left by over-optimistic clients in the almost invariably doomed hope that Aunt Julia's old seascape with cows might prove to be a long-lost Cuyp. She welcomed me with her usual pre-occupied smile, and indeed seemed in every way eerily unchanged: thin, unmade-up, dressed in jeans – a beacon of pure scholarship, on whose findings millions turned. From time to time, well-padded men in Savile Row suits, their hair a little long at the nape, could be seen gingerly advancing along these druggeted corridors in their hand-made shoes, carrying smaller or larger flat parcels. Months later, the papers would be full of some exciting new find in the world of art – a hitherto unidentified De Hooch, a lost Renoir, a ballyhooed sale filled with glitterati. Lindsay's name, however, would not appear in the news-paper reports. 'Well,' she said. 'So what's the mystery?'

I handed over my plastic envelope and explained that I'd rather not say anything at this point – I just wanted to know what she thought of the contents.

'*Very* mysterious. Aren't you even going to show me a photograph?'

Feeling rather stupid, I burrowed in my bag and pro-duced one. Lindsay reached for the rimless half-moon glasses that were lying on her bench and studied it intently. 'Looks like a Caravaggio, or that school. Is that right?'

'It may be. That's what I need to find out.'

'You do realize,' she said, looking at me over the tops of her glasses, 'that I can never tell you that anything defin-itely *is* something? I can tell you what it may be, and how likely, and what it certainly isn't. But in the end it's just varying degrees of likelihood.'

I nodded agreement.

She turned the envelope over in her hands. It contained a fragment of canvas and a flake of paint about three millimetres square – Uncle Francis had been laudably concerned not to damage other people's property. A minute amount, it looked, but we were talking microscopic analysis here. 'All right. You do know I charge for this?'

'Yes, of course,' I replied smoothly, though in fact the thought hadn't occurred to me. Somehow, like most people, I assumed university expertise came free. 'I've got a budget.'

She looked at me sharply. 'Didn't you say you're at the

190

National Gallery? Why don't you give this to them to analyse? If you've got a budget, presumably this is something official. They'd do it for free, surely?' One way or another, she seemed determined to refuse my piece of work.

I felt like a first-year again, explaining why I hadn't written my essay on time. In the wavy world of accreditation, Lindsay and her unbendable panoply of tests tended to have that effect. People might opine till they were blue in the face, but if the science didn't add up, all their opinions were worth precisely nothing. I agreed that the Gallery did indeed have its own experts. 'But it's a bit edgy politically. It's all quite OK and above-board,' I added hastily. 'But I just thought – I'd rather come to someone outside.'

She considered this, and laughed. 'Well, all right then,' she said. 'I'll give you a ring when it's done. OK?'

'There's just one more thing. You wouldn't happen to know someone called Tim Salisbury-Newall? Used to work for Sotheby's.' I knew Lindsay had connections at Sotheby's – she sometimes helped them when they needed something authenticated.

'Salisbury-Newall.' She stood lost in thought. 'It rings a bell. Hasn't worked there for a while, though, has he?'

'Not for years. I just wondered.'

'No ... but I'm sure I heard the name somewhere just recently. Let me think ...' After a couple of minutes, though, she shook her head. 'Sorry. If it comes to me I'll let you know.'

I was halfway down the corridor when she came running after me. 'I remembered as soon as you left the room. He's set up in business on his own account.'

'I don't suppose you know where?'

'I wouldn't swear to it, but I have a feeling it's in King Street, St James's. The shop's called Salisbury-Newall Associates. Give him my regards.'

By now it was gone twelve, so I decided I'd have some lunch then go straight on to King Street. If Salisbury-Newall was there, fine; if not, I'd make an appointment.

King Street is home to a number of old master dealers. Salisbury-Newall's shop was about halfway along, with a discreet narrow frontage and shiny black paint, its small window almost entirely taken up by a Dutch flower piece. I rang the bell, and a Sloane sitting at a desk towards the back of the shop eyed me suspiciously before deciding I probably didn't pack a gun and pressing the buzzer to let me in. A lady in a ruff stared down from my right, on my left hung a tiny view of Venice in an ornate black and gold frame. But I saw better every day of my working life. I concentrated on the Sloane. 'Is Mr Salisbury-Newall around?'

'Who should I say wants to see him?' she drawled.

I handed over my National Gallery card. The Sloane looked at it, then me, as if it were a passport. I said, 'There's something I need to know and Lindsay Hillier thought he might be able to help.'

Reluctantly she rose and vanished into a back room. When she re-emerged it was in the wake of a tall, pink-faced fellow in a close-fitting black and white tweed suit. He had brown slicked-back hair, balding on top and curling slightly on his collar, and a fleshy, small-featured squire's face out of a Gainsborough portrait. 'Dr –' he glanced down at my card – 'Lee? How can I help you?'

I said, 'It's a bit of a long story.'

'We'd better sit down to it then. Bring us some tea, can you, Venetia?'

Venetia, poor thing. I always think it's a bit tasteless to name your children after the place of conception. It makes it all seem so biological.

Tim S-N. led the way into the back room, sat himself down behind a large mahogany desk, and motioned me to an armchair opposite. Venetia appeared carrying a tray with a teapot, a milk jug, a sugar bowl, two mugs and a plate with four chocolate biscuits, and set it down on the desk. When we were both settled with a mug of tea and a biscuit Salisbury-Newall said, 'Lindsay Hillier. It's a good few years since I've heard from her. How is she?'

'Much as she was when you last saw her, I should think.'

192

'Yes, I can't imagine her changing,' he agreed. 'So how did she think I could help you?'

'Actually, that was a bit of a white lie. I wanted to find you and she kindly gave me your address. It's to do with an exhibition I'm trying to get together.'

'Fascinating,' he said politely when I'd described it. 'But I don't really see how I can help.'

I explained about Antoine Rigaut – his unexpected refusal to lend the picture, his even more unexpected death, my growing sense that the two were somehow connected.

'Really?' he said, even more politely. Clearly he thought me a total fantasist.

Now for it: time to broach the Swiss scam. A tricky topic – that much was evident. Neither Janet Colquhoun nor Freddie Angelo had wanted to talk about it. I couldn't see why the comfortable gentleman sitting so snugly opposite me, and now embarking on his second chocolate biscuit, should feel any more inclined to oblige. Whatever it had been for them, for him it had been, at least temporarily, disastrous. Still, that was why I was here. I took a deep breath and said, 'I came across a story that happened ten or twelve years ago that seemed as though it might have involved Rigaut. It was to do with Russian paintings coming into Switzerland.'

At the mention of Switzerland Tim Salisbury-Newall may have turned a slightly deeper shade of puce, though given his normal complexion it wasn't something I'd have liked to swear to. However, whether because he was more shameless than my other informants, or non-informants, or had less of a guilty conscience, he displayed no other sign of discomfort. Instead, biting into his biscuit, he said, 'No, no, *Antoine* didn't have anything much to do with that. Though having said that,' he mused, 'he did acquire one or two rather good things for his collections. And as I recall there was a very nice Poussin that I'm pretty sure he kept for himself.'

'When you say *Antoine* didn't . . .?'

'The one involved was his brother. Jean-Jacques.'

'*Jean-Jacques?*'

He nodded. 'Creepy fellow, don't know if you know him. Operator, though. Not that you need me to tell you that these days. But he was just an obscure provincial politician then. Mayor of his local town, something like that. When the Wall came down and the Soviet empire crashed, he went to Russia with some deputation of French local politicians to see if they could help, hands across the water kind of thing. And perhaps find something interesting among the pieces. And who should he meet there but some chap who knew his brother – curator of a provincial art museum, the usual kind of stuff, lots of gloomy Russian pictures of melting snow and a few more interesting things pinched from local collectors in 1917. I imagine the chap recognized the name and introduced himself – I know someone called Rigaut, don't expect you're anything to do with him but thought I'd just ask sort of thing. Anyhow, he spoke to Jean-Jacques and told his tale of woe – no money, worthless when it did come, everyone's pensions and salaries down the drain, don't know where the next meal's coming from, buildings falling down, collection suffering, the usual ghastly story. People were selling their grandma for a loaf of bread, and perhaps he hoped if he could get in touch with Antoine he'd be offered a job in the Louvre or something. Well, of course he struck lucky all right, but what Jean-Jacques saw was that if he played this right everybody stood to do rather well. So he said Leave it to me, or words to that effect, and when he got back home started to make a few inquiries. What he needed was an anchor-man – someone well-connected but not too overlooked and who wouldn't ask too many questions. And that's where Antoine came in. Everyone knew he'd made a few lucky finds through this chap Hegelius in Zurich. I don't know if Antoine actually put Jean-Jacques in touch with Hegelius or if Jean-Jacques simply went straight to him – it was no secret who Antoine's dealer was there. Anyhow, he went back to Russia not long after, and all this stuff began to pour out. The way it worked was, Rigaut paid for it in dollars, which Hegelius provided and Rigaut got sent out in the French diplomatic bag. I imagine someone that end passed them on – I never knew exactly what the arrangement was there. Realistically, I don't expect many of the dollars reached the actual chaps. Then when the stuff got to Zurich, which of course also took a bit of arranging, there was a private auction. And then a little while later bits and pieces trickled into the public auctions, and bona fide buyers paid lots of bona fide money. And everyone was happy. Some people did *very* nicely for themselves.'

'Until it was blown.'

'Ah, yes,' he said imperturbably. 'Well, nothing lasts for ever. The flow was drying up by then, anyhow. Though I seem to think Hegelius and Rigaut went on with it for a while in a private capacity, if you get my meaning. But by then I didn't have any more to do with it. Or him.'

'What sort of stuff was it?' I asked.

'Oh, this and that – all sorts, really. Not much of tremendous importance. That would have been too noticeable. But some nice pieces, some very nice pieces.'

'Did you buy any yourself?'

'One or two.' He smiled. 'Another biscuit? No? Then I'll finish them.'

And that, clearly, was that.

I thanked him very much, and we shook hands, and Venetia scowled as he saw me to the door.

Walking back along Piccadilly, I felt a certain satisfaction. We were getting closer. Here, at last, was something that connected the brothers. And it wasn't something Jean-Jacques the Presidential aspirant would want known. I wondered if Antoine had been blackmailing him in some way.

By the time I left King Street it was a quarter past three. At four I was due at a seminar at the Courtauld, which didn't end till six. The discussion went on over drinks till seven thirty, so that by the time I got home it was almost half past eight. As I was about to let myself into the house, two men crossed the street, one stocky and fair, in his mid-thirties, the other tired-looking, older and thinner, with receding dark hair. The stocky man said, 'Miss Regina Lee?'

I nodded.

He held out an ID tag. 'Detective Sergeant Edmunds, Metropolitan Police. This is my colleague Mr Lebrun from France. I wonder if we might have a few words?'

I felt the sweat start to run: panic, unspecific but nonetheless intense, flooded through me. 'What about?'

He nodded towards the house. 'Could we perhaps talk indoors?'

I opened the door, and Edmunds shut it behind us.

My house was once two cottages; the ground floor has been knocked through to make one big kitchen/living room. I led us to the sitting-room bit, wondering how I'd ever make it through to the end of whatever this was. The day already seemed to have been going on for an unusually long time, and now it threatened to stretch on into eternity. I took an armchair, Edmunds and Lebrun sat somewhat awkwardly side by side on the sofa. I repeated my question. 'What on earth is this all about?'

Edmunds nodded at Lebrun, who said in heavily accented English, 'I'm sorry to bother you, madame. Something has arisen and it seems you may be able to help us.'

I said nothing. Since Lebrun was French, this must have something to do with the Rigauts. Perhaps Olivier had published his piece and the police had been prompted to investigate Juliette's death.

Lebrun's next words indicated that this was indeed the case. He said, 'A Madame Juliette Rigaut was found dead on 25th August. I believe you knew her?'

I wondered how hard-pressed the British force would be to find someone who could speak French even as well as Lebrun spoke English. I said, 'Yes, I knew her. And I heard she'd died.'

Lebrun inclined his head. 'As I think you perhaps know, the circumstances of her death were not altogether straightforward.'

I said, 'I don't quite understand what you mean.'

Lebrun scrabbled in his briefcase, brought out a copy of Olivier's magazine and handed it to me. His was the lead story, headlined *Mystery Death of Minister's Mother*, with photographs of La Jaubertie and the Minister, and a blurred image of Juliette, obviously blown up from a small snapshot.

On August 25, Mme Juliette Rigaut, mother of Interior Minister Jean-Jacques Rigaut, was found dead at her home, the château de la Jaubertie, in the Dordogne. Mme Rigaut had not seemed unwell, but since she was eighty-eight years old, an age when death is hardly unexpected, no questions were raised. She was buried four days later in the family vault.

Mme Rigaut, widow of the famous Surrealist photographer Emmanuel Rigaut, had spent the day of August 23 in conversation with Dr Régine Lee, a scholar from the National Gallery in London, who hoped to borrow an artwork for a forthcoming exhibition. The conversation went on into the evening; at eight o'clock Mme Rigaut suggested it should be continued the next morning, August 24. It was agreed that Mme Rigaut would telephone Dr Lee when she was ready to receive her.

Just after nine next morning, Dr Lee's mobile phone rang. It was Mme Rigaut, saying that she was ready and that Dr Lee should come round.

Dr Lee at once set out for La Jaubertie, arriving about ten minutes later. But when she rang the front doorbell, nobody answered. As the door was open, she let herself into the house, thinking that Mme Rigaut was probably waiting for her upstairs.

Dr Lee expected to find Mme Rigaut in her study, where they had talked the previous day. But no one was there, nor did there seem to be any sign of life elsewhere in the house. She was about to leave when she heard footsteps approaching. However, the person who entered the study was not Mme Rigaut but her son, Jean-Jacques, the Minister of the

197

Interior. He assured Dr Lee that his mother could not see her and (despite their arrangement and the earlier phone call) was not in the house. He then ordered her out.

Naturally she left; equally naturally, she was worried and curious as to what could have happened. In the afternoon she thought she would try once more, in case Mme Rigaut had returned. However, when she got to La Jaubertie, the house was closed and shuttered, and it seemed clear that no one was at home.

On the following day, August 25, when Mme Rigaut's housekeeper Babette Lacour returned from a short holiday and let herself into the château, she found Mme Rigaut's body lying on her bed. She was declared dead of natural causes, and buried in the family vault four days later. But when had the death occurred? And did anyone look to see what she'd really died of?

Edmunds said. 'Don't tell me your phone hasn't been ringing off the hook.'

'I wouldn't know. I've been out all day.'

As if to prove Edmunds' point, my phone began to ring. I let it go through to voicemail, but the caller hung up when the message began to play. I went over to check: I had twelve messages waiting – at least one of them, doubtless, from the person who'd just hung up.

'May I keep this?'

Lebrun nodded. 'Would you say this is a correct account of events?'

'Yes, that's pretty much what happened.'

'Pretty much?' Lebrun repeated sharply.

'Obviously there are some details he hasn't included.'

'Such as?'

'Well, for instance, when Monsieur Rigaut found me in the study – I don't know if you've seen him, he always seems very calm, very in control. But he looked absolutely distraught. Panic-stricken. It struck me – I was astonished, I couldn't imagine what could have been happening to make him look like that.'

'Perhaps finding an intruder in the house,' Edmunds remarked.

'Perhaps,' I agreed. 'But we'd met before. He knew I'd been talking to his mother. He'd tried to stop it, but we'd gone ahead anyway. And I don't think I'm a particularly alarming figure. Would you say?'

'Why had he tried to stop it?' Lebrun asked.

'I have no idea.'

'I take it you were the source of this story.'

'I spoke to Olivier Peytoureau, yes.'

'So what are you implying? That Monsieur Rigaut murdered his mother?'

'I'm not implying anything. All I can tell you is what happened to me and what I saw. I made the arrangement with Madame Rigaut, to see her at La Jaubertie on the morning of 24th August. I wanted to look at a notebook – a diary kept by her father when he bought a picture I'm interested in. You probably know, I work at the National Gallery. We'd spent the previous day together and she'd shown me the notebook, but we'd been talking all day and she was tired, and I wanted to look at it more closely. So we agreed I'd come back in the morning, after she'd called to tell me she was up and ready. So that's what she did – called just after nine – five or ten past. But when I got there a quarter of an hour later, no one answered the door. I knew she was deaf, and might not hear the doorbell, so I tried the door – I knew it usually wasn't locked. And then I went along to the study. I assumed she'd be there. But she wasn't, so I got on with looking at the notebook. And then Monsieur Rigaut arrived, and told me she wasn't there.'

'Perhaps he just thought it would be the quickest way to get rid of you,' Edmunds said. 'I know I wouldn't be too pleased to come into my lounge and find someone fossicking around.'

'Madame Lee,' Lebrun said, 'would it surprise you to know that there are perhaps other interpretations of what happened that morning?'

199

'I'm not interpreting. I'm just telling you what happened.'

Taking no notice of this, he said, 'Clearly the assumption must be that Madame Rigaut died a natural death. She was old – eighty-eight – an age when it's natural to die, *n'est-ce pas*? But the implication of the article is that her death was not natural, and that Monsieur Rigaut knew more about it than he said. But in that case, the same could be true of you. If she was killed, why should it be Monsieur Rigaut that killed her? Why not you? You could have done it, why not? You were there.'

My mind whirled. 'Is that what he's saying? Have you spoken to him?'

'Naturally we spoke to Monsieur Rigaut.'

'And?'

'Madame, my business is to find out what *you* say. But it's always possible, *n'est-ce pas*, that when he said his mother didn't want to see you he was telling the truth? As I understand it, you seem to think that by the time Monsieur Rigaut found you, Madame Rigaut was dead. But why should that be? And if the house was locked when you returned there, is that so unusual? But whether it was locked or open, you were there that afternoon, you said so yourself. Who knows what happened then?'

'I've told you. Nothing. No one was there. The place was locked up.'

'That's what you say. But telling is not proof.'

I looked him in the eye. 'You can't seriously be suggesting I killed her?'

'I'm not suggesting anything. I'm simply saying that if – if – she was killed, it's not impossible.'

We stared at each other for a moment. Then he said, 'Were you a friend of Madame Rigaut?'

'I hadn't known her long, if that's what you mean. I'd been there a couple of times to discuss various things. I liked her a lot.'

'She had a picture you wanted to borrow?'

'That's correct.'

'And did she lend it?'

'No. She said she would – I can show you the letter – and then Monsieur Rigaut wrote to say she wasn't the sole owner and the other owners, of whom he was one, refused. I went back to see Madame Rigaut, and showed her his letter, and she said he was lying – she wrote it on his letter, I can show you that too. They'd had a big argument about it. The whole thing seemed very strange, and naturally I wanted to try and find out what was going on. That's how I met Monsieur Peytoureau. He comes from there, and the families know each other. I thought he might be able to give me a clue.'

'And did he?'

'Not really. I still don't understand it. But there you are.'

'How about Monsieur Rigaut? You know him?'

'I've met him a couple of times. I don't think he likes me, and I know he didn't like me talking to his mother.'

'When you left La Jaubertie that morning, where did you go, exactly?'

'I went back to Les Pruniers, the b. and b. where I was staying, and talked to Delphine Peytoureau who runs it. Olivier's wife. We'd become good friends. I paid her for the room, and she said did I want to come swimming in a lake where they go, but I said I wouldn't.'

'And then?'

And then, and then. Up to this point my story had involved other people, so it could be checked. But after that, I'd been on my own.

'I stayed at Les Pruniers for a while – it was a beautiful day and I lay about in the garden. And then, as I told you, I went back to La Jaubertie.'

'Why, exactly?' Lebrun asked.

'Because I was worried about Madame Rigaut. Wouldn't you have been? One minute I'd been talking to her and the next she supposedly wasn't there and didn't want to see me. Something very strange seemed to be going on. And I'd become fond of her. So I wanted to make sure she was all right. I thought I'd see whether Monsieur Rigaut was there, and if he wasn't, then perhaps she would be and we could have our talk. So at about two, two thirty, I went back there.'

'And what did you find?'

'Well, there were no cars there. Not that that meant anything – I hadn't seen any cars in the morning, either. So I got out and rang the bell. And no one answered.'

'As in the morning.'

'As in the morning. But this time when I tried the door it was locked. All the doors were locked, and all the shutters too. No one was there.'

'So you left?'

'Not before having a bit of a look round. The château's surrounded by woods, and on one side they come quite close in. I found a sort of old barn in a clearing there, with tyre tracks going to it. That must have been where Monsieur Rigaut put his car.'

'But you didn't actually find it there?'

'No, that was locked, too.'

Edmunds and Lebrun exchanged glances.

'Did anyone see you while you were there?' Lebrun asked. He looked exhausted: he'd probably started early, and now it was almost ten in the evening. Eleven, if he was working on French time. And it's always tiring operating in a foreign language. They'd probably only sent him over because he spoke English.

'I don't think so.'

'Madame Lee,' he said finally, 'are you sure that's all you know? This is serious, madame.'

'Believe me, that's it. And if you don't believe me that's still it. There's nothing more I can tell you.'

'How many other people have you told about this?'

'Only one.'

Lebrun said, 'Peytoureau,' and I nodded.

'Why him, particularly? To get the story in the press?'

I wondered how much he knew about me and Olivier. Our hillside embrace hadn't exactly been private. If Rigaut or one of his gorillas had seen us, he certainly wouldn't

202

have hesitated to pass that little detail on to the police. Not that it needed much passing – Rigaut's gorillas *were* the police, for God's sake. I felt sure, now, that that must be what had happened. What was it Rigaut had said? *I see you two are friends* – something of that sort.

'Yes, I met him through his wife. I told you, I was staying at their house – she does *chambres d'hôte* at St Front, near Meyrignac. The tourist office recommended her.'

He sighed and said, 'You realize the predicament you are in, madame? I'm afraid that for the moment I must ask you to remain available.'

Edmunds said, 'Perhaps you would give me your passport, Miss Lee. We'll keep it quite safe.'

Perhaps. How very British, to phrase an order as though there were some choice about it. I said, 'If you don't mind waiting down here, I'll call my lawyer.'

Edmunds shrugged. 'Of course.'

I left them sitting while I went up to my study and called Caroline on my mobile. She answered at once, and it struck me she was probably in bed. However, she was still awake, and for once David was there – he was working at home for a couple of days. She passed me to him, and I explained briefly what had happened. 'They want my passport. I can't imagine what they thought I'd do – skip the country?'

David considered for a couple of minutes. 'Did you have any foreign trips planned?'

'No, not immediately.'

'Well, if it's not going to inconvenience you, I'd let them have it. It'll keep them happy and we can always get it back. Have they been there long?'

'An hour.' I looked at my watch. 'No, actually nearly two.'

'It would probably have been better if we'd had someone there.'

'All I said was what happened.'

'Yeah – well, it should be OK. Keep in touch. Don't answer any more questions without someone there.' He gave me a number to call, and rang off.

Downstairs, no one had moved. Lebrun looked as though he might be asleep. I fished the passport out of my bag and handed it over. Edmunds wrote me out a receipt, then slipped it into a plastic envelope and stowed it in his briefcase. He asked for the number of my mobile, and when I hesitated, added, 'Otherwise I'm going to have to ask you to contact me if you're thinking of leaving London.'

I gave him the number; he noted it down and slid it into the plastic bag alongside my passport. When I asked where I could contact him he said simply, 'Paddington Green,' with a note of surprise that implied, Don't call us, we'll call you. Lebrun stood up and held out his hand like a sleep-walker. It contained a card. I took the card and shook the hand. *'Au revoir, madame.* If you need to contact me, that is my number.'

I closed the front door behind them, poured myself a large slug of whisky and told myself to forget all about it. But I couldn't, however hard I tried. Instead I spent the night wondering what French prisons were like, and hoping I wasn't going to find out.

18

Grounded: London, September

They say that even when you think you haven't slept you really have, more than you know. If so, the results were not discernible when I got up.

As soon as I plugged the phone back in it began ringing, so I pulled it out again and checked the voicemail. It kicked off with a message from Olivier telling me he'd done the story and would send me a copy. There was also a message from, of all people, Joe, hoping I was all right. His main concern was probably professional (though he had the grace not to actually mention our arrangement) but it was still good to hear him. Not so long ago, I'd have called him back instantly, wouldn't have had any peace until I'd spoken to him, but now other priorities were more urgent. The other messages, as Edmunds had predicted, were from the French and English press.

I deleted them, and wondered how best to contact Olivier. His mobile seemed the best bet. But when I called the number I was switched direct to voicemail. Perhaps he was having the same problem as me. I left him a message, and asked him to call my mobile. Relatively few people knew its number, so that at least should be safe from the press.

At the office, my phone was similarly swamped. Olivier's mobile still didn't answer, and he hadn't called. I tried his office extension, but there, too, I was switched direct to voicemail.

I couldn't disconnect the office phone, so I took it off the hook and tried to concentrate on the pile of work that as usual awaited me. But that was impossible, so I called Joe.

'Well,' he said, as casual as though speaking on the phone was something we did all the time these days. 'You've been and gone and done it this time. So what's all this about?'

'Are we speaking professionally or personally?'

'Personally, of course.' He sounded hurt. 'What d'you take me for?'

'A journalist. You can't imagine what it's like. The phone just rings all the time.'

'Poor old Reg. The only comfort I can offer is, it won't last. Eventually they'll move on to the next story. Seriously, though. What's all this about Rigaut? You aren't really implying he murdered his old ma, are you? On account of a picture?'

'I'm not implying anything. All I told anyone is what happened. And you'll never guess what happened after that.'

'No, I won't, so why don't you just go ahead and tell me.'

'They're charging *me* with the murder.'

'They've actually charged you?'

'Not yet, but they've confiscated my passport.'

'Fantastic. You've got to hand it to him.' He sounded almost admiring. 'This is his moment, and he isn't going to let someone like you mess it up. If you want my professional advice I think you should get away somewhere till it's all blown over. Go and see Caroline or something. And then when you come back we should meet up and discuss it, OK?'

OK for whom, exactly? But despite my jaunty assumption that I'd got over him I found I terribly wanted to see him. Olivier had helped me over the obsessive stage. But as soon as we actually spoke, the pull returned. 'OK,' I said meekly.

'And Reggie.'

'Yes?'

'Take care, all right?'

The television romance must be over, if it had ever existed. More likely it was just journalism – while a story's in progress, everyone associated with it at once becomes interesting. Still, what he'd said made sense. No one would find me at Caroline's.

True friend that she was, she urged me to drop everything and come at once. 'Take a couple of days off,' she advised. 'Tell them you're ill. Anyway, it's true – you'll have a nervous breakdown otherwise. It's a shame David won't be here – he's had to get back to town. But perhaps it's just as well. You need to take your mind off things.'

I agreed. All I wanted at that moment was never to think about Caravaggio or the Rigauts again. I put my head round Alice's door, told her I thought I was in for a bout of flu and was going to take a couple of days off. By eleven o'clock I was on the road.

Even the Forest of Dean couldn't entirely block out unwelcome snippets. The story didn't make the English front pages – other countries' political scandals rarely do – but it was there in the international news sections: *Mystery Death of Minister's Mother.*

'What I can't understand,' Caroline said, as we sat sipping coffee in the silent house (the girls at school, David in London), 'is why you told Olivier about it in the first place. You might have known something like this would happen.'

I tried to explain – how shocked I'd been to hear of Juliette's death, how filled with pure rage at Rigaut – how I'd longed to bring it home to him, to make sure that this time at least, he wouldn't get away with it.

She shook her head in disbelief – whether at my foolishness or the improbability of it all. 'This time? What else is he supposed to have done?'

'Any number of things. He's quite ruthless. It's obvious when you meet him.'

'Of course he is. He's a politician. Sounds just your type,' Caroline observed, and I felt myself blush.

I'd been there two days, and was reluctantly thinking it was time to take a deep breath and plunge back into the hot water, when my mobile rang. We were about four miles from the house at the time, making the most of a sunny day. I'd forgotten I'd even left it on, and for a moment didn't register the sudden bleating. Then Caroline said, 'Is that your phone?'

The caller's number wasn't one I recognized. I stared at it for a moment, then pressed the green button and held it to my ear. Olivier's voice said, 'Régine?'

I let out my breath, not having realized I'd been holding it. 'I thought you'd never get back to me.'

'Sorry, things have been hectic ... So what did you think?' He sounded jubilant, on top of the world.

'Of the story? I –'

But he was rushing on. 'It's fantastic. You'll never guess – they're giving me a tryout at *Le Figaro*. I'm covering the exhumation ...'

'They're exhuming her?' Despite myself it was impossible not to get drawn back into it all.

'Yes – next week.'

'And what does Rigaut say?'

'Oh, all for it – insists he's got nothing to hide.'

'Olivier. Listen. They're investigating me, as well.'

'You? What – they don't seriously think –?'

'I don't know. I don't have an alibi, it's my word against Rigaut's.'

'*Merde*, Régine, it never crossed my mind.'

'Nor mine.'

There didn't seem anything more to say on that subject, so I wished him good luck in his new job and rang off. At least somebody was happy.

When we got back to the house, David was waiting for us. Caroline had told him I was there, and he'd come back early so that we could talk before I left. I was touched: he was a busy man, and I was Caroline's friend, not his. As we spoke I kept remembering that every minute of his time ought to be costing me several hundred pounds. Still, he could afford it.

I told him more than I'd told Caroline. It seemed important that he should know everything, including my lapse with Olivier, which I hadn't confessed to her, not feeling strong enough, at that point, for more barbed remarks about my taste in men. David, by contrast, was every middle-class mother's dream, diligent, responsible, successful, not bad-looking behind his rimless specs, but not too devastatingly good-looking either. Altogether, a middle-of-the-road man. And middle-aged, ever since I'd known him. Now, well into the real thing, his mousy hair beginning to grey, the gravitas that had always seemed faintly absurd had begun to transmute into something approaching distinction. I even felt it myself, though I knew he wasn't any wiser, just older.

He remained professionally impassive throughout, taking notes now and then. When I finished my recital he said, 'Timing may be important. I wonder if there's any way we can prove Madame Rigaut rang you that morning?'

I explained, as I'd explained to Lebrun, that no one had been with me when the call came. And no one had been in the house with her except Jean-Jacques: not exactly a helpful witness. He seemed abstracted, then suddenly clicked his fingers. 'Of course, stupid of me – there'll be a record of the call. It'll show on her phone bill. So that's OK. Can't prove it was her, of course, but it'll show someone spoke to you from that number.' He looked at his notes. 'Sure you've told me everything?'

'Absolutely everything.'

'Then with any luck you've nothing to worry about. My guess is the exhumation won't find anything, otherwise Rigaut wouldn't allow it. He could stop it if he wanted to. Of course he knows you didn't do anything. If you ask me he just decided to give you a bad time. Serve you right for being so bloody stupid,' he added feelingly. 'What on earth did you think you were going to achieve? Honestly, Reggie, I do sometimes wonder.'

He told me to get in touch should there be any trouble retrieving my passport, and we left it at that.

I stayed on at Caroline's till Sunday morning. When I got back to Kentish Town my voicemail, which I'd emptied, had filled up again with eager reptilian inquiries, but most of them dated from the day I'd left London, and the phone had stopped ringing. There was also an email from Lindsay Hillier saying she'd finished her analysis. If I wanted to come round she'd give me the report.

As always, I found her at her bench. Maybe she'd been there all the time since our last meeting – it seemed not impossible. She turned and greeted me with her charming, unexpected half-moon smile. 'Well,' she said. 'Your mystery package.' If she'd seen my name in the papers she gave no sign of it. Perhaps she never read them. That, too, seemed not impossible.

'Did you find anything?' Over-eager as always.

'All sorts of things,' she replied reprovingly. 'Whether they're what you wanted or expected I've no idea. Generally speaking I'd hope to actually see the painting I'm working on. I warn you, all I can tell you from isolated samples like this is the most general kind of stuff.'

'I do see that. But I really didn't have any choice.'

'All right, then.' She turned back to her bench, pulled a folder from a pile, and extracted some papers from it. 'The canvas. Linen fibres, but that's what everyone used, so it doesn't help with the date. But it would suggest Italian, if it's early – they were using canvas in Venice much more commonly than north of the Alps – from the mid-sixteenth century onwards. Now the paint . . .' She glanced through the pages, stopping at a photograph of what looked like a slice of multilayered cake. She pointed at the lower edge. 'It's got a brown ground, d'you see – that's the sort of preparation they were using in Rome around the end of the Seicento. And the pigments, look at this green. Some nice size particles here, not the sort of machine-ground pigment you find in the nineteenth century. Quite a subdued palette, but generally the sort of quality you'd expect in the late sixteenth century. Together with the ground, I might tentatively put it there. But the paint layers are extraordinarily complex. Can you see that this green doesn't relate to the top layers at all? Of course, it could simply be that the painter changed his mind.' She pulled out a graph from the file. 'This is the most puzzling find though. It seems as if the painter has used some sort of protein for the final highlights, though the rest is in oil as you'd expect.'

I felt as though I was back in one of Lindsay's Materials Science classes, and failing to come up with the answers. 'Does that mean egg tempera?'

'Yes, that's just what it may mean,' she agreed approvingly, and I felt a warm flush of triumph. 'And if it does it's rather interesting. You thought your painting might be by Caravaggio – well, as far as I know only Caravaggio uses egg tempera in that way. For instance the white highlights in the *Boy Bitten by a Lizard* – it's in your Gallery, you should go and have a look next time you have a moment ... Anyhow, you read it. My bill's enclosed.' She handed me the folder. 'Is this some find you're authenticating, or aren't you at liberty to say?'

'There's no particular mystery. It's to do with an exhibition I'm trying to get together.' I explained about the different versions of the picture and how there seemed to be one too many.

'Interesting,' she said. 'D'you have some photos?'

'As it happens, I do. Of two of them, anyway.' I pulled my laptop out of its case and called up pictures of the Louvre version and the ones I'd taken at La Jaubertie. We put them up side by side.

'It's a very exact copy, isn't it,' said Lindsay. 'The only real difference is that little flower on the floor by the music – if you look, it's a bit further over in the Louvre picture, in the other one it's actually near the middle of the music book. Otherwise they're pretty much identical.'

'Pretty much,' I said. 'But there's something about them I don't quite understand. I don't suppose you know anyone in the Louvre's technical department, do you?'

Lindsay said, as I'd hoped she would, 'As a matter of fact I do, yes.'

'I don't want to be seen to be asking for a technical examination – I'm still hoping we may be able to borrow this, and it might give exactly the wrong idea. But it would be really interesting if they could do a few tests, and perhaps an X-ray. D'you think it might be possible to ask your friend just to take a discreet look?'

'I don't see why not,' Lindsay said thoughtfully. 'Leave it to me – I'll tell you what she says. I'll say it's for a friend of mine at the National Gallery, shall I?'

'I'd much rather you didn't. Could you possibly pretend you're interested in it yourself?'

'All right,' she agreed. 'It wouldn't be altogether pretence, either. I agree, there is something . . . It's nice to see all our careful training being put to some use for once.'

We copied the photos to disk so that Lindsay could refer to them. When I got back to the office, I looked through her report. Of course I already knew its broad outlines, but that didn't make it any less interesting. As she had been at such pains to emphasize, tests like these couldn't tell you whether a picture was by one artist rather than another. But if her findings were correct – and that they *were* correct, I had no doubt – then despite its dodgy provenance, the Jaubertie picture definitely was not a nineteenth-century fake. In which case it seemed likely to be the genuine Caravaggio I'd thought it from the start.

But although that was gratifying, it was also puzzling. If, as seemed almost certain, one of the pictures was 'wrong', that had to be the most likely candidate. That or Freddie Angelo's – but his proof seemed incontrovertible. Which left the Louvre and the Getty – both equally unimaginable.

Perhaps there really were four versions. But that, too, seemed unlikely. Caravaggio had often made more than one version of a picture, but four? He was a painter, not a factory.

Meanwhile, I had other things to worry about.

19

London, October

The body was exhumed the day after my meeting with Lindsay. Juliette had been buried in the little cemetery at St Front, with its cypress trees and glass-roofed tombs. She'd doubtless been stored in one of those stone drawers – did they cement you in? Would she have had to be chipped out? Not that anything would have set very hard quite yet . . . *Figaro*, which I now checked daily, carried a picture of gaping onlookers gathered around the police tent that had been erected over the Beaupré family vault. None of the faces meant anything to me. Oddly, the accompanying piece wasn't by Olivier. It wasn't anything very significant – merely a résumé of the proceedings to date – but even so, surely (if the *Fig* really was giving him a trial run) this was his story?

As always seemed to happen these days, Olivier's cellphone switched me straight to voicemail. So I called *Figaro*. The switchboard seemed to recognize his name, and put me through, but the phone at the other end rang and rang. No one answered.

I rang off and dialled *Figaro* again. This time I asked the switchboard to put me through to the news editor. When he answered, I said I was trying to contact Olivier Peytoureau.

'Ah, Olivier. He had some bad news – had to go back home.'

My mouth felt suddenly dry. 'Bad news? Not too serious, I hope?'

'His wife died,' the news editor said shortly.

'Delphine? *Died?*' I thought of cutting up melons together, and nearly wept into the phone. However would he cope? And his children, poor things. 'What happened? She wasn't ill.'

'No, it was a car accident, I believe. They called yesterday afternoon . . . Poor fellow's stunned, you can imagine. Are you a friend of his?'

'Sort of. Thanks, I'll try and get in touch with him.'

No. It couldn't be a coincidence.

Retching my breakfast into the lavatory bowl, I wondered how many people could say they literally turned their own stomach. I should never have touched Olivier. I'd known it from the first guilty moment: rule number one. When he phoned that morning I should have told him, no. Or met him in a restaurant. I didn't have to invite him round. And now Delphine had died. All because of me.

I rinsed out my mouth and held my face under the cold tap, and promised her ghost that I'd get the bastard.

My friend Alice, coming into the Ladies just then, looked startled. 'Did you say something, Reg?'

'No, no. Sorry. Talking to myself.'

'You look awful. Are you all right?'

'Had a bit of a shock. I'll be OK.'

A car accident. Well, it could happen to anyone. But the roads round St Front were as unthreatening as roads could well be in the twenty-first century – hardly any traffic, and none of it fast. Your most dangerous moment, generally speaking, would be trying to pass a combine harvester.

No wonder Olivier wasn't answering his phone. I ought to leave him alone. I must be the last person he'd want to speak to. But somehow, I had to find out more.

I pulled out my Meyrignac folder, flipped through it to see if anyone possible might suggest themselves – and came across the note Olivier's uncle Francis had slipped in with his package. It was scribbled on his builder's headed paper, and it gave his number. I looked at my watch – eleven o'clock: but of course France was an hour ahead. If I tried in half an hour, he'd be home for lunch.

He was. 'Laronze.'

'Monsieur Laronze, it's Régine Lee from London. I heard that Delphine Peytoureau was in a car accident. Is it true?'

'I'm afraid so. God knows how they'll manage, poor things. The funeral's the day after tomorrow.'

'What happened, do you know?'

'Hit and run,' said Francis laconically. 'He forced her off the road and she ran into a tree. Died instantly . . . They haven't caught him, the *salaud*. There's a red mark on the car, that's all they know. But there are a lot of red cars in France.'

I had a vision of Rigaut's red BMW. You wouldn't want a scratch on that expensive bodywork. If one appeared, you'd get it fixed. At once. I wondered if the same thought had occurred to Olivier.

I thanked Francis, then took a deep breath and tried the Les Pruniers number. Magali answered. I said, 'Hello, is your papa there?'

She yelled, 'Papa, it's for you.'

Olivier said, *'Oui?'* He sounded grave, distracted.

'Olivier, it's Régine. I heard . . .'

'I can't believe it,' he said. 'I just can't believe it. I don't know what I'm going to do.'

'They haven't found who did it?'

'No. I don't get the impression they're looking very hard,' he said bitterly.

'Your uncle said there was a red mark on the car. I was thinking of that red BMW.'

'Yes.'

'Do you think –?'

'No idea. Nothing would surprise me now.'

I remembered the mix of guilt, rage and impotence that had swamped me when I heard about Juliette. Olivier must be feeling the same, but raised to the power of a thousand. It was as if the spirit of Caravaggio, that unquiet and violent soul, had somehow infused itself into his pictures, as though anyone who touched them was condemned to experience something of his own lawless desperation.

'My God, Olivier. What can I say?'

'Not much,' he said. 'There's nothing to say.'

'I'll get that bastard if it's the last thing I do.'

'It probably will be,' he said, and rang off.

After the madness, my phone was now reduced to silence. Nobody called. And my passport remained in Paddington Green. Surely they'd have done the autopsy as soon as they'd exhumed the body? And surely, once it was done, I was entitled to know the results? Quite apart from anything else, I urgently needed, for both professional and personal reasons, to visit Paris again. Finally I lost patience and phoned Detective Sergeant Edmunds. Naturally he wasn't at his desk, so I left a message and awaited his call. Two days later it came.

'Dr Lee? John Edmunds here from the Metropolitan Police. I believe you wanted to speak to me. Is there something I can do for you?'

What a time to play silly buggers – as though he and I didn't know exactly what he could do for me. However, I recalled my father's maxim – always be polite to police and customs officials: they have the upper hand. So I said mildly, 'Oh, Sergeant Edmunds. Thanks for calling. I was wondering when I could have my passport back. They exhumed the body a while ago – there must be an autopsy report by now. I assume they haven't found anything suspicious or they'd have got in touch. '

'That's down to Lebrun,' he said. I waited for him to say, I'll give him a ring and get right back to you, but no.

Mildness was clearly wasted on Edmunds. 'Then please get in touch with him and let me know what he says. Or I'll ring him myself. Perhaps that would be better.'

That got him going. '*I'll* ring him,' he replied sharply. 'I'll get back to you.'

I told him, as evenly as I could manage, that I'd appreciate it if he did that, and the sooner the better.

Predictably enough, he did nothing of the sort. My sanity was saved, however, by an email from Lindsay Hillier. *Some results from the Louvre. Why don't you come round and see.*

When I rang she said she was free for an hour that afternoon, if I wanted to come. Glad of any distraction, I hotfooted it to Bloomsbury, where I found her deep in conversation about resins with a man I recognized from the Gallery's own technical department. I waited at the back of the room, where she kept the pictures she was currently working on – a stiff eighteenth-century portrait, a Russian-looking abstract from the agitprop period – and tried, inconclusively, to decide whether they were or were not what they purported to be. Finally the resins conversation drew to an end, and it was my turn.

'Ah, Reggie, yes. Something quite interesting here, I think.' Lindsay rummaged among her folders.

I tried to keep quiet but it was too much for me and I burst out, 'You mean it's a fake?'

'Not exactly.' She grinned, found the folder and laid it on the desk. It contained a list of pigments, a number of photographs, and various notes from the person at the Louvre. Lindsay scanned through it. 'The period seems right – the right pigments, and hand-ground. It's not on its original stretcher, so that doesn't help us much. But it's certainly not a modern forgery. But now look at this.'

She pulled out three photographs and laid them on the desk. One showed the Louvre picture, the next was an X-ray, showing where it had been blocked out in lead white on the dark ground. The third at first glance looked like another photo of the same picture, but when you looked more closely, you could see that it was slightly different. I recognized my own photograph of the Jaubertie picture.

'D'you see,' Lindsay said, 'there are no *pentimenti* on the X-ray.' It was true: no ghost limbs or vanished figures pointed to the usual second thoughts and overpaintings. 'Usually you'd say that pointed to a copy,' she went on. 'But of course that's not necessarily true with Caravaggio.

He often didn't alter his compositions at all, even when they were quite complicated.'

I remembered Freddie Angelo's demonstration. 'Perhaps it's because he used lenses.'

'Perhaps,' Lindsay said sceptically. 'But now look at this.' She produced a sheet of tracing-paper, on which were the outlines of the picture's main features – the Angel, St Cecilia, the lute, the violin. 'I traced this from your photo. And now –' She superimposed the tracing on the Louvre picture. It fitted exactly. 'That's strange for a start – when he made a new version of a picture he usually changed some of the details. But not this one. The only difference is the placing of that flower on the music. Everything else is identical. It must mean someone requested an exact copy of a particular painting. So, that leaves us with two possibilities. One, Caravaggio makes his picture, someone comes to see it while it's in his studio, or even when it's been hung in his patron's house, and likes it so much they want a copy. So he makes one. It's by no means unknown – he did it more than once.'

'And the other?'

'The other is, he refuses to do it, or isn't around, or maybe he's already dead. So someone else makes the copy. So in that sense, although it's not actually a Caravaggio, it's not a fake either. That's what I think seems to be most likely. It would explain the contemporary materials and the different quality. Look at the treatment of the fur here.' She pointed at the Jaubertie picture. 'It's so delicate and alive in this one, and so flat and heavy in the other. And her face – and his. The Louvre one's wooden by comparison. You could never prove it, of course.'

Of course. But now that Lindsay had offered a reasoned explanation for what had until this moment been no more than a feeling, the difference in quality between the Louvre picture and the Jaubertie one seemed so obvious, so glaringly apparent, that there could be no more doubt. Caravaggio could not possibly, even on a very bad day, have painted the Louvre picture.

'Here.' She gathered together the various items spread out on her desk, shuffled them back into their folder and held it out. 'Why don't you take them with you? They're more use to you than me. I'd have expected it to take longer, but Judith said it was apparently all to hand. Somebody had already had all this stuff done, all she had to do was find the file.'

That made me sit up. 'Really? Did she say who?'

'I'm afraid I didn't think to ask.'

Back at the office I pulled out my bulging Caravaggio file in order to add the folder to it. Something fell out, and when I bent to pick it up I saw that it was the *Partir, c'est mourir un peu, Martyr, c'est pourrir un peu* pamphlet. As I leafed through it, something caught my eye.

I looked again. Surely it couldn't be?

It was.

The photos in the pamphlet were not of the picture that hung in the Louvre now. They unmistakably showed the Jaubertie picture, with its little flower laid across the centre fold of the music book. At some point – presumably during the missing weeks between the picture's theft and its reappearance – the two must have been switched. Juliette hadn't said anything about this, whether by accident or design I would now never know (and what else, I again wondered, had she left unsaid?). But there could be no other explanation. After they'd abducted the picture they'd driven it round Paris, taking the photographs that they'd use over the next few weeks. Then they'd taken it to La Jaubertie. While the photos were being teasingly sent to the press, and the police were vainly setting dawn traps to try and catch the thieves, the picture was hundreds of miles away. And when eventually a different picture was returned, nobody, in the excitement, noticed the substitution.

Had Juliette known? Impossible to imagine she had not. The one essential detail, unmentioned.

I rang the library and inquired whether they had any old illustrated books on Caravaggio. Something pre-war.

219

Yes, they had one or two. If I wanted to come down, they'd get them out for me.

When I got there the librarian had two books waiting, one from 1907, one from 1928. Both were in German, but that didn't bother me – it was the plates I was after. Staggering under their combined weight, I took them to a table.

The 1907 book didn't show the St Cecilia, but the 1928 one did. It mentioned the three versions, the church's, Del Monte's and Doria's, but pictured just one, the one belonging to the Louvre. The photograph was black and white, but it was good enough. There was the little flower, crisp and clear, lying across the centre of the music book; and the Angel had two fingers extended. It was incontrovertibly the Jaubertie picture. QED.

A day passed, and then another: still no word from Edmunds.

Before the exhumation I'd become relatively calm, but now, perhaps irrationally, the jitters returned in full force. Naturally I knew I hadn't done anything, but in a battle with Jean-Jacques Rigaut mere innocence seemed a puny weapon. Who could have been more innocent than Delphine? When the phone didn't ring, which was most of the time, I couldn't concentrate, and when it did my heart leapt into my mouth.

Inevitably, when the call eventually came I was away from my desk. The caller wasn't Edmunds, but Lebrun. In his halting English, he left a number for me to call. I dialled it at once: it was engaged. I spent the next half-hour punching Redial, but it went on being engaged. Finally I got through. Somewhere in France, a phone rang. There was no reply and no answering machine. I dialled the number again from scratch, in case I'd got it wrong in the first place, but the same thing happened. In the split second between ending his previous interminable conversation and my getting through, Lebrun had vanished.

I tried again ten minutes later. This time I had better luck. The phone not only rang, but was picked up. 'Lebrun.'

I said, in French because it was easier and I really didn't feel like playing about, 'Monsieur Lebrun, it's Regina Lee. I saw that Madame de Beaupré's body was exhumed, and I wondered if there were any autopsy results.'

'Certainly,' he said. 'Over a week ago. Did no one say anything to you?'

No, I said. I'd heard nothing.

'There was nothing. She died of old age. A heart attack. The case is closed.'

'Then I can have my passport back?'

'*Bien sûr,*' he replied. '*Au revoir, madame.*'

Just in time, I remembered to ask him if he could send me an email to this effect. Then at least I'd have proof that this conversation had taken place. He said he would, and twenty minutes later it arrived.

By then I was dancing with fury. Edmunds must have known this all along. What did he think he was doing? Sitting there letting this hang over me, holding on to my passport, when all the time the results were there, the case closed. Spitting with fury, I called David to see what we should do next.

'Calm down,' he said. 'You'll do yourself no good.'

'But I'm sure he knew.'

'Whether he did or didn't, all you want is your passport back. Just concentrate on that, it's the only important thing.'

I rang Edmunds, but of course he wasn't there. Probably down at the pub with his mates or indulging in a few desultory stop-and-searches. I left a message to say Lebrun had told me the case was closed, and had sent me an email to confirm it, which I would forward. I was coming by Paddington Green in an hour, and I expected my passport to be ready and waiting for me to collect.

Paddington Green is the place they store all the really edgy prisoners, IRA bombers and terrorists of every stripe. It isn't nice. It's situated on possibly the nastiest site in London, just under the roaring Westway and immediately over a particularly squalid pedestrian underpass. I'd passed the building a hundred times, but never actually gone inside. However, I was too furious to be intimidated. I marched up to the counter and demanded Detective Sergeant Edmunds.

'Who wants to see him?' a harassed woman wanted to know.

I told her my name and explained that he knew I was coming by and should have left my passport to be picked up. She looked, but there wasn't anything. She rang his extension. Of course he wasn't there.

I asked her when he might be back.

'I'm afraid I can't say. You can wait if you like.'

I explained that he should have returned the passport a week ago, and that I needed it now as I was going to Paris in the morning. (Who knew? I might be – if I had a passport.) I produced my receipt and a copy of Lebrun's email: she studied them without much interest and said there wasn't anything she could do, I'd have to speak to him.

I suggested he must have a cellphone. She did not take the suggestion kindly. Those numbers were for use in an emergency. This was not an emergency.

By now I was beginning to actually shake with rage. I said, 'What's the name of his superior officer?'

'Please calm down, Dr Lee,' said the woman. 'Losing your temper won't help matters. I'll try his extension again. You never know, he may be back.'

As luck would have it, he answered. Back from the pub at last.

'John? I have a Dr Regina Lee here at reception. Something about a passport . . . OK.' She put the phone down. 'He'll be down shortly. Please take a seat.'

Steaming, I took my place among a disconsolate gathering of the marooned. It was twenty minutes before Edmunds ambled in. He was carrying the passport in its plastic bag. He nodded, handed it over to the woman, and, perhaps wisely, ambled out again without emerging from behind the protective counter. In fact I probably wouldn't have attacked him: even I could see that might be counterproductive. I signed for the passport and left before they took it into their heads to confiscate it again, then celebrated the return of foreign travel by booking a seat on next morning's seven twenty Eurostar.

20

Paris, October

My first destination was the Louvre, and an unannounced visit to Charles Rey. There were things I wanted to know, and even if he didn't want to share them, they might nevertheless be divined if I could confront him face-to-face. And that could only be achieved impromptu. If I tried to make an appointment, not only would the element of surprise be lost, but he almost certainly wouldn't agree to see me. Whereas if I just turned up, he couldn't escape.

London was being battered by October gales, but Paris, when I arrived there, sparkled palely under an autumn sun. I took the metro to the Louvre, and descended to the subterranean corridor that contained Rey's office. It was eleven forty-five – not lunchtime yet, there should be a good chance of finding him at his desk. I knocked, and Janine Desvergnes' voice called, '*Entrez.*'

I entered. '*Bonjour, madame*. Regina Lee from the National Gallery, we met in June. Is Monsieur Rey in?'

'*Bien sûr.*' Madame Desvergnes sat trimly at her desk. I wondered if she'd seen the story and noted my starring role. It seemed impossible she had not. 'Naturally I re-member. Is Charles expecting you? I don't seem to have anything written down.'

'No, I was passing by, so I thought I'd take a chance.'

She got up and opened the door that led into the inner

sanctum. 'Charles – Madame Lee from the National Gallery's here to see you.'

There was a short pause: I imagined him trying, unsuccessfully, to devise a way out. Eventually a chair was pushed back, and he appeared in the doorway. After the first brief shock the young man I'd known warped into the middle-aged figure before me. He'd got plumper, and his thick black hair had receded and thinned, though the terrifically unhealthy white complexion was unchanged. Presumably he was registering similar details. I dyed my hair so incessantly these days that its original colour was a mere flickering memory. Had my Ghent self still been a nut-brown girl? She'd certainly been a larger girl ... For a minute we stared at each other. Then, wordlessly, he waved me into his office.

Charles Rey and I were about the same age, but on Juliette's measurement – are you successful? – he definitely scored higher than me. Where I had only the most exiguous share of a communal secretary, he commanded an outer office complete with watchdog. This time, however, the system had unaccountably failed, and he was trapped. He looked sulky, there was no other word for it. He nodded perfunctorily towards a chair, closed the door, then slumped down behind his desk and waited.

'Nice to see you again after all these years,' I opened cheerfully.

He grunted, not actually disagreeing in so many words. 'Next time it would be better if you'd call if you're planning to visit. I might easily have been away from my desk.'

I didn't bother to remark that this was exactly the point. Why waste precious time telling him what he already knew? 'I wondered if you'd remembered any more about that Caravaggio, or Monsieur Rigaut,' I said sweetly. 'I was in Paris, so I thought I'd take a chance and drop by.'

'Uh.'

'I'm still hoping you may change your mind and lend it to us.'

He shook his head. 'Not a chance.'

225

'Give me one good reason why not.'

He looked at me, his elbows on the desk, his chin resting on his clasped hands. Then he leaned back and spoke as from a great distance. 'Just accept it. Some things are more trouble than they're worth. What are we talking about, some piffling little exhibition? Take my advice, give it up. It's not worth it.'

Trouble indeed. I wondered how much he knew about it. 'Perhaps it's worth it to me.'

'Then you're stupider than I thought.'

Temper, temper! This was obviously a sore spot. All the more reason, then, to probe it further. 'You must see, Monsieur Rigaut's behaviour was puzzling. First he said yes, then all of a sudden no. No reason, just no. But that's ridiculous. It can't have been simply a whim.'

'No,' he said grimly. 'I don't suppose it was a whim.'

'Fine, so there was a reason. And I thought, since you knew him, you might know what it was.'

He still didn't move, but the colour rushed to his face. 'No,' he said. 'I'm afraid I don't.'

I didn't believe him. Was that a bead of sweat on his forehead? He knew all right, but he wasn't telling. Why not? Because someone had told him not to? If so, no prizes for guessing their name. As for the leverage, that was easy. In France, museums are part of the state. 'Are you sure?'

'Are you accusing me of lying?'

'Of course not. But if something should happen to strike you . . .'

He shook his head and said, 'You'll just have to accept it,' then added, so softly I could hardly make the words out, 'otherwise you've seen the kind of thing that happens.'

Someone else had said that. Trying to remember who, I temporized. 'I don't know what you mean.'

'I think you do.' He was definitely sweating now, no doubt about it. He got up from behind his desk and held the door open for me. 'I don't think there's much more I can tell you. I'm sorry. Goodbye.'

I marched out past Madame Desvergnes, who kept her

eyes demurely on her keyboard. I hoped Charlie wouldn't take his annoyance, if that's what it was, out on her. It seemed unlikely. Not much doubt who was the boss there.

I glanced at my watch: twelve fifteen. My next appointment was at twelve thirty. If I walked fast, I should just make it.

On the way, I remembered who'd used that phrase about seeing the kind of thing that happens. Manu. It had been Manu.

When I'd rung his number last night, expecting either absence or the man himself, to my surprise a woman's voice had answered. For a moment I was disproportionately thrown – but why shouldn't an attractive young man have lady friends? I pulled myself together and said, 'Sorry to disturb you, I wanted to speak to Manu Rigaut.'

'I'm afraid he doesn't live here any more,' said the voice. 'But I can give you his new number, if you want.'

'That's very kind. If you would . . .' Obviously, now that Juliette had died, he'd been thrown out of his cushy digs.

Manu duly answered the new number. He didn't ask where I'd got it, nor did he sound particularly surprised to hear from me. As before, he merely acquiesced. I asked for his new address, and he told me 14, quai des Grands Augustins.

This was a part of Paris I knew well from the days when we used to visit our grandmother. Our mother had often taken us for walks along here on the way to the zoo at the Jardin des Plantes. Sam and I used to fantasize about what went on in the various buildings we passed, and when I got there I realized that number 14 was one we had particularly noticed. It didn't go straight up like its neighbours but was prettily domed on the top two storeys, in a gentle curve of silvery lead. As I remembered it had been the home of a rich princess that a mad scientist was holding for ransom up in the roof behind the dome. And the scientist's lair, it turned out, was exactly where Manu lived. 'Take the lift,' he said, as he buzzed me in. 'I'm on the top floor.'

The ancient lift wheezed and groaned up to a landing with two doors. Manu was waiting outside one of them. We hesitated between the formality of a handshake or the slightly more familiar double kiss: I solved the problem by kissing him. These days, I was all but part of the family.

'Well,' he said. 'Had you any particular reason for this, or is it purely a friendly visit?'

'A bit of both.'

He opened the door a little wider. 'Come in. Or shall we go out? I don't usually bother with lunch, but there's a brasserie a few doors down if you're hungry.'

'I'm always hungry at lunchtime.'

We ordered steak and chips and a couple of beers. I said, 'I thought you lived in the rue d'Assas.'

'I did.'

'Not any more?'

'No, now I live here.'

'It belonged to your uncle, right?' The address had been niggling me all morning, but when I'd turned into the quai I'd remembered.

He nodded.

'Won't you have to move once the estate's settled?'

'No,' he said. 'It belongs to me now.'

'Lucky you.'

'That's what they all say.'

He didn't seem inclined to say much else. We concentrated on our steaks. When we'd finished he said, 'Thanks, that was great. So. I've got to go somewhere in a bit. It might interest you. You can come, if you want.'

'That's very kind,' I said, laughing. 'Where to, exactly?'

'You'll see when we get there . . . It's not for a while, though.'

We wandered back to the apartment. The space behind the dome was every bit as splendid as Sam and I had imagined it all those years ago. The door gave on to an entrance hall, with parquet floors and cream and gold-painted panelling, from which a door opened into a large salon, similarly parqueted and painted, that overlooked the river. The outside wall was gently curved above the three windows that framed the spectacular view; the inner ones were covered with bookcases interspersed with pictures, including a magnificent Poussin landscape with a temple and a scatter of nymphs and fauns, doubtless the booty from Russia. 'Wow,' I said.

'Wow,' Manu agreed.

He wandered restlessly around the room, nervously pulling books from the shelves and replacing them. The summer had tanned him, his grey eyes burning out even more insistently from the even brown of his skin and hair: a beautiful young man. But there was no spark there. Perhaps he wasn't interested in women. Perhaps he wasn't interested in anyone, full stop. There was something hollow about him. Where he'd lived before, his grandmother's house in rue d'Assas, had felt quite impersonal, like a very expensive hotel. This, by contrast, was very much someone's home. Not Manu's, though. Perhaps he'd grow into it.

He made us some coffee, and I noticed he was left-handed. 'Your grandmother was too, wasn't she? I seem to remember noticing.'

He nodded. 'Yes, it runs in the family. Antoine, too.' He sighed. 'She said you'd been to see her.'

I waited for him to say something more – about the exhumation, about my part in the whole affair – but he fell silent and looked sad. Eventually he added, 'She liked you.'

'I liked her. I was very sorry to hear she'd died.'

'She was old, I suppose.'

I said cautiously, 'Lucky for me I got to her in time.'

He nodded. Perhaps, like me, he was thinking of the circumstances in which he'd given me her address, for he suddenly asked 'So how's your exhibition going?'

'Not very well. First your uncle wouldn't lend the picture I wanted, and then your father tried to stop your grandmother lending hers. And now it's his, so that's that.

He seems to have it in for me, your papa. I really can't imagine why.'

'Ah, my papa . . .' He pulled out a big, thick, heavy book – it looked like a dictionary – and stood weighing it in his hands, as though considering how far and hard he might be able to throw it. 'Believe me, you're not alone. I sometimes think he hates the whole world. Including me.'

'You?'

He nodded. 'Especially now. He was furious about this place. I think he thought maybe there was something between me and Antoine, and that this was a kind of pay-off. That I was some sort of tart.'

'Was there?'

He shook his head. 'Nope. Not that it would be any of his business if there had been. We were just fond of each other. Friends, you know? I miss Antoine so much. My father can't understand that. He doesn't have friends, just people he does or doesn't control. He doesn't do emotions. They're too complex. You're either for him or against him. And if you're against him you're an obstacle to be got out of the way. I've often thought he's actually autistic. High-grade, but autistic. I think maybe he was jealous of Antoine and me – we had something he thought he should have had, but he couldn't manage it. Another reason to hate us.'

'They didn't get on?'

Manu shook his head. 'Not even as children, apparently. Antoine was always the favourite, and my father was always jealous of him.'

I thought of Helmut Kopp.

'What about the place in rue d'Assas? Is that yours too?'

He shook his head. 'Fortunately, not. Though there were some bad moments when we were waiting to know what was in my grandmother's will. I really think he'd have gone mad if that had fallen into my lap too. Killed me or something.'

I thought this perfectly possible, but it seemed tactless to say so. Just because people are rude about their relatives doesn't mean you can be, too. Instead I blandly confined the conversation to property. 'So that's his now? The little house?'

He nodded. 'They can't decide what to do with it. My mother wants it for her town house, but my father wants to rent it for lots of money to Americans. Or sell it. He never has enough money. The amount they get through . . . I expect she'll win, though. She usually does. It's not much fun being married to Papa, but she makes sure it's a comfortable sort of hell.' So that must have been his mother I'd spoken to. 'Why are you so interested in my family, anyway?'

'Because they're interesting,' I said, which was certainly true enough. 'Not many people's fathers get to be President.'

He shuddered. *'Pas possible.* If people only knew . . .'

'So why don't you tell them, if you feel so strongly? It'd be easy enough. Every journalist in France would be fighting to talk to you.' I thought of Olivier, and then of Delphine. Not such a good idea, perhaps.

He shook his head and looked at his watch. 'Time to go.'

We left the apartment, creaked down in the lift, then set off at a brisk trot along the pavement. I scurried to keep up with his long-legged stride. 'Where are we going?'

'You'll see when we get there.'

We turned into a side street with a parking garage, and took the lift to the fifth level. Manu led the way to a silver Mercedes. Not this season's model, but still, a surprisingly lush if rather middle-aged vehicle for so young a man.

'Was this your uncle's too?'

He nodded and got on with the business of manoeuvring it down the ramps. We crossed the river and drove north towards Montmartre, then through St Denis towards the banlieue, the ring of suburbs whose poetic names – Mantes-la-Jolie, Aulnay-sous-Bois, Villiers-le-Bel – sit so ironically with today's grim reality. I tried to chat, but Manu, preoccupied with his thoughts, or perhaps simply with the nerve-racking business of manoeuvring through the traffic, did not reply.

At half past three we arrived at what seemed to be our destination, in a town whose name I hadn't registered as we turned off the autoroute. We drove through a labyrinth of grubby streets beside some railway sidings, fetching up in a district of dilapidated high-rises and heavily fortified shops, where veiled women hurried along the broken pavement and groups of loitering African and Algerian boys, unwanted debris of a dead colonial past, clustered around bus shelters and in rubbish-strewn stretches of unkempt grass. Manu seemed to know his way around – had obviously been here before. I wondered what had brought him – sex? The only other middle-class whites I could imagine in these streets would be social workers, and I certainly didn't see Manu as one of those.

We parked just off a shabby main street containing a municipal-looking hall. I noticed Manu didn't bother to lock the car. Perhaps he didn't care, or maybe he thought locking it simply a pointless gesture, no defence against the marauding youths. We joined a stream of citizens evidently headed for some event, and I noticed a poster informing us that at four o'clock today the Minister of the Interior, Jean-Jacques Rigaut, was due to address a public meeting in the hall. A cluster of blue police vans parked a little way down the street were presumably connected with this event – a visible presence intended to discourage trouble or stifle it should it occur. That there was potential for trouble was clear. At some point the groups of boys would get too big, or too close, the police would spill out of their vans and there'd be a full-scale confrontation of the kind they'd been rehearsing in the woods at St Front. For the moment the boys kept their distance, but groups of them were gathered everywhere you looked. For them Rigaut was the enemy, which of course was exactly why he had chosen this particular venue. His message was addressed to the other inhabitants of this place, the ones who'd been here before the tower blocks came, who inhabited leafy villas a few streets away and lived in terror of the roaming boys. If there was trouble so much the better – his support would only increase. I was surprised, at first, that the authorities had allowed him to speak here – such a person in such a place was so unequivocally inflammatory. But they probably had little choice in the matter. Rigaut, as Minister of the Interior, was ultimately responsible for law and order, and if he chose to come here it would be almost impossible to prevent it.

At the door, formidable-looking bouncers scrutinized all comers. It was pretty clear what – or who – they were looking for. No black or brown person would attend a gathering like this unless they had trouble in mind. Not that any seemed very keen to penetrate the cordon – they confined themselves to watching from a distance. The people in the hall reminded me of the marchers I'd seen near the Voltaire that day with Olivier, respectable small shopkeepers and functionaries, all lily-white. From time to time the bouncers stopped someone and conducted a random search. They stared at us, as they stared at everyone, and Manu stared back. They eyed him with what might have been suspicion or astonishment – his resemblance to his father was unmistakable – then nodded him through. I followed in his wake, head well down, wishing I wasn't there. If Manu had told me before we set off where we were headed, I certainly wouldn't have come. That, I imagined, was why he'd kept his mouth shut. Though why should he want me there? As a witness? To what? I couldn't think why he'd come – he must know exactly what his father would be likely to say, and it wasn't as if his hatred needed stoking. Or perhaps it did: perhaps he was trying to pump himself up for some confrontation, intended to embarrass Rigaut in some way. In which case the very last thing I needed right now was to be sitting beside him. If I wasn't careful my passport would be confiscated again on some pretext – suspected terrorism, perhaps.

The hall had a platform at one end and the inevitable town-hall rows of tubular steel and canvas chairs. To my horror Manu marched resolutely towards the front. The front row seats were all reserved, but he made his way to the centre of the second row. I'd have left then, had I known where we were or how you got out of it. But there definitely wouldn't be any taxis, and I didn't fancy waiting for a bus under the eyes of the bus shelter's habitual occupants, nor sitting alone for who knew how long in the car. I hoped it would still be in working order when we got back to it. Meanwhile all I could do was to tag reluctantly along in Manu's wake, and try to pretend I wasn't there.

Circumstances, however, were against me. Our row was empty except for us: the hall, as always, was filling from the back. As Manu no doubt intended, Rigaut couldn't fail to notice us. I said 'Can't we sit a bit further back?'

'Further back? Why? Don't you want a good view?'

I was still havering between leaving or moving to a less conspicuous seat when a stir in the crowd announced the day's main attraction and the Minister marched on to the stage. A claque at the back applauded: he acknowledged them with a raised hand. I waited for a catcall, but none came – this was a gathering of true believers. His gaze raked the audience: it settled briefly on us, but he remained expressionless. He was briefly introduced (as though we didn't all know who he was), and began to speak.

He gave what was clearly his stock speech, though now with detail appropriate to this bleak urban venue – dangerous streets, not enough jobs, the threat of uncontrolled immigration, the mob at the gates. It was old stuff – everyone there had heard him say it a thousand times. But as everyone knew, the words were beside the point. This wasn't a policy meeting. The real statement was his presence. He was their ally, he was with them in the continuing war against the threatening boys outside. That was what they wanted to know, that was why they would vote for him when the time came.

Beside me, Manu tensed. Whatever he'd come for was clearly about to happen. Then there was a noise – a sort of muffled roar – from outside, and as everyone turned to see where it had come from, a stone shattered one of the dirty windows that dimly lit the hall's left-hand wall.

Was that it? Had he had some warning that there would be a riot? There was a moment of shocked silence, then a buzz. Rigaut, whose speech was drawing smoothly to a close, added a coda about deprivation being no excuse for crime. 'The only thing to do with this rabble is sweep them off the streets, and with your help, that's just what we shall do,' he said, as another stone hit the window. A journalist at the far end of the front row feverishly noted down this last sentence, congratulating herself, no doubt, on being on the spot as the news broke.

I noticed Manu's hand – his left hand, the one beside me – sneak towards his pocket. And suddenly (idiotically, my head rang with Mae West's old line – Is that a gun in your pocket or are you just pleased to see me?) I knew why he'd been too preoccupied to talk while we drove, why he'd kept his coat on even though the hall was so warm – why we were there. I grabbed his wrist and held on to it as tightly as I could – if I couldn't make him drop whatever it was he was holding, I could at least prevent him aiming it.

He fought to free himself from my grasp, and since he was stronger than me, eventually succeeded. But by then the moment had passed. Rigaut had vanished, no doubt to take his place beside the police, ready for the television cameras that would soon be here, and another man – the one who'd introduced him – was standing in his place, telling us that fighting had broken out, that the building was a target, that the rioters had petrol bombs, that the Minister was anxious no one should be hurt, and that we were all to leave by the back exit. In an orderly way, he added, but everyone was too busy pushing their way towards the gangways to hear him.

We followed in their wake, as more stones hit the windows, and filed through a deserted kitchen into a sort of alleyway. There was a flash, followed by a bang, and I heard someone say 'They're setting fire to cars.' I prayed ours was not one of them. I had no idea where it was: from the front of the hall I might have found it, but from this unknown alleyway, never. I hoped Manu was not similarly disoriented.

He set off at a furious pace. To our left we could hear shouts and bangs, and from somewhere at the front of the building a flicker of flame was visible. Something acrid in the air made us choke – perhaps now they were firing tear-gas. We heard running feet. And then suddenly we were at the car, which seemed miraculously untouched. As we slid inside and locked the doors, a group of boys appeared at the end of the street. They ran towards us. Manu lay back in his seat, saying nothing, staring at the roof: I put my hand into his pocket – an oddly intimate gesture – and pulled out the gun. It was smallish, heavy and black: it looked lethal enough, though in my shaking hands it would probably be worse than useless. As the boys drew level with us, I tried feverishly to work out which was the safety catch. But before I could release it they were past, more concerned with getting somewhere, or perhaps getting away from somewhere, than stopping to attack even such a tempting target as the Mercedes.

Unable to think what else to do with the gun, I stowed it in my handbag. A wave of rage washed over me – at Rigaut, at his bully-boys, at the terrifying young men who had just thundered past. Since he was to hand, I directed it at Manu. 'You idiot!' I shouted. 'Are you mad? What good would that have done?'

'It would have got rid of him,' he muttered.

'Your recipe for a better world.'

'It would have *been* a better world. If you hadn't interfered –'

'So why did you bring me?'

'You're so keen to know about us,' he muttered sulkily. '*Et voilà. La famille Rigaut.*'

I waited for him to start the car, but he seemed lost in a dream, so I unlocked the doors, rushed round to his side and pushed him into the passenger seat. He slid glassily across, his coat snagging on the gear-lever as I set about putting distance between us and the riot. Eventually we hit a main street, and after a while there was a roundabout and a sign to Paris and the *périphérique*. Beside me, Manu still lay motionless – stunned, perhaps, by what he'd nearly done. After a while I said sharply, 'Manu, you'll have to tell me where to go now.'

Silence.

I hit him sharply, a backhander across the neck. 'Manu!'

His head jerked up. 'What?'

'Tell me where to go. I've never driven in Paris.'

He sat up, and mechanically issued instructions which I as mechanically followed. Eventually they led us to the parking garage. I slid the car into a slot and switched off the engine, shaking.

There was a bar opposite: we sat at a table near the back, and I ordered two double brandies. Behind the barman, the television news showed pictures of the riot we'd just escaped. In front of a burning car, the Minister talked about law and order and how the irresponsible few destroyed the lives of their fellow citizens.

'Why do you hate him so much? Is it just politics?'

'Just politics,' he repeated scornfully. 'His politics are part of what he is. You can't separate them. Don't you see that this is exactly what he intended? It's not just that, though. He's a murderer.'

'You mean Delphine Peytoureau?'

'*Delphine Peytoureau?* Your boyfriend's wife? What's she got to do with any of this?'

I felt myself blush. If even Manu knew about it, our only-too-visible embrace had evidently become a hot topic in the small world of St Front. I hoped Delphine herself had been spared the gossip, but it seemed unlikely – even my limited acquaintance with village life was enough to tell me that. I said, 'Someone forced her off the road and she hit a tree. They haven't found the driver.'

'What are you saying? That my father –?' Now that he was confronted by actual detail, he seemed stricken.

'Not him personally, no. But it seems likely he's connected. After Olivier published his story, he tried to get me accused of murder.'

'Of my grandmother? Of course I read the story.' He shook his head. 'Really, Régine, things are bad enough without letting your imagination run away with you.'

'You didn't see your father that morning. He was terrified. Utterly panicked. *Something* had happened.'

Manu said dreamily, 'As a matter of fact I asked him about it.'

That was something I hadn't expected. 'Really? And what did he say?'

Somewhat to my surprise, he began to laugh. 'He said it was all your fault.'

'*My* fault! That's too much. How could it be my fault? I didn't even see her. That was the whole point.'

'Ah, but you were the catalyst. The reason she died. He told me about it after the – the exhumation. I don't think that was easy, even for him. She was his mother, after all ... He rang, and we had dinner together. He wanted to talk. I didn't want to, but he really seemed almost desperate. One of his intervals of being almost human ... He said he'd arranged to call by La Jaubertie that morning to talk about the roof – you must have seen the mess there, they'd been arguing about it, there was something he'd forgotten to show her. He'd meant to get there around eleven, but then something came up and he had to make it earlier. He didn't bother to tell grand'maman – quite frankly, the kind of life she lived, it didn't make a lot of difference if a visitor arrived at nine rather than eleven. So he got there a bit after nine.'

'That must have been just after she'd called me.'

'Perhaps. Anyhow, he found her in her bedroom, and she told him he'd have to wait, she couldn't talk then, she had a visitor coming any moment. So he asked her who, and she said it was you. Naturally he got angry. He said he'd forbidden her to see you. And when my father forbids something ...'

'I still don't understand that. The very thought of her lending us that picture seemed to make him apoplectic. Did you know he tried to pretend she didn't really own it?'

Manu waved his hands in front of his face, as if to block out this fresh example of his father's paranoia. 'One thing at a time. So they began to argue, and then the doorbell rang, and of course grand'maman wanted to go and answer it. But my father forbade her, he said she wasn't moving from the room. He locked the door and wouldn't give her the key, and she got angrier and angrier, and then, this is what he told me, after a bit she refused to talk to him any more, said he made her ill, and she was going to lie down. So then he unlocked the door and was going to leave – it was obvious they weren't going to have a sensible discussion that day, and he took it for granted that by then you'd have given up. But when he looked out of the window he saw your car was still parked there, and there wasn't anyone in it. Obviously you were still around somewhere. And of course he knew grand'maman never bothered to lock the front door. So he thought he'd better check. And there you were, in the study, looking guilty. So he saw you off the premises, then went back to check on grand'maman, but she was still lying down, and she wouldn't talk to him. And he had to get on to his appointment. So he left her to it, left her to sulk were the words he used. He locked the place up to make sure no intruders would get in. And then of course it turned out she'd died. All because of you . . .'

It made sense. The autopsy had told the truth. He hadn't actually killed her – not in the sense of laying hands on her. When she said he'd made her ill, he'd assumed she was talking metaphorically: *You make me ill.* But in fact she really was ill. She was old and frail and he'd made her so angry and frightened that she had a heart attack. He'd scared her to death. And he knew all right, he knew. I'd seen him. But he told himself what he told himself, and let himself off the hook. It was the start of an election campaign, life was a string of urgent engagements – that was why he'd had to change his plans in the first place. It wasn't the moment to quibble about details.

And when I'd gone? What happened – or didn't happen – then?

I said, 'Yes, the front door was locked when I went back. The whole place was shut. I thought he must have taken her off with him.'

'Managed like a true politician,' Manu pronounced. 'Guilty as hell, but technically in the clear. To our future President.' He lifted his glass.

I said, half-jokingly, 'Let's hope he doesn't make a habit of it,' and thought again of Delphine.

'But that's the trouble,' Manu said. 'He does.'

I stared at him.

'My uncle Antoine,' he said.

'But I thought he committed suicide.'

'Maybe ... People don't just commit suicide like that. Why would he do it? He had a good life. Everything was going fine.' He picked up his glass again, but it was empty. 'Another?'

'Just a small one.' I noticed his hand was shaking. 'We should really get something to eat ... Are you saying that had something to do with your father?'

He shrugged unhappily. 'I don't know. What I do know is that Antoine was as horrified as me when it became clear he might really become President. We were in the apartment, watching television, when he announced it. I feel this is something I owe the French people blah blah. Antoine said, He can't, and I said, Oh yes he can, you just watch. So Antoine said, No, I'm going to stop it. I asked him how, but he wouldn't tell me. He just said he could. He said, This is something I owe the French people, and we laughed. But then, a few days later, when it came up again, he looked very serious and shook his head and wouldn't discuss it. All he'd say was, I can't bear to talk about it, your father is a very wicked man. And two weeks after that he was dead.'

'And you thought it was to do with the picture. Isn't that

240

why you gave me your grandmother's address? You'd promised your uncle you wouldn't, but you felt that let you off the promise.'

Manu sighed. 'The thing is, I heard them arguing about it. Antoine and my father. It was some family do, a wedding, those were the only times we all met. Antoine mentioned the Caravaggio, there was obviously something he wanted to do, and my father was shouting at him. Whatever it was he wasn't having it. He was really angry. Have you taken leave of your senses, don't you understand what that would mean, telling him it wasn't his to do what he liked with, it belonged to the whole family, on and on. But I can't bear that kind of thing, so I went off and left them to it.'

'When was that?'

'It must have been when my cousin Jeanne got married. Sometime in May.'

'This year?'

He nodded. 'Why, what difference does that make?'

I was thinking. May. That figured. TM had given me the go-ahead in March. I'd been in touch with the Louvre and the Getty, and they'd both said yes. Subject to conditions, obviously, but in principle, yes. And then, at the beginning of June, the Louvre's permission was withdrawn. Just like that, no reason given. Of course Antoine Rigaut must have suspected I'd be round, trying to persuade him to think again. And it was not impossible I'd find my way to Manu. So he'd exacted his promise.

Yet in April he'd been all for it. That phrase in his letter about having some suggestions to offer – it must mean he'd intended to send me to St Front. So what could have happened between April and June to change his mind?

What would you do, if you were Rigaut and a letter like mine arrived, requesting the loan of a picture for an exhibition? It's obvious: unless it was very familiar, you'd take a look at it.

I was willing to bet that it was a while since Rigaut had spent any time in front of the Louvre St Cecilia. Caravaggio

241

wasn't one of his main interests. True, he'd grown up with another version of that very picture, but that didn't mean he was particularly fond of it.

So perhaps this was the first time he'd looked at it hard. He would quickly have seen that it wasn't actually very good, and being human, would surely have felt rather pleased that the family version was better. But once he'd got interested he probably wouldn't have left it there. Could that really be a Caravaggio? All artists have their off-days, but ... He'd have had some tests and X-rays done, and he'd have done some reading round. The Louvre must have had a copy of the Surrealist pamphlet – Rigaut probably had one himself, perhaps more than one. After all, it had been put together by his uncle and his father. And looking at it again, perhaps more attentively than before, he'd have noticed the flower detail, and realized that the pictures had been exchanged, and that the substitution must have happened when the Louvre picture was 'borrowed'.

If that was true – if the picture hadn't been borrowed but stolen, and an inferior picture, the one bought by his grandfather, substituted for it – his position was potentially rather awkward. However, before making any move, he'd have wanted to be absolutely sure of his facts. The obvious thing would be to do what I'd done, and check in old books to see if there was any record of the picture between its acquisition and the theft. The Louvre library would probably have the book I'd found – I could ask Marie-France, or check in the catalogue. If he'd seen that, the last vestige of doubt would have been removed. There was the picture he'd grown up with at La Jaubertie, and there was the caption – *Caravaggio, St Cecilia and the Angel, The Louvre, Paris*.

In such a situation, what would any conscientious curator do? All the ones I knew would have given the same answer. He would want to exchange the pictures back again. A member of his family had committed a crime, and he was in a position to set it right. No scandal, no lawsuits, no unpleasantness – just a quiet switch. Or perhaps not so quiet. It was just the kind of story to draw in the customers: new light on a famous Surrealist exploit.

But Jean-Jacques wouldn't want that. He was planning to run for President – to run as an independent, if necessary – and where was the money coming from to finance his campaign? He wasn't a rich man, and he led an expensive life. When you move among the wealthy and powerful, you need to keep up appearances. If other wives dress at the couturiers', so must yours; you must be seen in the right places, live in style, entertain as you are entertained. No mere salary, however relatively generous, would be enough – let alone to support the expenses of an independent election campaign. And there, hanging on the wall of La Jaubertie, was the answer. What did a Caravaggio fetch these days? Five million? Ten? Twenty? Enough, in any case, to set him up nicely, even after the roof had been mended, even if the proceeds had to be shared with his brother.

Had Antoine shown him the pamphlet? Probably – that was the proof of what Robert de Beaupré had really done. If he really had proposed switching the pictures back, how appalled Jean-Jacques must have been! And even if he could be dissuaded, the exhibition I proposed would put everything together, side by side, including the pamphlet. *A particularly interesting small show*, my letter had said – and so it was, more interesting than I'd ever imagined. Thousands of people would see it all laid out there, the whole story before their very eyes. Anyone might draw the obvious conclusion. It was virtually certain someone would.

So the show must be stopped. And that wouldn't be hard. No hint of the Jaubertie picture, no loan from the Louvre – *et voilà*: no show. He'd leant on Antoine, and the family had been warned: if I came sniffing round, they were to keep quiet. No hints, no interviews. Nothing.

And then Antoine died, and Manu declared open season on his father.

'How exactly did Antoine die?'

'Shot himself. The gun was found by the body. There was no note. Some homosexual scandal. That was the story,' he added contemptuously.

'Is that so unlikely?' I thought of Charlie Rey, who had the apartment key, and Manu's own assumption that his father had suspected him of being Antoine's boyfriend.

'I suppose what I mean is that these days it's hardly a matter of life and death. But scandal seemed the only reason he'd do something like that, what else was there? Not money, certainly not paternity ... And there was no sign of violence, no sign of an intruder.'

'So how can you say your father did it?'

'Like my grandmother. You don't have to actually commit the crime.'

It made sense. Keeping his hands clean had to be better in every way – less unpleasant, easier to live with. And safer. Get rid of Juliette: that would get him the money. Get rid of Antoine: he wouldn't have to share it. And there'd be no danger of embarrassing revelations.

But why should Antoine oblige?

'Did your father have some hold on Antoine? Any way he could say, If you do this I'll make sure they know that?'

'That's what I've been asking myself. There was some old scandal they were both involved in ...'

'To do with pictures from Russia?'

He nodded. 'I remember years ago some book came out and everyone was very nervous. But it all blew over and nothing happened.'

According to Tim Salisbury-Newall, Jean-Jacques had been far more involved with that than Antoine. But perhaps Antoine had dipped in deeper than his virtuous public pronouncements let on. Jean-Jacques might have had proof to that effect – a letter, a tape – he wasn't a man to let that kind of evidence slip through his fingers. He'd have kept it and, where necessary, used it. Maybe the brothers had played a game of mutual blackmail – threat and counter-threat: if Antoine put a spoke in Jean-Jacques' political wheel and destroyed his presidential prospects, Jean-Jacques would take his revenge and get Antoine ejected from his job.

'How important was the Louvre job to your uncle?'

'Everything. It's the top job in that field. There were hints he might quite soon be nominated for the Académie Française.'

Betray everything he believed in, or lose it all. Faced with a choice like that, suicide might easily seem the logical way out.

'What's going to happen to the picture? Is your father going to sell it?' In my mind I was already running through the possible buyers for such a thing and wondering how amenable they might be to an approach. We wouldn't get it, that was for sure – it would fetch about five times our annual purchasing budget. Possibly more.

Manu burst out laughing. 'You're not going to believe this. It's the only really good thing to have come out of the whole ghastly business. My grandmother left it to the Louvre!'

21

Proof: London, October

By the time Manu and I stopped talking, I'd long missed the last train. I spent a sleepless night on one of his several sofas and crept out of the apartment before he got up. At 7 a.m. the building was silent. But the concierge was visible, a thin, overalled woman in her late fifties, putting out the rubbish bags. As I'd hoped. We exchanged Bonjours, and I asked her to keep a bit of an eye on Manu. 'If he doesn't appear for a couple of days, perhaps you could find some excuse to go up and check he's all right?'

She agreed she would, and added, 'Very like his papa, isn't he?'

'Does he come here? The Minister?'

'No, no, but you see him on the television. As far as I know he's only been here the once. Not long before his brother died. Monsieur Antoine. What a nice man. Tragedy, really.'

'You mean the Minister was here before his brother was found?'

She looked at me uncomprehendingly. For her, of course, Antoine's death and the finding of the body were one and the same event. 'Two days before, yes. I'd never seen him but I recognized him from the television. He was just leaving. He was in such a hurry I don't think he even noticed me, but you'd know him anywhere, wouldn't you?'

'Did you tell anyone about this?'

'No, why would I?'

Why, indeed.

Remembering Delphine, I took particular care crossing the road. But no one seemed anxious to run me down, and soon I was in the metro headed for the Gare du Nord. As the Eurostar swayed northwards, I thought about the concierge's revelation. However superficial, there must surely have been some sort of inquiry into Antoine Rigaut's death? If someone is found dead of gunshot wounds, then the police are brought in. And in that case, surely they'd ask the concierge about who'd come and gone at the relevant time?

Not if the verdict was suicide. Why would they?

So leave it alone, said a voice inside my head – David's voice, I recognized it at once, ballasted with the successful lawyer's weary, unshockable calm. Learn a lesson, why don't you? So Jean-Jacques Rigaut seems always to be on the spot when a close relative dies. Fine. What's that to you? You weren't there, you aren't a member of the family, you aren't even French, so he won't be your President. You're English, and your job is to curate pictures. You've just discovered something rather significant in the curating line. And now that the Louvre owns both the pictures, why shouldn't they lend them?

'Charles? It's Reggie Lee.'

'I thought we'd had this conversation. I can't help you.'

'Ah, but things have changed. D'you know what I've just heard? Madame Rigaut left her picture to the Louvre.'

'So I understand.'

'Well, then, there's no more problem, is there? You own them both, you can lend them both. Monsieur Rigaut hasn't got anything to do with it any more.'

'I'm sorry, Reggie,' he said flatly. 'The answer's still no. Don't ask why. You'll just have to accept it. It was bad luck, the wrong moment, these things happen. That's the way it is, and too bad.' And he rang off.

The wrong moment? Still? For what? For Charlie's career, was what it came down to. Even now it was more

247

than that career was worth to reverse the decision without checking back. I wasn't unsympathetic. The prospect of asking Rigaut to change his mind on this particular topic at this particular moment would have daunted a better man than Charles Rey. In his place I'd probably have done the same.

Unlike Charlie, Joe sounded gratifyingly pleased to hear my voice. 'Recovered from your little misadventure?'

For a moment I couldn't remember which misadventure he was referring to. 'I've got my passport back, if that's what you mean. Look, I'm on to something rather interesting. D'you want to meet up?'

'You're still pursuing this Caravaggio stuff?'

'It's connected.'

'How about the Rigaut story?'

'It's connected with that, too.'

Joe said he'd buy me lunch and I could tell him all about it. I explained that I'd been away from the office a lot recently – a long lunch at this juncture might not be tactful.

'So make it dinner. Eight? I'll see you at Sapori's,' he said.

Sapori's, an echoing ex-warehouse in Drury Lane that combines considerable discomfort with the best casalinga cooking in London, had been one of our favourite haunts in the dear dead days. It isn't exactly the venue for romance, but if you want a private conversation it's got a lot going for it – there's so much noise that you can hardly hear what the person opposite is saying, let alone anyone at the next table.

Joe was there when I arrived, making inroads into a bottle of Montepulciano and dipping raw vegetables into a little dish of olive oil, which he was spreading liberally over the table. It was odd, seeing him and knowing he was waiting for me. I'd run across him once or twice since we'd split up – at a couple of parties, across the room in a pub – and each time my stomach had done a sort of somersault. Now, however, it stayed put. Olivier's doing? Or perhaps its previous antics had been the result of unpreparedness.

Joe waved, wiped his fingers, stood up and kissed me formally on both cheeks, mwa mwa. He'd put on a bit of weight, though not enough to make him discard the ancient brown corduroy suit I'd tried so often to chuck out. I sniffed its well-remembered bouquet with a mixture of annoyance and nostalgia.

'Well,' he said. 'Exciting life you're leading these days.'

'Much too exciting,' I agreed. 'If I fall asleep don't take it personally.'

'You won't,' he assured me. 'Not in these chairs.'

He poured me a glass of wine and we considered the menu. As usual, I chose the seafood spaghetti. 'Nice to see some things don't change,' Joe said. He ordered the same thing himself and asked for a half-bottle of white Orvieto to go with it. When the stuff about twenty-one units of alcohol a week being the healthy maximum first came out, and we tried comparing it with his normal intake, we just laughed. Hollowly, and slightly tipsily. 'OK,' he said. 'Shoot. Tell me all.'

So I did.

By the time I finished, our table was littered with dead bottles, most of the other customers had left, and I felt so tired that I had no idea whether or not I'd spent the entire evening talking gibberish.

Joe signalled for the bill. 'I don't know if I've got the detail right,' he said, 'but if half of this is true that's your man's career up the spout.'

'Not so's you'd notice. That's the terrifying thing.'

He sat with his elbows on the table tapping his teeth with a teaspoon, a signal that he was deep in thought. 'There must have been an inquiry into Antoine's death. An old lady of eighty-eight's one thing, but he was a public figure.'

'That's what I thought.'

'Thing is, how do we get hold of it?'

'No idea.' Now that I'd stopped talking I was fading fast.

'Poor old Reg, you don't look as though you've got much idea about anything just now. Let's get you home.'

Drury Lane is undoubtedly one of the nastiest streets in London, but fortunately it's always full of taxis that will take you somewhere nicer. When we got to my house Joe didn't suggest coming in, but kissed me chastely and said, as I'd hoped he might, 'Why don't you leave it with me and I'll look into a few details?' Then he rolled away into the city, a happy journalist in pursuit of a hot new story, while I fell into my bed and a dreamless sleep.

For the next week I got on with my work and tried to put Caravaggio, the Rigaut family, and everything associated with them, out of my mind. Then Joe phoned, and all that good work was instantly undone.

'OK,' he said. 'Things may be moving.'

'Things?'

'I've been beavering on your behalf,' he said. 'To prove your gratitude you can make me dinner this time. What sort of wine shall I bring?'

It seemed we were back on terms, though exactly which had yet to be negotiated. I wasn't sure that any of them included the assumption that I was automatically available just because he happened to have a spare evening. 'How do you know I'm free for dinner?'

'Aren't you?'

I sighed. 'As it happens I am.'

'Fine, then I'll bring a St Emilion.'

He arrived just after nine, with the wine in one hand and a rather unattractive bunch of flowers in the other – those spray chrysanthemums in dreary white and pink that look half-dead before they've begun. I have rules about things like that. There are the fruit salad rules – no oranges, no apples or pears, and absolutely, under any circumstances, no bananas – and the bunch of flowers rules, in which pink spray chrysanths figure in the banana position. Still, the wine looked excellent.

He put his burdens down and looked around, checking to see what had changed since he lived here. Then, for the first time in over a year, we kissed. Properly.

I'd dreamed of this moment, its absence had for months

reduced me to despair. And now my wish had been granted – but as in all the fairy stories, there was a catch. The kiss was too late: delightful and familiar, but not, as once, liquidizing. *Amour*, perhaps irrevocably, seemed to have transmuted to *amitié amoureuse*. I wondered if Joe felt it, too. Perhaps that was what he'd been waiting for before making contact again.

We let each other go; he looked at me quizzically, but didn't say anything. Instead he made for the drawer where the corkscrew lived (that at least was still the same) and opened the wine. 'What are we eating?'

'Lamb chops.' In the supermarket on the way back from the tube blankness had struck, and lamb chops were the result. I knew he'd be disappointed. A lamb chop is – well, a lamb chop. Eat one, you've eaten them all. But just for the moment, culinary imagination was beyond me.

'Anything else? It's a really good wine, this.'

'Potatoes.'

He sighed. 'OK, are you going to ask me what I've found out?'

'What have you found out?' I wished I didn't feel so tired.

'Well, I got in touch with my friend Pascal. I can't remember if you met him? Does the kind of thing I do, for *Le Monde*. Anyhow, he knows people who know the examining magistrate – he was at the Ecole Nationale d'Administration, and bingo, that's it, even though he cut loose and became a journo. The top of that pyramid's ridiculously small, if you make it that far the whole of French politics just seems like an old boys' reunion.'

'Nice for some. And?'

By now Joe had poured himself a glass of wine and settled into what had once been his usual armchair. He pulled a notebook out of his briefcase. 'Hang on a mo . . . Yeah. The inquiry into your boy's death.'

'Antoine Rigaut.'

'That's the one. Apparently it was squashed. Orders from on high. The examining magistrate somehow

251

gathered that if he was too persistent it wouldn't do his career a bit of good. So he brought in a verdict of suicide and everyone was happy.'

I chopped some mint and mashed it with lemon juice into a lump of butter. I always enjoy economy, whether of thought or action, and mint butter served two purposes: it raised the gastronomic stakes, and making it was conducive to contemplation – rhythmic, without urgency. I thought of Charlie Rey, how he wouldn't lend the picture, and wouldn't say why – how he hated talking about it. He, too, had his career to consider. I wondered what he'd found, that day in Antoine Rigaut's apartment. There must have been something, or Jean-Jacques would have left the examining magistrate alone. When, as with his mother, there'd been nothing to find, he'd been only too delighted for the law to take its course. Tampering is a risk even for the powerful – they have so much more to lose if it comes out.

'How well does your friend Pascal know whoever told him this?'

'No idea. Why?'

'I just wondered if there might have been some photos. There must have been, mustn't there? When the police first got there they must have taken some. They ought to be in the file. If the file still exists.'

'You're asking him to ask his mate to steal the *file*?'

'Not the file. Just a photo . . . He needn't even steal it. He could just copy it. Then we might be getting somewhere. Why don't you see if he can work something out? Tell him there might be a big story in there. Come on, dinner's ready.'

The photo arrived five days later. It was in a manila envelope with an English stamp and a central London postmark, the address computer-printed, no sender's identification. There was no covering note, just the picture. The subject was viewed from above, the body of a man slumped forward over a desk. The right-hand half of his

252

head was covered with blood, as was the desk. Near his right hand, on the desk, lay a pistol.

That evening I rang Manu. I didn't bother with niceties but dived straight into the meat of it. 'Manu, it's Reggie. Do you have a computer?'

'Yes,' he said, sounding puzzled.

'OK, I'm going to email you a picture, and I want you to tell me what you think.'

I sent it off, and when, half an hour later, no answering email had appeared, rang him again. He sounded tetchy. 'Yes?'

'Did you get it?'

'Yes.'

'It's your uncle, isn't it?'

'Yeah, it's him. I was going to get back to you but it kind of got to me.'

'Sorry. Yes, of course.'

'Also there's something wrong, and I've been trying to work out what it is.'

'And?'

'At first I thought the print might be the wrong way round, but then I went into the room and it isn't, the window and everything's in the right place.'

'Yes.'

'The thing is, the pistol's by his right hand. And my uncle Antoine was left-handed.'

22

Jean-Jacques: Paris, October

'You realize what that means,' Manu said.

'Of course.'

I'd been thinking about it ever since I first saw the photo. The sight of the gun had brought to mind that other gun, the one Manu had tried to pull – with his left hand; hadn't he told me left-handedness ran in his family? There were doubtless other forensic matters – the angle of the shot, whether it could have been self-inflicted – that only an expert could identify. But no one could argue with this. When you pick up a gun to kill yourself, the hand you use, unless it's been cut off or otherwise disabled, is the one that comes naturally.

Of course this didn't prove who had done the deed – only that it hadn't been the dead man. If anything, the photo argued against rather than for Jean-Jacques' guilt – he and Antoine had grown up together, he surely could not have forgotten such an obvious detail? But he wasn't, at least to my knowledge, accustomed to actual face-to-face murder. Perhaps it had been messier than he'd bargained for, and he'd had to make the best of a bad job. And in the end it wasn't so risky. You'd have to know a person very well to register that particular anomaly – it certainly wasn't the kind of thing to strike an examining magistrate. I wondered if he knew the concierge had seen him, and hoped, for her sake, that she was right and he didn't. Better not mention that conversation even to Manu.

'What are you going to do?' he said. 'Tell the police?'

'I don't think so. They weren't much use last time, were they? Listen, I want to ask a favour.'

'What?' He sounded suspicious.

'I'd like to get in touch with your father, but it won't be easy – he'll have walls of guards fending people off. So I need the number of his private line. He must have one.'

'Régine, we've been through this. What's done's done. Just keep away from my father. Let it go. He's a dangerous man.'

'And I'm a grown-up woman. I can look after myself. Why don't you just give me the number.'

After a little bullying he gave it to me, as I'd known he would. He was weak, poor Manu. Flattened.

It sat on the table in front of me now, daring me to dial it. Every sane instinct advised against. What I had in mind wasn't just scary, it was wrong. Mad, dangerous, immoral, on every count a no-no. So why was I doing it? Perhaps wickedness is like death – contagious. You want to keep away from it for fear of infection. Unfortunately it had come to find me. Though there as in all other respects, I wasn't in Jean-Jacques' league. Ambition, ruthlessness, greed – you name it, he had me outclassed. Disreputable, that was the word for what I proposed. That was more my level.

I knew what I *ought* to do. Failing the police – and that the police would fail I had little doubt – I *ought* to tell Joe what I'd found and leave the rest to him. What could be more important than to bring a criminal to justice?

Nothing. And I would. Oh, yes. I owed Juliette and Delphine nothing less, not to speak of the ones I'd never met – Antoine Rigaut, and who knew how many others? But in St Augustine's immortal words, not yet. Between Jean-Jacques and me, things had got too personal. I needed to finish them off in my own way and my own time.

The number began with 06 – a cellphone. I wondered whether it would work. He probably had it arranged so that different ringtones indicated different callers. In which case I'd never get through directly.

I dialled; the phone rang – and switched to voicemail. I said, 'Monsieur Rigaut, this is Régine Lee. I'm in possession of some interesting facts regarding the provenance of your Caravaggio, and various events surrounding it, and also some information regarding your brother's death. I'm thinking of publishing it. If you're happy with that, fine. If not, we can discuss it.' I left my own number, and rang off.

The call came a couple of hours later, while I was watching the television news. Naturally it wasn't the great man himself. The speaker was a young man, some secretary or gofer. 'Madame Lee?'

'Yes, who's this?'

'I'm speaking on behalf of Monsieur Jean-Jacques Rigaut. I believe you phoned him.'

'Yes, I did.'

'Perhaps you would like to tell me what this is about.'

'I told you. Or rather, him. I don't have any more to say than that. Except to him, that is. If he wants to arrange a meeting, I'm happy to fit in with his timetable.'

'Madame, you perhaps don't understand how busy he is . . . the elections coming up . . . I'm sure this can be settled over the phone.'

'Unfortunately not,' I assured him crisply. 'It's up to him. If he doesn't have time to meet, then please assure him I shall publish, if not this week then early next.'

'I'll get back to you,' said the voice and rang off.

Half an hour later he rang again. 'Tomorrow ten o'clock. He can give you half an hour.'

'Where would this be?'

'Paris. His office at the ministry.'

Not allowing myself even to think about the monstrous fares bill I was racking up, I said, 'I'll be there.'

Ten o'clock! Well, I was lucky he hadn't said nine. Or even earlier . . . Whatever, I'd have had to go along with it. I checked the Eurostar timetable. There was a five twenty-four that got me in just after nine. Or I could fly – any number of flights left later and arrived earlier. But there'd be all the bother of getting out to the airport, and then back in to Paris during the rush hour, to say nothing of possible delays. Better to take the train, however uninviting. I booked a taxi for four fifteen.

Given that I was going to get up in the middle of the night I ought to go to bed at once. Before that, however, there were still a few things to do. I wrote a précis of what I now knew regarding the two French St Cecilias, together with instructions as to the whereabouts of the file that contained all the backing paperwork – the pamphlet, Lindsay Hillier's reports, the xerox of the photo in the 1928 Caravaggio book – and emailed one copy to David at his office, one to Tony Malahide, and one to Joe. After that, I wrote an account of my suspicions regarding Antoine Rigaut's death, printed off two copies, left one with a copy of the photograph in an envelope on my desk addressed to Joe, and slid a similar envelope, addressed to myself at the office, into the postbox on the corner. Finally, when everything was in order, I rang Joe.

'Reggie, hi, I've been meaning to call you. Any movement on the story?'

'Quite a bit, actually. I think we may have what we're after. Look, I'm going to see Rigaut tomorrow morning, in Paris. At his office in the Ministry of the Interior. I've sent you an email with all the art stuff and left you a note with everything else on my desk at home – Mrs Walton next door's still got the key. If you can't get in I sent a copy of it to myself at the office. If I don't get in touch by six tomorrow evening it's all yours. OK?'

'Are you crazy? This is serious, Reg. Not the moment to piss about with melodramatics.'

'I'm not pissing about. We have different priorities, that's all.'

'Different priorities? What are you talking about?' After a moment he said disbelievingly, 'You can't still mean that bloody exhibition of yours?'

'It's very important to me,' I said primly. 'It's going to be the making of my career.'

'If you're not careful it'll be the unmaking of your *life*. Fat lot of use your career'll be then.'

'Listen,' I said. 'This is my story. Eventually you'll have it. I promise. But in my time, OK? If the worst comes to the worst, tomorrow evening. Otherwise, later. It's no use going on about it.'

I was so keyed up that sleep was a long time coming, and the consciousness of an early start meant that I woke long before I had to and spent the next hour and a half consulting my watch at five-minute intervals. By the time the train reached Paris I felt flattened, and doubtless looked it, too.

The Ministry of the Interior occupies the Hotel Beauvau, in the Faubourg St Honoré. During World War II it was the headquarters of the Gestapo; the unfortunates who were summoned there then – among them, doubtless, many associates of the current Minister's father – must have felt much as I did now. I gave the address to the taxi driver, and sat back exhausted while he negotiated the traffic-choked streets. The slower the better: as far as I was concerned, the ride could happily have gone on for ever. Only too soon, however, I found myself standing outside the Ministry. This was Rigaut's home ground – no shabby provincial château, but a grand seventeenth-century palace, its pillared façades surrounding three sides of a huge *cour d'honneur* designed to contain the horse-drawn carriages of the rich and powerful, several abreast. All around busy *fonctionnaires* came and went, in animated conversation with their cellphones.

Silently repeating my mantra – *knowledge is power, knowledge is power* – I penetrated the wrought-iron gates and approached the vast reception desk.

'To see Monsieur *Rigaut*, did you say?' The receptionist sounded distinctly unconvinced – disbelieving, even. It struck me that, having got me here at such effort and expense, my quarry was about to fob me off with some underling. I was instantly filled with invigorating fury. Fine, I thought – just let him try. He'd soon see what happened.

Almost to my regret, these fantasies were interrupted by the receptionist's fluting 'Yes, that's correct, to see Monsieur le Ministre.' She summoned an official to take me through the usual procedure of badges and searches, and at ten precisely we stood outside a pair of imposing double doors, almost three metres high and elaborately gilded. The official knocked, then opened one wing of the doors. And I stepped inside.

The Minister's office had once been the grand salon. Mirrors set in gilded panelling reflected an elaborate Louis XVI escritoire, and many side-tables, armchairs and silk-upholstered sofas in the same style. A matching arrangement of white and gold lilies perfumed the air with a faint scent of corpses. Four immense windows, of the same proportions as the door, looked out on to the *cour d'honneur*. My man was seated at the escritoire, looking over some papers. When I came in he glanced briefly up, said, '*Bonjour*,' and went on with his paperwork.

I said, '*Bonjour*,' and went to wait by the left-hand window.

'*Asseyez-vous*,' he said, not looking up, and I took my place on a sofa, which was quite as uncomfortable as it looked.

'Well,' he said after we'd been sitting like this for a while, 'I understood you had something to say to me.'

'Absolutely,' I agreed.

'Then please say it.' He looked at his watch.

I started out on my recital. The two pictures, the slight differences between them, how I'd realized what must have happened, and so on.

'Most interesting, I'm sure,' he remarked. He still hadn't looked at me – was still shuffling through those papers. '*Et alors?*'

'*Et alors*, Monsieur le Ministre, suddenly a lot of things fell into place.'

'Very possibly, but art history, however fascinating, isn't exactly at the top of my agenda just at present.' He looked me levelly in the eye, his confidence so absolute that it felt almost physical, a barrier to be scaled.

'Then let's move on to something else,' I offered. 'Your brother's death.'

'Ah, yes. My brother . . . Madame, excuse me for asking, but what can the circumstances of my brother's death possibly have to do with you?'

'*Eh bien*, monsieur, it's the same old story. The picture. And then one thing led to another.'

We sat staring at each other, holding each other's gaze as lovers do. What lay between us, I shiveringly understood, was not so very different from what had bound me, briefly, to Olivier.

'*Et alors?*' he said again.

In reply I pulled the photograph from my bag and put it on the desk, on top of his pile of papers. He studied it, still expressionless.

'May I ask where you got this?'

'It came in the post. I've no idea who sent it.'

'Really?' he said coldly.

'Really.'

He looked at the photo again. 'My poor brother. It's a mystery why he did it, who knows what goes on in a person's head? But since you didn't know him – I believe that's so? – I don't imagine you can cast any light on that.'

'Forgive me, but why he did it isn't really the question,' I said. 'It's whether he did it at all.'

'Please don't speak in riddles.' He was frowning now, his impassivity ever so slightly ruffled. Everything had been so securely tied up – what could possibly have gone wrong?

'I believe the magistrate found that he committed suicide. But there's a problem. If you look, the photo shows the gun by his right hand. And he was left-handed.'

Did he flinch? If so it was the merest flicker. Nor did he argue. What would have been the point? Instead, like the seasoned campaigner he was, he moved on to the attack. 'Really? If that's all you have to say, madame, I'm afraid I shall have to terminate this interview.' He looked at his watch. 'I can give you just two minutes more.'

'Fine. I'll get to the point. I have several copies of this photo, Monsieur Rigaut, and a number of my friends know I'm here today with you. I haven't told them why – or only the art history. But if anything happens to me, I've made sure they will find out.'

'How very melodramatic,' he said, echoing Joe. 'And why should anything happen to you?'

'I've noticed that things do tend to happen to people who get in your way. Your brother. Your mother. Olivier Peytoureau.'

'Ah, your little boyfriend. Did something happen to him? How unfortunate. I wasn't aware . . .'

'His wife died in a car crash. Forced off the road. The other car was never found. All we know is, it was red.' *Just like yours.*

'Indeed. I still don't understand what all this is about.' He removed the photo from his papers and began to go through the next one on the pile.

'I'm quite sure you do,' I said. 'I'm here to strike a bargain. If you don't give me what I want, I'll publish what I know. Think about it, Monsieur le Ministre.'

He studied me for a while. Unlike Manu his lips were thin and firm: when as now he pressed them together, they almost vanished. 'Ah, now I understand. This is a blackmailing exercise.'

'You could look at it like that,' I agreed. 'But then, you should know.'

His head jerked up. '*Moi?*'

'You said a minute ago that no one can know what's going on inside another person's head. Well, I think you knew pretty well what was going on in your brother Antoine's head the day he died.'

He didn't reply at once, but got up and, profiled in the many mirrors, turned to look out of the window. Then he turned slightly, and in those same mirrors our eyes met. After a minute he said coldly, 'So what exactly do you want from me, madame?'

'That's easy. What I've wanted all along. I want the pictures for my exhibition. All you need do is give the Louvre the green light.'

That surprised him. He'd been expecting – what? Political lectures, demands that he drop out of the presidential race? At the very least, the promise of his brother's old job at the Louvre. A surprise appointment . . . And now – this puny little request. Art history. What sort of person was this, who would go to such lengths and then so signally fail to take advantage of the opportunity when it arose? Our eyes met again. 'You did all this just for *that*?' he said softly.

'That's my job,' I said. 'I do pictures, not politics. It isn't as though I'm being asked to vote for you. I noticed that that little riot you started did wonders for your poll figures, by the way.'

He turned and approached the sofa where I was sitting, his hands clasped in front of him, visibly restraining himself from – what? Hitting me, strangling me? I wondered what it would feel like, and what would happen then. Suddenly, disconcertingly, I felt that familiar, insistent tingle between my legs. What would happen if I took those hands and directed them to the spot? I thought of that President of the Republic who died *in medias res* with the mistress of the moment . . . Rigaut was behind me now, so close that I could feel the warmth of his body. If I looked up our eyes would meet –

With an effort I pulled myself back from these fantasies. For all I knew he had the place covered by hidden cameras: tit for tat, and *au revoir, madame*. If you show mine, I'll show yours. Sitting up very straight I said, 'In any case, there's no reason not to lend them now. They both belong to the Louvre, there's no money in it for you any more.'

He moved away. 'True enough, unfortunately. So why not just say so to begin with?'

'Sheer pleasure,' I said. 'I wanted to enjoy a little power, for once. You of all people should understand that.'

He raised his hands in dismissal, or agreement.

I rose to take my leave. 'So no more obstacles to those loans. *Entendu?* And no black marks hanging over any-one's career.'

He nodded. 'Not that that kind of thing is anything to do with me.'

'Of course not. But even so ... And don't forget what will happen otherwise.' Now we'd got so lovey-dovey, it seemed a good idea to reinsert a little chill. I held out a hand. '*Au revoir*, Monsieur le Ministre.'

He ignored it, turned on his heel, returned to his desk and reapplied himself to his papers. He must have had some sort of bell-push there, for a second later the door opened to reveal the official who had guided me here. 'Please take Madame to reception,' Rigaut said, not look-ing up. '*Au revoir, madame.* Good luck with your show.'

Back in London, I notified Joe of my continued existence. And then I put in a call to Charlie Rey at the Louvre. The redoubtable Madame Desvergnes tried to deflect me, but I told her it was essential to Charlie's career that I speak to him and, on the off-chance I might be telling the truth, she put me through.

Charlie sounded furious. Doubtless he'd hoped never to think about the St Cecilia or hear my voice again.

'Correct me if I'm wrong,' I said, 'but I believe I'm right in thinking a certain obstacle has just been removed? Do tell me if it hasn't, and I'll get through to the person in question and let him know you didn't get the message.'

That did it. As in a dream, I heard him admit that yes, something of the sort had indeed happened.

'So we can go ahead after all?'

'I suppose so. Please deal with it through my assistant. You'll excuse me, I've got a lot on my plate just now.'

23

Exhibits: London, June

The Director laid out the various items I'd brought and studied them intently. 'Extraordinary,' he said, more than once, as I told him my story – the pamphlet, the switched pictures, Lindsay's reports and the one from the Louvre, the xerox of the 1928 photograph. I explained that at one time there had been a little difficulty regarding the loans: Antoine Rigaut's unfortunate death had held things up at the Louvre while the 'owner' of the real Caravaggio had been afraid that if the story came out he'd be forced to exchange his excellent picture for the inferior copy. But now, by a happy chance, both belonged to the Louvre, and there were no more problems. Dr Rey, the acting head of pictures, ('Charming fellow!' the Director put in, and I didn't contradict him) – Dr Rey had assured me that all difficulties had been overcome, and that both his St Cecilias were at our disposal whenever we might choose to borrow them.

'Well, what shall we say? How about, I don't know, a year next June? It won't take up very much space, even with all the ancillary stuff – just a room, really, isn't it? That would give you eighteen months, a bit more. We don't want to leave it too long – don't want any of this leaking out before we're ready, do we? And you won't want to wait indefinitely to publish ... Think you can do it?'

As we both knew, an exhibition of this kind, even a

264

small one, takes a good deal of setting up, even after everything's agreed. Insurance and transport must be arranged. A catalogue must be prepared, its essays commissioned, its pictures selected, its printing scheduled. The exhibitions department must select a space and prepare a design. But he was right. Both for the reasons he'd outlined and for others of which he was happily unaware, we didn't want to delay any more than was necessary.

So there I stood, on a warm June evening, dressed in my best and waiting for the first guests to arrive. Behind me and on either side, four St Cecilias gazed up at four Angels, who extended one, three or (in two cases) two fingers in blessing. Of the four, Freddie Angelo's, the *originario*, was the finest, with a quality of detail unmatched in the other three, though the Jaubertie version ran it close. The Getty's picture, the last to be painted by Caravaggio himself, seemed by comparison a little faded, as though by then the artist had been running out of steam. Even the Angel looked slightly tired, while the Saint, poor girl, appeared exhausted. Along the remaining wall the abducted picture conducted its photographic dance across Paris. In a dark booth interested punters could sample the optical effects about which Freddie had written such an informative essay for our catalogue. And in a central glass case lay the pamphlet itself, along with contemporary newspaper cuttings and photographs of the protagonists. Emmanuel Rigaut, at twenty-two, looked unnervingly like the grandson who now bore his name. Robert de Beaupré, fiery dark eyes burning out of the photo, seemed tragically young. Juliette appeared twice, once in her convent girl's uniform, looking anonymous, and again as a full-fledged beauty, in one of the famous photos taken by Rigaut soon after they were married. She looked divinely happy, leaning back on a hillock of sand and laughing in the sunlight – a happiness that would soon be obliterated, and never truly regained.

This was the day of the first opening party, the one for the VIPs, the people who had made the exhibition possible and a few illustrious others, to be followed by dinner. Tomorrow there would be a press show, with information packs prepared by the publicity department, then a couple of Friends' days, and finally the show would open to the public.

Even before the exhibition opened, it seemed clear its effect was going to be all I'd hoped and more. I'd already given a number of interviews – to the Sunday broadsheets, *Vogue*, the *Art Newspaper* – and *Front Row* was booked for opening day. There had been television inquiries from people wanting to do drama-doc reconstructions, and invitations to give keynote papers at two conferences. We were all set for a big hit. Caravaggio's Angel had remembered our long friendship. Just one more detail, and we'd be quits.

The party was due to begin at six thirty, with speeches at seven. Several hours ago it had been six fifteen; now it was six sixteen. 'Relax,' said a voice in my ear.

I jumped several inches off the ground, nearly braining Joe, who had arrived early.

'I am relaxed.'

He took my hand and gave it a squeeze. 'So you are. Can't wait to see our boy.'

'You promised to be discreet, remember.'

'Oh, I will, don't worry.'

We spent a lot of time together these days, at his place or mine. What went on in the intervals? We didn't ask. Here, after all, we still were.

'Looks good,' he said, indicating the exhibits.

'Thanks. My big night.'

The guests were arriving now – the Director of the Getty, who happened to be in London, the Italian cultural attaché, the Director of the Tate, a couple of television pundits, the author of a recent book on Caravaggio, a famous painter, a few of the ultra-rich and ultra-generous. I'd asked Manu, who hadn't replied, and Olivier, who had – very sorry, he couldn't make it, too far (he was working in Bordeaux for a PR company), no time. And very little inclination, I'd have thought. I didn't blame him. I wondered if he'd found a new partner – he hadn't said anything about that – and how the kids were doing. Nothing had ever been found out about Delphine's death: the other driver had vanished (had anyone ever looked for him?) and she'd become another road-accident statistic. My very own. If I hadn't been so clever-clever, dropping my little bombshell in Olivier's ear, she'd still be alive now. If, if. If Olivier hadn't pursued me, or my story, to London. If Jean-Jacques Rigaut hadn't been a psychopath . . . I'd sworn never to forget her. But to my shame, she kept dropping to the back of my mind. From time to time, in a rush of guilt and sorrow, I thought of her, but those moments were already less frequent. Soon, despite my best intentions, she'd recede into a shameful oblivion, interspersed with sporadic moments of painful remembrance.

Here now was Charlie Rey. We exchanged a cool little airkiss before he moved hurriedly on to more congenial company. He was followed by Freddie Angelo, pink cheeks shining, red braces just visible beneath a tremendously chalk-striped jacket. In his wake stepped a grey-suited Japanese, perhaps – why else would he be here? – the mysterious owner of the fourth Caravaggio, though whether the one for whom Freddie had been acting when we met, or a buyer subsequently found, I didn't know and could not, just at that moment, ask.

'Freddie! Lovely to see you!'

'Darling, wouldn't miss this for anything. Isn't it wonderful? Congratulations. Let me introduce Mr Furuichi, Reggie Lee. You should have seen her face when I showed her your picture. I can tell you, she's an absolute *terrier*.' Or was that terror? Mr Furuichi looked bemused. He gave a little bow.

Waiters were circulating with champagne. I took two glasses and handed one to Mr Furuichi. I noticed Freddie's eyes sliding round the room, checking who was here, and felt mine insidiously follow. Charlie Rey was deep in conversation with TM. And there were David and Caroline!

This was a big day out for Caroline, the girls were staying with friends, she'd bought a new dress specially. We waved frantically and I rushed over to them. What do they always say – *Without X and Y the show/book/film could never have happened* . . . But we'd hardly had time to remind each other of the fatal school fair when, inevitably, I was whisked off to meet some financier, a big contributor to emergency appeals who had to be kept sweet and who wanted to know all the detail – what came from where, how I'd found it all. And suddenly, as I was in the midst of giving him the edited story, it was time for the speeches, an opening few words from the Director, followed by the catch of the evening: the French presidential hopeful, Jean-Jacques Rigaut, who was of course (I heard someone whisper to his wife) Emmanuel Rigaut's son. Didn't you know?

When I looked round for him he hadn't seemed to be there, though his office had confirmed that he was coming. They'd been enthusiastic – just the kind of thing to do his image good, remind people of the Surrealist connection, a bit of cultural resonance, always goes down well in France, one of the few countries where intellectuals actually go into politics – Poincaré, Malraux. Wonderful what the right gloss can do for the innately flaky. Not that Monsieur Rigaut could be described as flaky. On the other hand, he was sometimes in danger of appearing rather – well, brutal. But brutes don't open art exhibitions, do they? Firm yet wide-ranging, that was the message. They'd send a photographer.

The Director tinkled his glass, and everyone fell silent. 'My lords, ladies and gentlemen . . .' He gave his usual urbane and polished performance, deftly thanking all concerned, outlining the show's *raison d'être*, and finally introducing – yes, there he was after all, how had I missed him? A head taller than the rest of the crowd, snappily dressed today in a white silk polo-neck under a perfectly cut navy suit, Gallicly elegant. I wondered if he spoke English. It didn't matter – most of this crowd probably understood French.

'Mesdames, messieurs . . .'

In fact, like most French politicians, he spoke English with impressive ease. He made the obligatory remarks about how flattered to be here, then moved on to the pictures – quite a detective story, we should congratulate Dr Lee (here he caught my eye and bowed slightly, while people clapped and I blushed and acknowledged him). And yes, damn it, the rush was still there: in spite of everything, and after all this time, I still fancied him like mad. And could have sworn, as we exchanged complicit smiles across the room, that he fancied me right back. Not that there would be much opportunity to test that out now.

Appropriate, he went on, that both pictures should now be safely at the Louvre, or perhaps safe was not quite the right word (polite laughter). Then he talked about his father – how tickled he'd be to see himself enshrined as Official Art. He did not, I noticed, mention his mother, though she'd originated the joke, if joke was the word, that had, after all these years and so many adventures, landed us all here in this room today. Meanwhile he was delighted to declare the exhibition open – rather, it struck me, as though it was a garden fête.

Soon it would be time for the restaurant party to leave. There'd be thirty-five of us, what with spouses and partners. Rigaut was coming, his office had informed us, though he'd have to leave early. We'd booked tables at the Oxo Tower, where even if you don't like the food or the company you can enjoy the wonderful view. The publicity girl began rounding people up, telling them where to go.

'Will you be coming?' I asked Joe.

'Of course. Why ever not?'

'I thought you had to file –'

'Oh, that!' He laughed. 'I did it before I came. Gave Pascal the nod, too. Though there was a bad moment when I thought our man hadn't made it . . . Not that it'd have mattered, but we'd have had to change things round a bit and it wouldn't have been so poetic. They're really going to town. I got them to do me a mock-up. Want to see?' He scrabbled in his pocket and brought out a folded sheet.

'I can't look at it now!'

'Just the headline.'

I saw a photo of the St Cecilia surmounted by a head-line: *Caravaggio's Killer Picture*. The opening lines read: *The publicity surrounding the new Caravaggio show at the National Gallery has concentrated on a Surrealist jape involving two of the pictures. What has not been told is a far more sinister story* . . . I wondered what Pascal had done. Knowing *Le Monde*, something more restrained and intellectual. And of course more political. It was his country, after all.

'He'll kill me.' The cliché took on a sudden terrifying new life.

'You're the last person he'd kill. Too obvious.'

The publicity girl shepherded us into a fleet of taxis, and ten minutes later we arrived at the restaurant. We'd booked tables out on the terrace, and half London glittered beneath us. For any number of reasons I'd have liked to be seated as far as possible from the star guest, but the publicity girl had insisted. 'It's your show! You put it together. All this stuff about his father – he's sure to want to talk to you about it.'

'No, he won't. It's the last thing he'll want to talk about.'

'Don't be silly, Reggie, of course he will. All right, I'll put you on the opposite side of the table, if that's what you really want.'

'How about Joe?'

'Sorry, he's not a VIP, he'll have to go on one of the other tables.'

There was the usual milling about while people identified their namecards. At the other end of the terrace, a party of cityboys was in full bray. Suddenly I found myself beside Rigaut. He nodded, and we shook hands.

'*Bonsoir, madame*. So, you have your exhibition.' He still had my hand in his, and now gave it an extra little shake.

'I'm most grateful, monsieur.' All I could think of was the contact of our two hands.

'Grateful!' He laughed and finally let me go. 'You should go into politics. A formidable operator. My *chef-de-cabinet*, perhaps!'

People were taking their seats now. The Director came over. 'Let me show you where you're sitting,' he said to Rigaut.

'Ah yes, though I'm afraid I shan't be able to stay long.' He turned to me. 'Madame Lee – aren't you coming?'

'I don't think they've put us together.'

'Ah, non, quel dommage, j'insiste!'

That was a strange evening – one of the strangest I ever spent. Having insisted on my sitting beside him, Rigaut hardly spoke to me, as TM busily introduced him to the rest of the table. But as we exchanged pleasantries with the other guests, our attention was concentrated on each other. First, as if by chance, our legs brushed, then finally, all ambiguity abandoned, remained in a contact so distracting that all other activity – conversation, eating – became almost impossible. Once I felt his hand on my wrist. And through it all I knew (though he did not) that nothing further would ever happen between us.

Lying beside Joe later that night, enveloped in post-coital drowsiness, I thought of Rigaut. To tell the truth I'd been thinking about him ever since we'd said our goodbyes, his face imposing itself upon Joe's just as mine, I was willing to bet, haunted his dreams. He'd be in Paris now, in his own bed – perhaps (though this seemed improbable) beside his wife. They might even be lying in that very bedroom, in the rue d'Assas, where his uncle had lived and died. And tomorrow he'd wake up and do whatever it is prime ministers do on a Sunday – read papers, attend to urgent business, play golf, meet his mistress. But by then Pascal would have published his story. By midday it would be the lead on the television news. Journalists would be ringing Rigaut's office – soon he would be besieged. The inquiry into Antoine's death would be reopened, the question of Juliette's revived, perhaps

Delphine's as well. And that would be that – disgrace, maybe even prison. The end.

What would he feel? Fury, resignation? Chiefly, I suspected, surprise. The dead were dead – buried in the hectic flurry of present life, necessary rungs on the ladder. Why resuscitate them? Although for a moment I'd had him rattled, the possibility that they might rise again was something he'd never seriously considered. All that had been dealt with: we'd struck a bargain, last night's dinner the final flourish on the signature. He'd done his bit and he hadn't a doubt that I'd do mine. Didn't he have me entranced?

But there he was wrong. That was the Angel: true keeper of my heart.